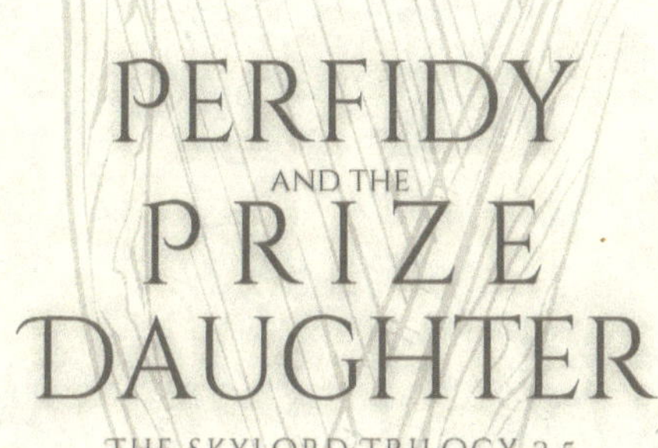

# PERFIDY AND THE PRIZE DAUGHTER

THE SKYLORD TRILOGY 2.5

KELLY FARINA

Book Cover by Kelly Farina

Chapter headers, title page, and scene breaks designed via Canva.com

# Contents

*For those who endure.*

*Perfidy and the Prize Daughter* contains material that may not be suitable for all readers. This includes death, torture (physical and psychological), gore, allusions to sexual assault, and animal death.

While there is no sexually explicit content in this book, it is intended for an adult audience.

With careful consideration,

Kelly

# Prologue

I always resented the notion of being someone's treasure to be protected. The finely molded walls of plush society loomed over me like the omnipresent bars of a gilded cage, cutting off my airflow and sapping me of inspiration. The vivid floral paintings that hung in our library became dull and gray. The melodic hum of my father's violin sounded flat—every note the same as the last. Then, my mother died, and so did my last hope for joy.

Such were the conditions that shaped me as a young woman. I remained passive as my attendants dressed me in the finest silks and rubbed me with exotic perfumes. I stared aimlessly through eyelids dusted with shimmering powder, glowing to offset the death in my eyes. In my frantic attempts to feel something—*anything*—I turned to a piercing needle. But two years and fifteen ear piercings later, the faint effect dimmed. Despite the distraction of my academic studies and musical training, I felt nothing. I cared for nothing. My senses abandoned me to a life of utter despondency.

The whispers of Father's friends always made their way to my bejeweled ears.

*"Prize daughter."*

*"Perfect poise."*

*"Guard her closely, she will attract many advantageous suitors."*

Every word was a hammer to the glimmering cage they'd built around me. The one from which I yearned to escape.

How spoiled and foolish I was, then.

## *Chapter One*

# BRINE

Saltwater flooded my lungs, throat, and nose, filling me with its prickling burn. I watched as my friends' ship sailed away, propelled by the powerful gusts of a windwalker.

*Levick.* My *windwalker.*

My dreams went with them, snatched away and fading into the darkness. Leaving me alone with Maksim and his new Skylords.

*I'll face that problem later.*

Levick's wind gusts also unintentionally summoned massive swells in the angry sea. And I'd fallen overboard.

Though I was a decent swimmer, the waves fought to pull me into oblivion. I broke the surface again, only to be met with torrential winds blowing sheets of rain into my face. I gasped and coughed, flailing in the tumultuous waters.

*Dear, Echna—I'm going to drown! After everything that's happened today, I'll be killed by water.*

A chorus of indistinct shouting met my waterlogged ears, but it was distant. Everything was distant. A new swell was rising, and I was going to sink again.

*How long can I maintain this before my body gives in?*

My heart pounded in my chest as the water rose. Some feral part of me broke free, and I kicked with all of my strength.

*I will not die here. I will not die here.*

A muffled bursting sound echoed through the dark, cloudy waters. My head spun around, trying desperately to find the source of the noise. My salt-stung eyes were met only with darkness.

Then, a set of strong arms hauled me to the surface.

The rough, callused hands of a seasoned fighter held me tightly enough to leave bruises. He hauled me away from the soldier who'd caught me in the water, dragging me over the edge of a dinghy to a nearby chorus of hollers and cheers. The sideways rain persisted, beating against me and falling into my burning eyes.

"Pin her arms, Stepan," commanded a voice as cold as steel. "Gently, of course."

Still gasping for air, I turned to face the speaker. I immediately recognized him.

*Maksim.*

There was nothing but pure resentment in his icy eyes. Wet hair of frosted flax stuck to his brutally chiseled face, long and unbound. His crimson military coat was soaked through and dark, contrasting with the northern pallor of his skin.

My brutish handler grunted his compliance and proceeded to haul me onto his lap. He was built like Ress—an adamant wall of muscle.

"Let me go," I hissed, squirming futilely against him. With my arms pinned against me, there was no hope of using my windblade. Though Levick had taught me rudimentary hand-to-hand, I was woefully outmuscled. Defenseless.

Stepan's massive arms tightened around me, further restricting my movement. "Would you look at that," he laughed in my ear. "They're leaving you behind."

I jerked my head around, almost colliding with Stepan's chest. Just as he said, Levick's ship was shrinking. Our ship was shrinking.

*Good. They have a plan. They'll find the Dawning Flame and reclaim Friese.*

Though I knew it had been the right thing to do, my heart sank at the sight of my friends sailing off into the horizon.

*My friends... my love.*

Suddenly, the grim reality of my situation crashed into me like a hurricane. My friends were gone. Everyone I knew and cared about. A wave of irrepressible nausea filled my gut, and I reached vainly for my mouth.

Mocking laughter echoed through the rain.

"Hold her over the rail if you want to save your boots." Maksim's voice was scornful and completely devoid of sympathy.

At his command, Stepan slid over to the edge of the dinghy. The small boat rocked as he draped me unceremoniously over the side, and the movement sealed my fate. I heaved and retched into the sea.

For an impulsive moment, as my burning throat gasped for air, I entertained the thought of throwing myself over the edge and swimming away.

*Maybe if I'm quick enough—*

As if sensing my thoughts, Stepan dug his thick fingers into my arms. My body tensed.

"Don't even think about it. We don't catch and release," he growled in my ear. His fetid breath made drowning seem appealing.

After I heaved the last drop of seawater from my stomach, I looked up to see Maksim seated directly across from us.

There was something about his stillness—the unnatural calmness he exuded—that was distinctly unnerving. Despite his powerful build, his high cheekbones jutted out at harsh angles, giving him an air of skeletal aloofness.

His appraising stare ran over every inch of my body, and I wished to Echna I was wearing a thick dress instead of my thin wrap top and trousers. Even if a thick dress would have dragged me to the depths.

"Where would you go, little gull?" Maksim asked, his eyes hard as diamonds. "There is nowhere to run, and your wings have been clipped."

He leaned forward and cocked his head at me. I tried to back away, but the attempt only sent me scooting further onto Stepan's lap. Someone whistled suggestively, and my captor laughed. Though Stepan's strength was intimidating, his leader's mere presence made the mocking laughs and leering stares seem benign. I'd accept the vile comments if it kept me far away from Maksim's heartless, vacant eyes.

A smile pulled at his serpentine lips, sending the rain flowing in rivulets over his chin. "This kingdom is mine. And now, so are you."

*Chapter Two*

# Monotony of Darkness

After Maksim's dinghy made it to shore, I was shoved into a carriage for the ride to the palace. I thanked Echna that I was left alone for the ride. I was well aware of the reputation of Trenican men.

Though my social life hadn't been as vibrant as most of my peers, I still attended one palace ball every year—my father in close proximity, of course. Compared to many Friesian structures, the palace was an ancient construction, filled to the painted ceilings with rich history and culture. The main ballroom dwarfed every other in Friese, barring the Exleys'. There were two smaller ballrooms that were said to be used for more private—and politically intentional—entertainment.

Staircases leading from opposing sides of the palace joined and led down into the main ballroom, which was inlaid with countless starry tiles. They'd been painstakingly arranged in breathtaking patterns, occasionally broken up by reflective silver marbling. I'd often wondered how they managed to keep the blue so deep and the silver so bright.

Contrary to many of Friese's major houses, most of the palace's fine filigree was accented in a dazzling mixture of platinum and silver. Much of the molding, the delicate furniture, even the frames around the paintings gleamed with cold, white silver.

But my knowledge of the Fresian palace was limited to those few public spaces. I had never seen the private wings, nor had I ever paused to consider what lay below my dancing feet in the dark and hidden places. The existence of a subterranean dungeon was knowledge I would've gladly gone my entire life without learning.

Beneath putrid labyrinthine halls and damp corridors was a place of such vile conditions that I was bewildered such a thing could exist in Friese at all. The dirty stone ceiling hung portentously like a premonition of a dark fate. Endless rows of wrought iron bars divided up the cavernous space, lending very little room for each prisoner.

But as far as I knew, there was only one prisoner to be found in the Friesian dungeon. All other Skylords had been massacred. A Trenican prince sat on the throne of Friese, and over eighty of his most elite, cutthroat officers wielded windblades. I was the only remaining Friesian with a windblade, except for my friends who were heading north.

For the first two days, my hands were kept tightly bound against each other. It made any kind of hygiene or maintenance incredibly difficult, but I refused to ask for assistance. I'd rather soil my tattered clothing than ask a Trenican man to help me disrobe. So I fumbled my way through basic tasks, doing my best to ignore the blooming ache developing in my restricted joints.

On my third day of capture, I was outfitted with a set of metal gloves. They were a clever set of engineering specially designed to prevent use of my windblade, while lending me enough movement to perform basic tasks. They looked like a pair of fingerless steel mittens linked at the sides with metal hoops. They were terribly uncomfortable, but were certainly a better alternative to having my hands tied flat together. Such contraptions clearly weren't thrown together in a matter of days. They'd been carefully designed in preparation for the invasion.

Soon after my gloves were placed, I made an attempt to throw my windblade at the wall. To my disappointment, the complete restriction of my fingers rendered the channeling impossible. I'd known that finger mobility was important to the throwing of a windblade, but I'd hoped it wasn't vital.

I was granted no human interaction save for a few brief moments with the guard who delivered my meals. Every one of my questions and requests were met with nothing but silent sneers. I demanded to speak to Maksim, to take a walk outside, anything but the suffocating monotony of the darkness. It was all met with derisive, but wordless, glares.

After days in the torch-lit seclusion, I tried baiting my guard with inflammatory comments.

*"You're just going to stand there? Staring at the wall? So useful. I'm sure your commander values you greatly."*

When that was ignored, I moved on to snide insults about his appearance.

*"It's too bad about your hairline. If not for the pathetic wispiness adorning your skull, you might be seen as alluring to someone with low standards."*

Finally, after running out of ways to call my guard hideous, I resorted to degrading comments about his ancestors.

*"If only your mother had been more beautiful. But I suppose an ogre can only beget another ogre. Your father must suffer from blindness. Such an affliction might've been a mercy."*

He gave no reaction. If he hadn't previously exchanged words with another guard, I might've thought him deaf.

Five long days later, I decided to simply scream like a banshee and hope to be enough of a nuisance to merit Maksim's attention. My only reward was a raw throat.

I paced my cramped cell and did some bodyweight exercises in an attempt to maintain some remnant of athleticism, but as time wore on, I knew it was futile. It was gradual, but my hope was dwindling.

I had just scratched the fourteenth tally mark into the grimy stone wall when I heard footsteps descending the staircase. The flickering light of a torch bathed the cavernous walls as they came closer. I raced to the gate, mindless and parched, only to notice the footfalls sounded different. Rather than a guard's heavy booted stomps and clanging scabbard against the wall, these steps were soft and rustling. It was someone new. I was so starved for human interaction that my fingers danced with excitement against the dirty metal bars.

My visitor turned a corner, and my excitement turned into cold dread. Platinum blond hair fell against a cruel face, smiling faintly at me. He was dressed from head to toe in vivid red, accentuating his pallid features. As he got closer, I noticed spidery blue veins running under the skin of his face and neck. He couldn't have been much older than me, but something about his demeanor seemed ageless. He hadn't visited me in my two weeks of confinement, and I'd forgotten the severity of his presence.

I backed away but he came closer, only stopping when his boots almost touched the cell bars.

"I hope your cage has treated you well."

"Are you going to let me out of here?" I asked, choking on my hoarse words.

Maksim reached into his pocket and produced a rusty key. "That depends," he said, twirling it in his fingers.

My jaw tensed, and I backed further away. No one accompanied him. The two of us were alone, and my glove cuffs rendered my windblade useless. I was completely at his mercy. I tried not to think about the lecherous, insatiable reputation of Trenican men, but the rumors burned in the forefront of my mind.

*Your grisly fate has been sealed. You knew what awaited you in Maksim's court of eternal debauchery.*

Maksim's cheek twitched, and his smirk spread knowingly. "How presumptuous of you. But alas, I must disappoint."

He unlocked the door and stepped into my cell, stopping a few feet away. "I have plenty of willing and," he paused, his lip curling in disgust, "clean women at my disposal."

I hardly noticed the insult through my relief. "Then why are you here?"

Maksim ignored my question and looked me up and down, dissatisfied with my grimy state. His expression soured further until his eyes finally met mine again, hard and unyielding.

"The ship you were on. Where was it going?"

It was a question I'd expected weeks ago, immediately upon my capture. I'd wondered why he hadn't yet interrogated me about it, but decided to accept it as a small blessing among my cursed circumstances.

"I don't know. We were just trying to get away," I said, lying through my teeth.

Considering the speed at which Levick was propelling the ship, I knew they'd already made it to Trenica. Maksim likely assumed as much, but his sudden interrogation after two weeks gave me hope that Trenica had lost all leads on their whereabouts. Had they veered off course? Or were they lying low in Trenica, evading capture as they searched for the Dawning Flame? A spark of hope burned in my chest.

Maksim's lethal smile faded, but his glare remained razor-sharp. "How interesting that you were kept in the dark. Convenient, wouldn't you say?"

A pit opened in my stomach, and I slowly moved away until my back met with the dingy wall. But with my every step backwards, Maksim stepped closer. Fury burned in his light eyes, but his hands remained at his sides. They were balled into fists, as if he were restraining himself.

"No matter," he whispered. "I can find other... uses for you."

Terror gripped my heart, locking me in place against the wall. My mind played out all of the degrading and violent *uses* he might find for me.

*Please, Echna. Spare me from this.*

But Maksim said no more. He simply turned and walked out, leaving me in gut-wrenching suspense.

I flinched at every noise for the next week, waiting to be dragged upstairs and tortured. I would lie awake on my hard cot, terrified of what Maksim had in store for me. But he never came, and my days returned to how they were before.

*What does it even look like up there?*

I'd been isolated in the dungeon since the takeover and had no idea what was going on in Friese. Every day I would say a prayer for the people of Friese, particularly the women. The threat Maksim had made towards Opal Droughton repeated in my mind. During the final battle, I'd arrived in the throne room moments before the lecherous men of Frost Company could descend on her.

*If I had arrived a few minutes later...*

I shuddered at the thought. Having their blood on my hands gave me no grief. I only wished I'd killed all of them.

Maksim didn't visit again. I'd begun to think he'd forgotten about me. I wondered what use I was serving him, languishing away in a dungeon.

*Better than an execution.*

There were thirty-one tally marks on my wall when I was removed from the dungeon. A pair of guards simply beckoned me out and led me upstairs, not bothering to give me an explanation. I followed along on shaking legs, trying to fight the feeling that my ascendance would damn me.

# *Chapter Three*

# Ascension

I was brought upstairs and thoroughly bathed. Female servants scrubbed every spot of dirt away with impressive determination, only omitting the portions of my hands encased in metal gloves. They brushed my hair, perfumed my skin, and lined my eyes with dark blue powder. I thought of the rumors surrounding Trenican gatherings, and found myself missing the layers of potentially protective grime I'd worn. I felt like an animal being fattened for slaughter. The mid-morning sunlight shone through the windows, making me feel completely exposed.

A dress of pure white fell over me in a precarious display that could easily be sabotaged by one awkward step. A Trenican servant fastened the smooth, weighty fabric around my neck. It fell over my front, barely covering my breasts. A small metal diamond shape connected the top of the dress with the skirt, which fell to my ankles. The result was a sad excuse for a dress that hardly maintained my decency.

The scars on my back were entirely exposed. It felt like a lifetime had passed since my home's glass ceiling rained down on me, tearing my skin open. The markings weren't deep, but they were still very visible. I briefly hoped Trenican men were averse to scarred women.

"What is the occasion?" I asked my attendant in an inconspicuous probing. I hoped it wasn't a private meeting. She simply rolled her eyes at my inquiry.

We stood in an elaborately decorated bedroom, covered in breathtaking paintings of primordial warrior-women engaged in perilous battle with one another. My eyes lingered on a dark queen with raven-black hair, preparing to plunge her sword into the back of a foe. The unsuspecting woman was facing away, unaware of her impending fate.

"Where am I to be brought next?" I insisted, forcing evenness into my tone.

My young attendant's eyes found mine and flashed knowingly. A coy smirk played at the corners of her thin lips. "The throne room."

A rushing sigh of relief escaped my lungs.

*Good. Not his bedroom. That's a good sign.*

*Right?*

The sapphire eyes of my servant gleamed. "You think you know His Excellency."

I remained silent. It wasn't a question—she was baiting me. Her pin-straight blonde hair brushed my arm as she leaned forward to adjust my dress.

"Any nature of summoning from your viceroy is a privilege." She leaned in closer than necessary. "But *that* sort of summoning? It would be an honor."

My lip involuntarily curled up at her sycophantic words. "Sounds like he has plenty of options, then," I muttered, meeting the young woman's eyes with an icy stare of my own.

She backed away, looking me over. "You are ready," she said, her voice back to its practiced monotone. "Follow me."

I followed her out of the luxurious bedroom and into the hallway, doing my best not to step on the trailing fabric of her skirt. Rather than her native Trenican velvet, she wore the shining silks of Friese and Corlaea.

"What is your name?" I asked.

"Yla," she answered without turning. I raised my eyebrows at the unusual name, but repeated the *eye-luh* pronunciation in my head.

A sudden curiosity tugged at me. "Why were you brought here?"

*What kind of army brings an untrained young woman along while they wage war?*

She paused, and I barely managed to side-step before walking on her skirt.

"Some of us volunteered to be a part of the occupying force. Friesian maids and servants can't always be trusted."

I bristled but didn't respond.

We walked under the gleaming silver molding that adorned the vaulted ceilings, and I briefly wondered how they managed to dust it.

*Levick could make quick work of it.*

A smile fought its way onto my lips, but died before it reached my eyes. It had been an entire month since he left, and I had no idea where he was or if he was safe.

*Please be safe.*

I pushed any thoughts of Levick out of my mind. It would do me no good to enter Maksim's audience while crying.

A dense pit of unease opened inside my stomach as we approached the throne room. Seven months ago, in that very room, I had placed the crown of Friese atop Arturian Exley's head. One month ago, I killed a dozen men there.

*Does Yla know what I've done to her countrymen?*

*I bet they all know... and want to kill me for it.*

I had dropped a chandelier on most of Maksim's elite Frost Company. A shiver went up my spine.

*That's why he's summoned me. For vengeance.*

The hairs on the back of my neck prickled, and I knew someone was following us. I dared a backward glance and accidentally met the cool gray eyes of the man who'd held me on the boat.

*Stepan.*

His white-blond hair fell in unkempt curls over his shoulders—a stark contrast to the brutal crudeness of his face. He made no acknowledgment of me except for a slight tilt of his lips. I quickly looked away.

"Quickly, *zuka*," Yla said, beckoning me forward.

I clenched my jaw, but the words slipped out anyway. "I have a name, and it's not *prisoner*."

Yla spun around, her hair flipping over her shoulder. Her pale eyes fell wide upon me, and I tried to suppress my satisfaction at seeing her so surprised.

"What is it, *ulestya? Cuvolest c'er veya*?" I asked. Stepan laughed from behind me.

My Vynesic wasn't perfect, but most Friesians had trouble understanding it, let alone speaking it.

Yla's face went red, but she haughtily spun back around without a word.

I was almost jogging to keep up with her by the time we got to the throne room's heavy double doors. She turned to me, not bothering to hide the hate in her expression.

"You will address the viceroy as *Your Excellency*, no less. You will kneel, kiss his ring, and do anything else he requires of you."

Despite the fear coiling itself through my gut, my anger overpowered it. "I'll do no such thing."

Yla looked over my shoulder, shooting an exasperated glare at Stepan. "Tell her, soldier. Tell her she must kneel."

A scoff escaped my lips before I could stop it. "I rather think you do that enough for both of us, no? Or has Maksim not bestowed that *honor* upon you, yet?"

Before she could even react, an explosion of pain erupted over the back of my head, and I fell to my knees on the unforgiving stone tiles.

"You're funny, *zuka*. I admit that." Stepan chuckled.

I groaned and attempted to stand, but my vision was swimming.

His voice returned to me in muffled waves. "But your pedigree won't protect you here."

A new, tearing pain bloomed over the back of my head as I was crudely lifted to my feet. Stepan had my hair wrapped around his palm and began dragging me towards the doors.

My screams and shouts echoed through the room, accompanied by Yla's smug laughter. I scrambled to my feet and tried to pry his hands away, but he was unshakable.

*Dear Echna, he's going to break my neck—*

Stepan yanked the doors open and threw me into the room like a child's toy.

## *Chapter Four*

# The Viceroy and the Gull

Glossy blue constellations sprawled beneath me, shining in endless stars under the candlelight. They were cool and damp under my fingertips. Friese's summertime humidity stuck to the tiles like a waxy sheen, and I could almost see my eyes in their distorted reflection.

I looked up, only to realize the wet tiles weren't distorted. *Everything* was.

A dozen thick pillars lined the throne room, each inlaid with intricate engravings I couldn't decipher in my addled state. My gaze followed each pillar until my blurred vision rested upon a rectangular shape sitting in the middle of the room.

"Already pushing your luck, little gull? I thought the Yorkes were known for their intellect." The familiar voice echoed from the central shape—the throne. "Come here."

My neck burned with pain and my head was still swimming, but the sound of Stepan's approaching footsteps spurred me to action. I stumbled to my feet on shaking legs, my metal-gloved hands clacking on the floor. My fingers tugged at the straps of my dress, as if that could somehow extend it to cover me completely.

As I got closer, I realized Maksim wasn't alone. Doressa Stokes—forever an opportunistic Friesian courtesan—sat on his lap, her hand resting on his shoulder. Though my vision hadn't completely cleared, it was obvious she was unshackled and composed.

"Go upstairs, Doressa," Maksim muttered, shooing her away like a dismissed pet.

Doressa smiled—*smiled*—at him, then curtsied. "As you command, Excellency." She walked away, hips swinging under her flowing silk nightgown.

I seethed at her, but she was already gone.

*Traitor. So quick to switch bedfellows.*

Maksim tracked my glare. "Jealousy doesn't suit you."

"I would never," I said through a grimace, my voice a hateful whisper.

"Don't judge so quickly. War creates desperate times," Maksim said. "In fact, I have a proposition for you."

He somehow managed to lounge upon the ancient throne, leaning on his elbow. He forewent any formal attire, and instead wore a partially buttoned shirt the color of Corlaean wine and a pair of gray trousers. A half-eaten platter of fine meats and shining silver cutlery sat beside him on an end table. The familiar, relaxed look was more terrifying than if he'd worn his full royal uniform.

I stopped in front of the throne, using every ounce of my strength to remain on my feet. "What do you want?"

An indignant growl echoed from the back of the room, followed by hurried footsteps. My heart dropped, and I waited to be knocked down again.

"No, Stepan," Maksim said, his voice betraying no upset. "This young lady is my guest. You are forbidden from further harming her."

His words brought me instantaneous relief, but it didn't last long. While I hadn't had many interactions with Maksim, my limited experiences were disquieting. He seemed like a man who deeply enjoyed toying with people.

"Surely you've noticed the treatment you received today?" he asked, studying my expression. "You've been bathed, perfumed, dressed, and kept separate from everyone else. Your hair smells of juniper rather than grime. You're wearing fine silks instead of tattered rags. I've treated you well, have I not?"

My eyebrows rose at his characterization. He'd kept me wasting away in solitude and filth for a month. My confusion grew as I tried to intuit what he could possibly need from me of all people. I didn't want to betray my ignorance, so I remained silent.

He beckoned me closer. I hesitantly complied, climbing the low steps to the throne.

"Ah, the famous Yorke manners. I hope you're not always so withholding." He leaned forward. "Because I'm in need of something only you can give me."

My throat tightened and the blood drained from my face. I took a small step backwards, but I stopped when I nearly toppled over the stairs. Maksim leaned closer until he had to crane his neck to look up at me. His hot breath warmed my skin, left exposed by the winds-damned dress he'd made me wear.

He met my eyes, and I suppressed a shudder. Behind that icy gaze lurked an evil I'd never seen, unbeholden to anything or anyone. Vein-riddled circles ringed his eyes, giving a manic air to his unnatural stillness.

"I won't sleep with you," I said, the words barely audible.

A playful smile spread over his face, showcasing a set of gleaming white teeth. "Dear Miss Yorke, so presumptuous. Age-earned wisdom has not yet outweighed your spoiled, conceited upbringing."

My lip curled up at the clear condescension in his words. "If age is what earns wisdom, I fear you preclude yourself. Though I'd argue that the method in which wisdom is earned is irrelevant if none is ever displayed. The wisest man in the world will remain unrecognized if he indulges every one of his debased urges."

Maksim's eyes lit up, and he leaned back on the throne. Though his stare never left my face, I could feel him picking at me. Like I was an orange waiting to be peeled, and he was starving.

"I need you, little gull. Not in my bed, but in my army."

My jaw fell slack.

"You are the last remaining Friesian with a windblade. A *Skylady*." He scoffed at the word. "I need you to train my men. To train me."

I clenched my fists at my sides as I processed the request.

*Train him? Train my enemies?*

"No," I said, my tone firm despite my clear disadvantage. "I will not assist my enemy."

Maksim's eyes hardened. "I thought you might say that, but it's too bad. I truly hate to waste."

He brought his thin fingers to his lips and whistled. The shrill sound made me jump, and I nearly fell down the steps for the second time.

A banging sound echoed through the room. My eyes darted around until they landed on the newly opened double doors. Feminine screams erupted through the room, bouncing off the walls.

"No, please!" a young woman cried, but she was already being thrown into the room.

The guards shut the doors behind them.

The girl screamed again and raced for the doors, pounding on them with bound wrists. Pitch-black hair fell over her shoulders in wiry tangles. Her uniquely bronze skin told me she was likely East Corlaean.

"Let me out! Please!" she shrieked.

"What is this? What are you doing?" I whispered to Maksim, who'd leaned over to see past me. A mildly bored smile tugged at his lips.

"My skill with a windblade is atrocious. My aim is awful." He rose to his feet and stepped up beside me. Drawing close, he whispered, "But don't take my word for it. I'll show you."

"No!" I shouted, but he was already flinging his arm forward, directly at the terrified girl. She screamed and jumped aside as the windblade sliced into an Exley tapestry. It fell to the floor in a dusty heap.

"See what I mean?" Maksim asked with an amused smile.

I grabbed his arm to stop him, but he shoved me backwards. I tumbled down the steps, barely slowing my fall. He continued to throw his windblade at the young woman, who screamed and attempted to run away.

*There is nowhere to go.*

My mind raced as I tried to discern a solution.

"You can still change your mind," Maksim called over. He didn't even bother to look at me. My mind kept waiting for the sick squelching sound of evisceration.

*How did I end up here? A prisoner yet again?*

I wanted to cry. I wanted to scream. I wanted to tear everything apart until it all stopped.

"I'm growing tired of this." He threw again but missed. He massaged his shoulder.

The young woman cowered behind a pillar, but I could hear her cries as clearly as if she were right beside me.

"That's it." Unbothered, Maksim fell back onto the throne. "Stepan, take care of it."

My heart dropped into my stomach. Maksim's massive soldier began stalking towards the sobbing young woman. She shot to her feet and raced towards the edge of the room.

"So wasteful," Maksim mumbled, plucking a glass from his table and taking a sip. My eyes followed the movement, catching on the dull gleam of a stained steak knife.

*Echna, help me.*

I stood and drifted towards Maksim, hands splayed and eyes desperate. He cocked his head and slowly lowered his hands. He opened his mouth to speak, but I'd reached the table. Before anyone could react, I had the knife in my hand and was bolting down the steps.

Maksim called to Stepan but he was too late. I was upon him. I leapt and plunged the knife into his back.

## Chapter Five

# The Misfortune of Rynne Wemberley

The grease-covered steak knife cut through layers of muscle and tendon, just as it was created to do. Though this particular cut of meat was eager to fight back.

Stepan roared and clawed at his back, but I'd already jumped backwards, out of his grasp. The young Corlaean woman shrieked at the violence, but she didn't cower from me as I ran for her.

Guards burst through the doors at the commotion, rushing for me. I slid to a stop and covered the girl with my body. Blessedly, she didn't fight me off.

"Thank you," she whispered, then closed her dark eyes. I did the same, then waited for the inevitable consequences.

*They'll kill me for this.*

Footsteps echoed louder.

*I'm sorry, Levick.*

"Stop." Maksim's voice rang through the room, cutting through the noise. The footsteps ceased.

My heart pounded in my chest, but I was too scared to look up. I only saw Stepan from the corner of my eye, stretching and clawing at the knife lodged in his back.

"I don't know why I expected less," Maksim said, his voice drawing closer with every faint footfall. The young girl trembled under me, but I only held her tighter.

"Especially from the woman who crushed half of my favorite guards with a wave of her hand. You continue to surprise me."

"He's going to kill me," the girl whispered repeatedly. I shushed her but she was beyond comforting.

A pair of black boots entered my vision, and a shiver went up my spine.

"Please," I whispered. "Don't kill her because of me."

The shadows in my periphery distorted, and I knew Maksim had crouched down. "Look at me."

I didn't move.

"Look at me, little gull."

I held still as a statue.

A deep sigh escaped Maksim's lungs. Then, I felt it. A cool finger sliding over my skin, tracing my ribcage. My body began to tremble, but I didn't move from my protective position over the whimpering girl.

He leaned closer, and I could sense his gaze trying to capture mine. The faint aroma of spruce needles drifted from him, along with a citrus scent I couldn't quite place.

A fingernail scraped against my skin. "Don't make this harder than it needs to be. I want our arrangement to be amicable."

I clenched my jaw, willing bravery into my bones. "There will be no *arrangement*, usurper."

His fingertip crept closer to my navel. "I know what you need," he whispered. "A little bit of fun."

His finger hooked around the diamond-shaped clasp that held my dress together, and yanked on it.

I gasped, shooting up and sliding towards him to keep him from fully pulling my dress away. He tugged harder, and I had no choice but to get even closer. I could either follow the pull of his fingers, or back away and expose myself to him and every guard in the room.

Though his grip was unshakeable, he touched me nowhere else. A glint of manic excitement flashed in his eyes. His white-blond hair fell over his shoulder, so close that it laced with mine. To my unending discomfort, our blonde strands were indistinguishable.

"Have a drink with me."

He rose to his feet, bringing me with him. The girl whimpered behind me, but Maksim indicated to his guards that she was not to be touched. Stepan grumbled and stalked from the room, blood dribbling from his right shoulder. The blade was short, unfortunately. He would survive it.

Maksim didn't let go of my dress as he led me back to his throne. I prayed to Echna that he'd been genuine when he offered the drink, and it wasn't just a ruse. He climbed the steps but stopped at the last one.

"Sit," he commanded, motioning to the step.

I hesitated, disliking the idea of sitting at his feet like a supplicating subject.

He noticed my pause and raised a brow. "There's only one chair up here, little gull. Sit on the step, unless you'd rather share with me." He punctuated his last words with a suggestive twitch of the lips. I dropped down and sat on the stairs.

He feigned a pout, but turned and sat on the throne. "Rynne," he called out.

I perked up.

*Rynne Wemberley?*

My eyes darted around the room until they landed on a small servant's door in the back of the room. A beautiful redhead walked in, dressed in a maid's uniform and carrying a tray set with two metal goblets. Her blue eyes were wide but fixed on the floor, and her bottom lip trembled.

Maksim groaned in impatience. "Any day now, servant."

Rynne shuffled faster, the goblets clinking together as she came closer. Her red curls were pinned back in an understated bun, and her attire was much more modest than what had been selected for me.

Her name escaped my lips in a soft whisper, and her eyes shot up.

"Eliandre?" she asked, her mouth falling open. "You're alive."

"Bring me my gin," Maksim said, his tone betraying his thinning patience.

Rynne snapped up and crossed the remaining distance in eager steps. She placed the tray down on the table and handed a goblet to Maksim. He took it without even looking at her. His eyes remained locked on me.

I accepted the goblet Rynne offered. She made to leave, but Maksim held out a hand. "No. Stay here."

She swallowed nervously, but did as she was told.

Maksim took a long drink. "Well? Aren't you going to try it?"

I hesitated. "I don't drink."

His lips twitched. "That is a lie if I've ever heard one. Go on. Try it."

My pulse quickened as I peeked down into the metal goblet. The clear liquid smelled of juniper—similar to the perfume he'd selected for me.

"It's only gin," he whispered. His stare turned incredulous, as if he couldn't imagine why anyone would suspect him of malicious intent. "I could always give it to a more appreciative guest," he said, his eyes briefly darting to the Corlaean girl still hiding in the corner.

"No," I hissed, bringing the goblet to my lips. A refreshing, biting tang bloomed over my tongue. It tasted like the coldest days of winter—crisp, refreshing. It was as if someone took the essence of snowy pine trees and created a drink of it. I wanted to hate it, but couldn't.

He noticed my expression.

"Not bad, hmm?"

I shook my head and took another sip.

"Common ground doesn't seem so out of reach anymore, does it?" Maksim asked. "Be rational, Miss Yorke. I have your kingdom. I have your friends."

"No, you don't," I muttered, a hint of a smug smile growing on my face.

He raised a brow. "Is that so?"

With stunning speed, Maksim stood and grabbed Rynne by the fabric of her dress. She struggled against him, but he was strong.

I shouted and stood up, but he held his hand out as a warning.

"You showed me your weakness when you ran to protect a girl you've never met. I wonder what you'd do for a woman who you know personally?" He reached up and grabbed her throat. She flailed and fought, but no noise escaped her mouth.

"Stop, please!" I shouted.

His head jerked over to me. "Why? Why should I stop? You have something I want. I have something you want. How about a trade?"

My mouth went dry. To assist the enemy was unfathomable. I couldn't give Maksim and his generals the skills to fight and kill my friends.

"Train me and my generals," Maksim said, all pretense of politeness gone. "Or I will marry off Miss Wemberley and the Corlaean girl to the remaining leaders of Frost Company."

Rynne jerked against him at the threat, and the girl in the corner screamed.

He didn't even let me answer before throwing Rynne to the floor in front of me. "You have three days, little gull. This is your life, now. It's time for you to accept it."

## *Chapter Six*

# Bonding as a Leverage Tactic

I sat in the corner of my grand bedroom, cowering under every layer of robe and blanket I could find in the adjoining dressing room. It was larger than most bedrooms and was stocked with dresses of the latest fashions.

The guards had dragged me away and locked me inside, but I hadn't fought them. Being locked alone in a bedroom seemed like the best possible situation at the moment.

An impossible choice stood before me. If I trained Maksim and his men, I would be giving them the means to retain the kingdom. To kill everyone I cared about. Levick, Francie, Eadlin... even Arturian and Harley.

But to refuse?

My throat tightened at the thought. My anxious mind showed me images of Rynne walking down the aisle on shaking legs, wearing a tattered and torn wedding dress. Her emerald eyes wide as she beheld the wicked face of her future husband. Not to mention the Corlaean girl, who must've been only a teenager. Not even old enough to get married by Friesian laws.

*That certainly wouldn't stop the Trenicans.*

I pulled my blankets tighter around me. The plush lavender bed on the other side of the room seemed to taunt me. It was such an unnecessarily luxurious room.

*Where is Rynne sleeping? Is she safe?*

My stomach turned, and for the hundredth time, I reconsidered my choices.

Wind rushed through my hair, whipping it into knots over my back. I didn't care. Nothing else mattered in that moment.

In *our* moment.

The Exley estate shrunk below us as Levick carried me through the sky on winds of love and magic. I pressed my face against his chest and tried to savor the sensation. To remember what it felt like to be held by a man of such strong spirit.

He looked down at me, and I could've sworn I saw the future in those forest green eyes. I couldn't look away.

*"I love you, Eliandre."*

His words were lost to the torrent spinning around us, but I didn't need to hear it. I felt it. I knew it.

*"I love you, too."*

I still remember how his eyes lit up. He almost seemed surprised by my confession. As if he was unsure of how I felt, even as he carried me through the sky like a prince of the air. I slid my fingers over the soft linen of his shirt, then tugged at him. He leaned in and pressed his lips to mine. In that moment, I knew I'd do anything for him. I'd fight, injure, or kill.

I'd do anything. Even if that meant throwing myself to the wolves.

I woke up on the floor with a pounding headache and aching shoulders. A wave of nausea rolled through me as I remembered where I was. I closed my eyes again, willing the dream to return. The *memory*.

*Please be safe.*

I sent a dozen prayers to Echna before pushing myself up into a sitting position. The carpet was soft and surprisingly comfortable to sleep on, but I doubted I had been out for longer than a couple of hours. Afternoon sunlight streamed through my window. It hadn't even been a full day since I was brought up from the dungeon, but so much had happened since then.

*I wish they'd left me down there.*

A muffled clicking sound came from my door, and I jumped to my feet. My eyes darted around the room in a desperate search for anything that could be used as a weapon, but it was predictably bare. Before I could form another plan, the door opened, revealing Rynne Wemberley and the young woman from the throne room.

My brows furrowed at the shocking sight.

"How did you get—"

Before I could finish my question, they both stumbled forward, as if they'd been pushed. Behind them stood a tall and lean Trenican man. One side of his head had been shaved, and the other side sported elaborate braids and knots, falling past his shoulders and chest .

"His Excellency reminds you that your time is running out," he said through a strong accent. "And he requires your presence at his revel tonight. Be ready in one hour."

My jaw fell open, but the man shut the door behind him before I'd even processed it.

"Eliandre!" Rynne gasped, racing for me. She threw her arms around my shoulders and hugged me tight. "Winds! I thought you were dead! I thought you were—" Her words were cut off by her own sobs of relief.

I wrapped my arms around her and patted her back gently. "I'm alright, Rynne. I'm okay."

The Corlaean girl remained in the middle of the bedroom, staring at us.

"Have they hurt you?" Rynne asked, suddenly pushing away to examine me. Her eyes widened upon seeing the array of cuts and scars I'd accumulated in the lost war for Friese.

"I already had these," I said.

She nodded, but her expression darkened. "Have they... *hurt* you?"

The hair on the back of my neck stood up. "No. What about you?"

Rynne shook her head, and I almost cried in relief.

"They don't need to force themselves on anyone," she said, her tone full of resentment. "Almost our entire court has thrown themselves at the Trenican men in the most shameful display of side-switching I've ever seen."

I almost laughed at the words. To be scorned by Rynne Wemberley for being too forward with men was a severe indictment, indeed.

"I saw Doressa." I shook my head.

Rynne released a wry laugh. "I'm not surprised. She tried to weasel her way into Arturian Exley's heart for the last six months. I knew she didn't care about him. She just wanted to be bedded in the Royal Chambers. But it doesn't matter—Maksim will tire of her quickly. I only hope he doesn't kill her when it's over."

A shiver ran up my spine. I didn't respect or care for Doressa Stokes, but I certainly didn't want to see her dead.

"Excuse me," a small voice said from behind Rynne.

I peeked over her shoulder at the Corlaean girl. She was very young—maybe fifteen—and quite short. Midnight black hair fell past her shoulders in a disastrous mess, and her clothing looked like it had been left on a clothesline during a summer storm.

I rose to my feet. "What is your name?

"Kiera." She curtsied. "I wanted to thank you for what you did earlier. You saved my life." Her voice was a faint whisper, choked by heavy emotions.

My heart ached at the words. "You're welcome, Kiera."

"I wonder why they put us all together?" Rynne pondered, standing beside me. "There are countless rooms in this palace."

I knew why. Maksim knew that if I spoke to these women—shared closeness with them—I'd be much more likely to cave to his deal. To train him in order to protect them from marriage to the evil brutes in Frost Company.

"It doesn't matter right now," I said. "There are clean clothes in the dressing room. You two should change and get some sleep. I'm not sure how much longer we'll be left alone in here, and I doubt either of you have gotten much sleep recently."

They nodded and went in search of clothes. The sounds of soft chatting escaped through the cracks in the dressing room door.

*Echna, what do I do?*

*Train my enemy to fight my friends? Or doom these women to abuse?*

If I refused to help Maksim, I could only hope that my friends would return before the weddings. In my heart, I knew it was unrealistic. The voyage to Trenica took two weeks—maybe one, at their speed—and they still needed to find the Dawning Flame before their return. It would be *months* before I could hope for rescue.

Kiera emerged from the dressing room wearing a modest, sunshine-yellow dress that fell to her ankles. It was simple—not eye-catching. It was a wise choice. The color complimented her skin tone, and the fashion-forward heiress in me was impressed. I'd never seen anyone wear yellow so well.

*Does fashion really matter, right now?*

I shook the frivolous thoughts away.

"You look lovely, Kiera," I said.

She thanked me and approached the bed, but instead of lying down, she turned and sat on the floor. Her back rested against the bed, her hair draped over the comforter.

"Are you alright?" I asked, sliding closer.

She turned to look at me, her tangled hair blocking much of her face. "They killed them. Right in front of me."

My throat tightened. "Your parents..."

"They're dead. I'm now the last living Bruckton."

I suppressed a gasp. The Skylord of House Bruckton, Kurt, was married to a Corlaean princess. It explained Kiera's unique features.

"I've never been to my mother's kingdom... East Corlaea. Now I never will," she said, her voice cracking on the last words. She hid her face in her hands. "I'm going to die here. Just like they did."

"No," I whispered, scooting closer and leaning against her. "I won't let that happen, Kiera."

She leaned on me and cried against my shoulder. I wrapped my arm around her, regretting how cold my metal glove was against her trembling skin.

Rynne reappeared in the doorway of my dressing room, wearing a light green frock. Her eyes fell upon Kiera, and her usual vapid expression faded away to reveal something more genuine.

*Grief.*

"Where is your family, Rynne?" I asked.

Her eyes shot up to mine. She looked like she wanted to say something, but the words wouldn't come out.

"If I say it out loud," she began, tears welling in her eyes. "It will be real. I'll have to face it." She brushed a strand of curly red hair away from her face, then came to sit on my other side. "I can't."

I nodded and wrapped my free arm over Rynne's shoulders.

"I suppose you understand," she whispered.

My father's face flashed through my mind. The gray hairs at his temples, the wrinkles at the corners of his eyes. The tears running down his cheeks as he coughed and drowned in his own blood.

"You know the saddest part of it all?" I asked. Rynne and Kiera both looked over at me. "I'm glad they died first. I'm glad they didn't have to see their beloved kingdom descend into chaos. Lost to an enemy." A tear ran down my cheek. "Or see their daughter like this," I finished, motioning to the dress I still wore. I couldn't bring myself to undress to change it.

"They're saying Arturian is dead. Our king," Rynne said, her voice breaking. I almost corrected her, but thought better of it. They didn't need to know. If they were questioned—or, winds forbid, *tortured*—the information could be devastating to Levick's mission in the north.

"Is it true what they said about you?" Kiera whispered. "That you have a windblade?"

I nodded, and a smile spread over her face. It looked dangerously close to hopeful.

"Who cares about that," Rynne scoffed. I shot her an incredulous glare, but she wasn't done speaking. "Are you the windwalker's lover?"

Kiera gasped and covered her mouth with her hands, giggling.

I rolled my eyes, but couldn't suppress the smile pulling at my lips. "Also… yes."

Rynne squealed in excitement. "Winds, Eliandre!" she hissed, her voice thankfully still a whisper. "Betrothed to the king, only to fall for the Caelator?"

Kiera sighed wistfully. "It's so romantic."

My thoughts strayed to Levick again, and my heart ached. I felt the ghost of his touch against my hands, my face, my waist. A flush crept over my neck.

"Did he take you flying?" Rynne asked, her eyes twinkling with excitement.

"He did. A few times."

Rynne suppressed another squeal of excitement. "Oh, how magical! Why won't a handsome windwalker kidnap *me*? Some girls have all the luck."

I couldn't help but laugh. "It wasn't very fun at first, you know. He broke our glass ceiling and it fell on me. My back got sliced up."

Kiera winced. "I hope he made it up to you."

Rynne snorted. "Oh, I'm sure he *more* than made up for—"

The door lock began clicking, and we flinched.

"No, no, no," Kiera hissed, huddling closer to me.

The door swung open to reveal the guard who'd delivered Rynne and Kiera to my room. He glared, his eyes boring through me.

"I told you to get ready," he grunted. "Stand."

My stomach dropped. I'd forgotten about the revel.

"I'm already dressed," I murmured as I rose to my feet.

The guard hummed in consideration.

"That's fine. Come with me." He presented a tattooed hand. "They stay."

I glanced behind me at Rynne and Kiera. Rynne had wrapped her arms around the younger girl protectively, and was running her fingers through the tangles in her hair. I shot her a grateful look.

"We'll be fine," Rynne whispered.

I nodded and walked towards the door, ignoring my captor's outstretched hand. His eyes darkened at the slight, but said nothing as he followed me out and shut the door behind us.

## *Chapter Seven*

# Dance or Duel

The braided guard led me down the dark halls of the Friesian palace. He said nothing as we walked, but morbid curiosity ate away at me. I had no idea what I was walking into. Trenicans had a reputation for wild revels that could last for days. I wanted nothing to do with them.

A shadow appeared around a corner ahead, and I froze. My escort grabbed my wrist and yanked me behind him, brandishing a knife.

"Who goes there?" he growled. "Show yourself."

A feminine chuckle reverberated off the walls. Yla emerged from the shadows. She was draped in blood red silk and her hair was freshly washed.

"*Truseva*, Lukyan. It's only me." Yla slunk up to us, eyes narrowed and scrutinizing.

"*Ess*," my guard hissed. Then, in beautifully poetic Vynesic, he described her as a snake coated in pungent perfumes.

I bit back a chuckle at Yla's expense. Apparently I wasn't the only one who noticed Yla's serpentine qualities.

"Careful. That one understands Vynesic," Yla said through a scowl.

Lukyan shot me a glance, his unusually dark eyes sharp.

"Let me see her," Yla said.

Lukyan moved aside. Yla's ruthless eyes scanned me from head to toe, narrowing in dissatisfaction.

"She looks disgusting. I need to fix this."

Lukyan's jaw twitched. "No, Yla. There is no time. His Excellency expects her."

She crossed her arms and raised indignant eyebrows at him. "Surely it is better to deliver an alluring woman late than a repulsive one immediately."

"The lady is not repulsive, and you are clearly provoking. Be gone." Lukyan placed a hand on my back and pushed me forward. I walked on, sparing no look for Yla as we passed her.

"He likes his meals clean. I won't be punished for this," she called after us.

I shivered at the word.

*Meal.*

Lukyan didn't respond to her as he firmly pushed me along, but the implication in her words sent fresh panic into my blood.

*He said he didn't need me in his bed. Surely he meant it. He has his pick of Friesian defectors.*

Nevertheless, my legs grew stiff. Ragged, panicked breaths escaped my mouth.

*Walk on, Eliandre. Don't falter now.*

My throat began to tighten.

*Think of Kiera. Think of Rynne. You have to be strong. For them.*

But my feet failed me. I tripped and fell to the floor.

*I can't do this. I can't.*

Lukyan's boots entered my field of vision, and I braced myself for the pain. I waited to be hauled up by my hair or kicked in my side.

Instead, a callused hand appeared beside my face.

"They prey on weakness. On despair."

I looked up at him, and my eyes widened. There was pity on his face. It was subtle, but undoubtedly there.

"Stand up, *Elucia*."

I furrowed my brow, not recognizing the Vynesic word. "What did you say?"

He sighed, thrusting his hand closer. "Stand up. The moment they see your tears, they will come for you. They want to bathe in them. To taste them."

*Who is this man? He speaks like a poet, not a simple guard.*

"The northern rose does not wilt during times of hardship. It holds fast."

I nodded, unsure of what to say. But I hesitantly slid my fingers over his and let him help me up from the floor. I nearly jumped when I felt his finger on my shoulder, sliding my strap back into place.

He shook his head at me like a disappointed governess, then resumed leading me down the hall. "Try not to let your clothes fall off. You may be able to get away with that among your Friesian men, but not among my countrymen."

The telltale sounds of a lively gathering floated through the hallways, filling me with dread. Bawdy laughter, violins, and singing. I'd never been so loath to hear sounds of celebration.

Lukyan said nothing more as we approached a set of open double doors. They led into one of the palace's smaller ballrooms, meant for more private entertaining. Inside I caught glimpses of candlelit dancing and drinking. Flashes of shining fabric and swinging legs made my stomach drop.

My guard stopped and turned to me. "His Excellency awaits you at the Throne of Indulgence. At the head of the merriment."

I searched his expression, trying to glean his meaning from the words.

*What is intended for me? Why have I been summoned?*

A muscle over Lukyan's lean jaw twitched, and my stomach twisted.

"Hold fast, rose." He pressed a firm hand to my back and pushed me into the room.

I stumbled into the small ballroom, tripping over someone's boots. I mumbled an apology, but he'd moved on already. Trenican soldiers swarmed the room, crimson uniforms unbuttoned and swords lying about. Dozens of candelabras were arranged through the room, casting their amber flickering light over the chaos. I kept my head down and weaved through the crowds, hoping no one would notice me.

"You wouldn't do it," someone shouted, his Vynesic words slurring together. Following closely was the sharp ring of a sword leaving its scabbard.

A girl screamed, but a chorus of masculine laughter responded. "What's a duel between comrades, sweetness?"

The crowd separated a bit, and the ordeal came into view. A young Trenican officer had shed his coat and wielded his sword at another officer, who laughed at him.

"Please, don't!" A young Friesian woman begged, her light brown hair falling in her face as she shook her head desperately.

"I won't lose," the officer said before rushing at his comrade. The duel commenced to loud cheering, and I used the distraction to sneak behind the crowds to the edge of the ballroom.

From the perimeter, I gleaned a clearer sense of the debauchery that took place in front of me. Most of the soldiers were accompanied by Friesian women. Some trembled beside their partners, wincing at every unwanted caress or flirt. But many of the women took an attitude more similar to Doressa Stokes.

A few horse-lengths away a copper-haired girl sat on the lap of a Trenican soldier. A gown of draping teal silk hung over her curvaceous body, flaunting Friese's usual standards of modesty. She ran her fingers through his white-blond hair and laughed at everything he said. Near the edge of the dueling commotion a black-haired Friesian woman grabbed a soldier by his coat and yanked him against her. Even with the fighting and shouting erupting around the room, the scandalous treachery went on unrestrained.

I averted my eyes, unable to stomach it any longer. The women had completely surrendered. Some were terrified but compliant, and others were simply seizing their opportunity to potentially wed a Skylord. Even if that Skylord was a murdering usurper.

*Can you blame them? What power do these women have to fight against this? Their fathers are dead and their windblades stolen.*

A dark pit of helplessness formed inside me, threatening to poison me with despondency.

My fingers traced the grooves of the pillar behind which I hid, feeling every notch and crack. The cool sensation of the ancient marble soothed my nerves.

"I summoned you to *me*, little gull. Not to this pillar."

My stomach flipped upside-down. I turned around and backed away from the voice, my back pressing against the pillar. But Maksim stepped closer, an amused smile playing at the edge of his mouth. He was dressed entirely in black, except for the silver crown atop his head. It rose and fell in harsh swoops of elaborate filigree, coming to ten spiraling points.

When my eyes drifted back to Maksim's face, a knowing satisfaction flashed in his eyes.

"Royalty is quite alluring, is it not?" he asked.

My lip curled up at the question. "A crown is nothing but a piece of metal if it is worn by a thief."

"Interesting words coming from a woman who was betrothed to Arturian Exley."

I bit down an impudent reply. "Why am I here? I thought I had three days to consider your *deal*."

"You do," he said. "But what kind of host would I be if I barred you from our celebrations?"

His words painted false chivalry, but I saw the true maliciousness in those pale blue eyes.

"I'd like to return to my room."

"Dance with me."

I tried to suppress it, but my shock was regrettably obvious on my features. "There are only two kinds of dancing that are taking place in this ballroom: the dance of dueling, and the sway of seduction."

His mouth stretched into a lascivious smile. "So sway with me."

"Doressa will sway with you. As for me, I would rather duel."

"I'm sure we can find a middle ground." He raised his hand above his head and snapped his fingers.

A booming voice erupted from the crowd.

*"Sol ves!"*

The commotion halted, and an unnerving stillness fell over the room.

Maksim spoke clearly, but never looked away from me. "Clear the floor."

The crowds immediately shuffled to the edge of the ballroom. I could almost feel the weight of their curious stares on me. My face. My body.

Maksim lifted a hand to me. "What shall it be? Dance or duel?"

"I can do neither with hands encased in metal." I lifted my hands, the metal pieces ringing against each other.

His eyes darkened. "Ah, you could sway, though."

"Duel it is, then."

To my shock, Maksim threw his head back and laughed. "I should expect no less from a woman with the blood of a dozen men on her hands."

Though he didn't mean to insult by the words, they tore through me all the same.

*Much more than a dozen, hateful prince.*

He reached between us, grabbing my hands. I made to step away, but he produced a key from his pocket and held it up.

"This room is filled with Friesians and Trenicans alike. Scores of innocents." He brought the key to each lock, inserted, then turned. My gloves broke free and fell to the floor.

I rubbed my knuckles and stretched my fingers. They ached, but instant relief flooded through me.

A split second later, a smooth hand slid over my upper arm. Maksim came closer until his mouth was beside my ear. I tried to back away but I was standing against a pillar, and there was nowhere to go. His crisp scent of spruce wafted over my face, suffocating me.

"If you harm me or any of my men," he began, his tone more reminiscent of a lover's whisper than a threat, "you doom your friends. I have half a dozen guards outside their door right now, waiting for any signal or commotion. You would never get there in time."

My skin prickled at his words. His closeness. He was as stiff and frigid as a pillar of ice. Immovable. Unreachable. I pushed against him, but he held firm.

"Don't be so hasty, little gull. You are young, beautiful, and unmarried in a palace full of northern men. Think carefully. I am their leader."

I glanced up, and every set of eyes was trained on us. Men staring in curiosity, and women glaring in unmasked jealousy.

He was right. I was a sheep in a palace full of wolves. But if the alpha had his teeth on my neck...

The others wouldn't dare touch me.

Maksim ran light fingers over my waist. "Do you understand?"

My mouth went dry. "Yes."

He pulled away, a contentedness in his light eyes. "Good."

I fought the revulsion threatening to spill over. I hated him so much. Every light brush of his skin. Every seductive look.

*Levick, forgive me. Please.*

I took his hand, and let the prince of treachery lead me in a waltz.

## *Chapter Eight*

# The Curse of Foolish Relatives

The crowd eventually joined us in the waltz, providing some buffer to the stares. The quartet played an unnerving tune, unlike any I'd ever heard in Friese. The tempo was consistent, but the key was off... unnatural. It paired well with the nightmare to which I was shackled.

"What now, demon?" I asked just before Maksim spun me out. "Shall you threaten me again?"

He chuckled, the sound grating on me like a nail dragging over slate. "Was I not thorough enough?"

I scowled as I collided with his chest. "Your proposition is untenable. I will not assist my enemies."

His hand returned to my bare waist, tightening over my skin. "Then perhaps we amend it?" he asked before dipping me low.

I gazed upon the detailed bosses on the ceiling and wondered how I never noticed them before. The glaring gargoyles, the dancing dragons.

Maksim pulled me into his arms again. "I want you to meet someone."

My brows knit together, but he spun me out again. Only this time, he let go.

I jerked my head around, looking for him, but ran head-first into someone else.

"Eliandre!"

The familiar voice made my heart drop.

There, holding my hand, was my cousin Louis. His dark, wavy hair looked as if it hadn't been washed in days. His pupils were dilated beyond reason.

"There you are, cousin! I'm so glad you're alive!" He laughed, unhinged and disturbed.

My eyes narrowed on him. "Louis, what's happened? Did you drink something?"

He scoffed at me. "You shouldn't worry about me. That's my job, as the leader of our House."

I raised my brows. "Louis..."

Before I could remind him that it was I who held the heritage windblade of House Yorke and not he, Louis pushed me away in a violent spin. I stumbled through the crowd of dancers only to land back in Maksim's arms.

"How was the family reunion?" he asked, softly tracing his fingers over the scars on my back.

"What did you give him?"

"Nothing he didn't take willingly." In his free hand, Maksim lifted a goblet in front of me. "Have some gin. Maybe it will open your mind."

*When did he get that?*

I pushed his hand away, but he insisted. "I have your last family member. I have your friends. The least you could do is have a sip of my drink."

I bit the edge of my tongue as I grappled with my options. He had every bit of leverage over me, and I had none.

"What's in it?" I asked.

"Gin. What else?"

"You tell me."

We stood silently for a long moment, two stone statues in the middle of a swaying crowd. I knew he wasn't going to tell me, and I knew I had no options. So I took the goblet and drank the smallest sip I could manage.

Pleasure exploded over my tongue. Stars and fire burned in my eyes, and I wondered why I had resisted.

*Dear Echna...*

Maksim smiled, his teeth gleaming in the candlelight. "Do you like it?"

"Do I..." I muttered.

Maksim thrust the goblet towards me again. Before I knew it, more of the liquid was running down my throat.

He finally withdrew the cup, then downed what was left.

"This isn't only gin, is it?" I asked, but my question was answered as the ballroom transformed in front of me.

The previously stable pillars began growing up from the floor, twisting and wrapping around themselves as they went.

Flowered vines burst from the tiles and started winding their way up the pillars, over the walls. Some of the vines even began climbing unsuspecting revelers, gracing them with crowns of flowers and leaves.

My mouth hung open as I scanned the mystical display.

"Don't tell me you've never had appertonic."

The voice pulled me from my distraction. Maksim still stood before me, but he'd changed. A loose shirt of crisp white hung open at the collar, exposing his fair chest. His platinum hair—which had previously sported traditional Trenican braids—was now woven with strands of gleaming silver.

He reached out for me, and I cocked my head. Something told me I should've been scared of him, but there was no logic in it.

*How could such a wondrous creature be dangerous?*

His thumb brushed my bottom lip, wiping something away. Then, to my shock, he lifted it to his mouth and ran his tongue over it.

I recoiled, gasping at the horrific sight in front of me. Maksim's tongue was black. And dripping with blood.

*Echna above, what is this? What's happening?*

My reaction seemed to amuse him, as a foul smile spread over his face. "What do you see, little gull?"

I tore my eyes away from the blood dripping down his chin, only to watch the ballroom transform yet again. The previously colorful vines had turned black. Glistening silver teeth erupted from each flower petal, snapping and biting at passersby.

"No, no, no," I whispered, rubbing my eyes.

A black mist appeared at our feet, rising and thickening with every passing second. Massive dark plumes rose at the center of the ballroom and began transforming in front of me. They took an animalistic shape, contorting and dissipating until they resembled a pair of hellish horses. They cantered through the air, snorting and rearing as they went.

"Come with me," Maksim muttered, once again looping his finger through the metal diamond shape at the center of my dress. I let him tug me away, lost inside the chaos of the revel.

"Where are you taking me?" I asked, but my words didn't sound right. They sounded empty. Dead.

"I'm going to show you why I summoned you here tonight."

There was no fight in my body. My thoughts screamed and cried, but they didn't make it to the surface. There was only the deadly enchantment he'd placed me under.

The crowds separated for us, and I couldn't help but notice how they reacted. The Trenican soldiers wore looks of smug satisfaction as they glanced back and forth between me and Maksim.

*So proud of their dear leader for capturing one of the enemies. For parading me through them, degraded and humiliated.*

The women glared, their gazes judging my every imperfection as their ravenous flower crowns snapped at me. Their whispered words infected the air I walked through.

*"Whore."*

*"Backstabber."*

*"Disgusting."*

Maksim reached back and slid a cold hand around my waist. His touch against my skin made me nauseous.

"It's a great irony, isn't it?" he asked, lingering beside my ear.

The glares intensified, darting to where his hand rested.

"You're making it worse," I hissed.

His only response was a wicked laugh.

The last of the crowd parted, and something in the distance caught the candlelight. It was a grand silver harp, sitting on the edge of the ballroom. I breathed a deep sigh of relief.

*Music. He only wants me to play music.*

The closer I got, the more detailed the harp became. My eyes widened as it evolved in front of me. The reflective silver dulled, replaced by the flat white of exposed bone. Smears of bright red blood ran in messy handprints over its frame.

Maksim pulled the stool from behind the harp, and my breathing stilled. It was affixed with a set of golden chains. All the calmness I'd mustered disappeared in an instant.

"But you took my gloves off!" I hissed.

He only smirked at me. "You can't play the harp with your fingers bound. But you can certainly play with your *hips* bound."

I panicked, backing towards the crowd. "I can't be chained again. I can't—"

Maksim closed the distance between us in determined steps. He reached for the diamond on my dress, but I swatted his hand away.

"No! I won't be locked up—"

Maksim reached up and grabbed my throat in his hand. His bloodshot eyes were deathly serious as he squeezed tighter, bringing black spots to my vision. His fingers were an inescapable snare.

"You will do as your viceroy commands."

He swung me around and threw me to the floor. I landed beside the harp in an undignified heap, burning pain shooting through my hip and elbow. When I looked up, Maksim was gazing down at me with feigned pity. But all I saw was a demon prince and his acolytes jeering at me. Enjoying my humiliation.

My hands shook underneath me. I wanted to kill them.

*I could do it. I could paint this room in blood.*

The smoky horses multiplied in the air, galloping in chaotic circles and whinnying.

*Why shouldn't I? Why shouldn't I bring this entire place down with me?*

I pushed myself from the floor, a new determination filling me. Maksim's eyes flashed, recognizing my resolve.

Hateful tears fell down my cheeks. For a delicious moment, I fully intended on clearing the room. On taking every last one of them down with me.

But Maksim glanced meaningfully at the guard beside the doors.

My throat tightened as I realized what I'd been about to do.

*Rynne. Kiera.*

My eyes caught on a handful of Friesian women standing together near a pillar, watching me timidly. If violence broke out, they'd surely be reduced to collateral damage.

The impossibility of my situation fell upon me in a crushing weight, and I sank back to the floor. Mocking laughter echoed off the marble walls, burning through my ears and into my soul.

Maksim's boots appeared beside me. He grabbed a fistful of my hair and yanked my head backwards.

"You belong to me."

A pair of guards dragged my shaking body onto the stool, but Maksim impatiently motioned them away. He came over and fell to a knee before me. The crowd whistled and clapped.

He slid the golden chains over my legs and waist with the gentle care of a groom removing his bride's garter. There was no urgency in his movements. If anything, he was intentionally drawing it out. Fresh tears pricked at my eyes, but I restrained myself. I couldn't wither and die in captivity. My friends needed me. Levick needed me.

*Hold fast.*

Spectating soldiers hollered and cheered when Maksim finally made it to the lock resting on my lap. He was about to fasten it shut, but looked up, fixing me with his detached gaze.

"Remember this moment," he said. "Remember who has bound you, Eliandre Yorke."

He snapped the lock into place.

## *Chapter Nine*

# Harrowing Harmonies

I don't remember which songs I played. They could've been anything. But whatever I played, it seemed to entertain the partygoers. They swung around in lustful dances, moving together in questionable rhythms. I tried not to look at them.

For all of my determined avoidance, I couldn't ignore Maksim's stripping gaze. He sat upon his Throne of Indulgence on the opposite side of the room, but no distance was far enough. A rotation of Friesian women entertained him, giggling and perching on his lap. But even as his hands explored their bodies, his eyes remained focused on me.

Bitter hatred coursed through my veins.

I don't know how long I played. Many partygoers came and went—retreating upstairs for rest or a dalliance—only to return a few hours later. Whenever I began to falter, a guard would grip my jaw and force more appertonic down my throat. The visions continued, growing increasingly macabre as the night wore on.

In one vision, I watched Levick float around the ballroom, waving and smiling as he went. It wasn't long before everything twisted, turning my love into a terrifying specter of death. Sometimes Francie Hanover appeared, cutting through enemies with her windsword and freeing innocents from their hateful grasps. That one always ended with Harley Ainsworth embracing her, only to then duel Arturian Exley to the death. Even Eadlin made an appearance once, but she did nothing but scream. Hers was the most unnerving of them all.

My fingers hurt. The calluses I'd formed during my time at the Exley estate were weakening. I'd never played for so long. But Maksim's guards made it clear that I had to keep playing. After a few hours, I started begging for reprieve. I didn't know how long it had been. Five hours? Ten?

A guard forced my jaw open and poured more appertonic-spiked gin down my throat. Not long after that, my fingers started bleeding.

"Eliandre, dear! It's time to practice your reading."

I ran down the staircase, almost tripping at the bottom. Mother's new plush rug slid under my feet, but I managed to recover in time. I turned a corner and came upon my mother sitting beside a burning hearth.

"I know you're tired from your music lessons, but reading is important for a growing six-year-old," she said through a soft smile. She patted the seat beside her, beckoning me over.

I giggled and rushed to her side, cuddling against her.

"'The snow fell…'" I began, doing my best to enunciate each word perfectly. "'On the…'"

After a few moments of silence, Mother cut in. "'Mountai n.'"

I scowled, hating that I needed help. "What are mountains like anyways, Mama?"

She brushed her fingers through my hair, snagging on the blonde tangles. "A mountain is where people go to breathe the purest air in the world. They jut into the sky like magnificent palaces of earth."

My curious eyes darted to her. "Are mountains taller than our palace?"

She smiled at me, the firelight bringing warmth to her cool complexion. "Yes, sweetheart."

I scooted away, fixing her with a serious stare. "Let's go to a mountain! I'll climb all the way to the top, and be taller than Prince Harley!"

Mother laughed and pulled me back onto her lap. "Maybe someday." She cradled me in her arms like I was an infant again, and bopped me on the nose. I was too young then to notice the melancholy in her next words.

"I miss them."

Tearing pain burned my throat, and I opened my eyes. I was in my palace bedroom. The drapes were open, but it was dark outside. A few dim candles bathed the room in a flickering glow. Despite its faintness, the light sent a throbbing pain through my head.

*How long has it been?*

I turned my head, and blessedly, there was a glass of water on the nightstand. My muscles ached as I turned over and pushed myself up. I reached out for the glass and brought it to my lips. I'd taken a few gulps before noticing the red covering my fingers. They peeked out of the familiar metal gloves, coated in dried blood.

I gasped, nearly dropping the glass. Upon inspection, several of my fingers were bleeding and cracked.

"Eliandre," someone whispered from behind me.

I flinched before reason reached me.

Rynne Wemberley sat up in the bed, just behind me. "Are you okay?" she asked, leaning over. Her eyes widened on my gory fingers. "Echna's breath, they're still bleeding!"

Kiera shot up from behind Rynne, tangly black hair standing in every direction. "Is Eliandre awake?" she whispered.

"I'm up." I slid out of bed, but wavered on my feet.

Rynne rushed to my aid, wrapping an arm around my shoulders. "I'm sorry, I tried to clean your fingers when that braided guard dropped you off. I thought they were done bleeding. What happened?"

"He had me play for them. The harp," I whispered as I slowly made my way to a small cabinet near the window. Rynne followed along, supporting my every step.

"For how long?" she asked.

"Long enough."

"Why?"

"Because they're vindictive animals," Kiera said, a frown pulling at her mauve lips.

I continued towards the cabinet, knowing that hopelessness would crush me if I paused for too long. The wooden door creaked softly as I opened it and peered inside. After scanning the shelves, I found a pitcher of water and a towel.

"Let me do that," Rynne whispered, taking the supplies from my shaking hands. She helped me sit on the floor, close to the brightest candle. My fingertips burned as she gently dabbed at them, wiping the blood away.

"I'm sorry," I said, my voice thick with restrained sobs. "I can't protect you. I can't protect us."

"Oh, Eliandre," Rynne said, shushing me. "That was never your responsibility."

*Yes, it was. It still is.*

I clenched my jaw, working hard to bite down the despair that threatened to break free.

*Is this all hopeless?*

A trembling tear slid down my cheek. There was no way Levick and the others would make it back in time. Rynne and Kiera might soon be married off, then subjected to unspeakable abuse.

*I've doomed these women. I cannot train my enemies.*

A ringing tapping sound came from the window, making me jump.

"What was that?" Kiera hissed, scrambling further back onto the bed.

Then, we heard it again. Three taps, a pause, then another tap. Rynne's arm tightened around me.

"It's probably a bird, right?" she whispered, her voice shaking.

I shook my head. "No."

We heard a third sequence of taps, just like the others.

*All of my enemies are in this palace.*

I rose to my feet, surprising Rynne.

"What are you doing?" she asked, grabbing at my dress.

But she was too late. I'd already made it to the window and pushed it open.

I looked out, and the breath rushed from my lungs. Just outside our window, crouching on a spire like a gargoyle, was Captain Coran Trust.

## *Chapter Ten*

# EMPOWERMENT

*How?*

Coran was dressed from head to toe in black, and scruffy stubble peppered his jaw. The look was so different from the clean-cut uniformed officer I'd known.

"Captain?" I whispered.

"Miss Yorke?" he breathed, leaning closer.

"How did you know I was here?"

"I was informed that you were removed from the dungeon, so I came to find you."

I blinked in confusion.

*Informed by who?*

We remained silent for a long moment as I tried to make sense of it all.

"Why don't you come in?" I whispered, offering my hand.

He winced at the blood on my fingertips, but gently took it and climbed through the window. As soon as he got inside, he dropped to a knee in front of me.

"Miss Yorke. I am so relieved to have found you." He spoke in the formal tone of a subject appealing to royalty.

My lips parted in surprise, and I glanced over at Rynne. She seemed just as confused as I was, her blue eyes dancing with intrigue.

"You don't have to do that, Captain. I'm not royalty," I said, reaching down for him.

He cocked his head at me, then glanced at the other women in the room. "You don't know what's happening?"

Kiera, Rynne, and I looked back and forth at each other.

I shook my head. "No, they tell us nothing."

"Your name is something of a battle cry. Many Friesians have been calling you *Princess of the South* because of your wartime heroism and your—" he hesitated for a brief moment, "association with the Caelator."

My brows must've risen into my hairline, but I chose not to argue it. "Who else is alive? What's going on out there?"

Coran rose from his knee and ran a hand through his jet black hair. "There's a coalition hidden in the south. Some surviving soldiers and members of the Red Legion. There's unrest—the populace hasn't taken kindly to foreign occupation. Maksim has tried to gain favor but it's going about as well as you'd expect."

The words did nothing for my confidence. "What are your plans?"

He stilled at my words, his bright blue eyes especially serious. "Well, the king," he began, his words quieting. "Have you heard the rumors? He died during the invasion."

I bit my lip and tried not to look anyone in the eye. Arturian was very much alive, but I'd kept that information from Rynne and Kiera. There had been no reason to reveal it when we had no real hope of resisting. But Coran was alive, and there was an organized resistance to Maksim's rule.

"He's alive," I whispered. "He escaped with Levick. Along with Francie, Eadlin, and Harley. But this knowledge can't get to the Trenicans." I gave Rynne and Kiera a meaningful look. "They'd torture you for information."

The women's mouths fell open in shock.

"He was on the ship?" Coran stepped backwards, falling to sit on the edge of the bed. "Thank the winds."

My heart ached for him. He was the captain of Arturian's guard, and had thought his own king was dead. He thought he'd failed.

"Then our plans are not in vain," he muttered.

I perked up. "Plans?"

Coran looked up at me in surprise, as if he'd forgotten I was there. He pursed his lips and took a deep breath.

"This information is very sensitive. It's the sort of knowledge that could get you killed." He looked back and forth between Rynne and Kiera. "It cannot be spread."

My friends nodded gravely.

"We have people on the inside. In the palace. They're going to help us steal something that could liberate Friese." He paused, pinching the bridge of his nose in his fingers. "It was going well until we hit a snag."

"What happened?" I asked, but Rynne spoke at the same time.

"Who are they? Your insiders?"

Coran gave Rynne a look of incredulity, but his stare softened after a few seconds. "I can't expose the identities of my insiders. I'm sorry." He turned to me. "They aren't close enough to Maksim. He doesn't trust them and won't share the location of his inventories."

My heart sank. "They can't try to get closer?"

He shook his head. "There's already some distrust there. Pushing it would only put them at risk."

My mind raced at the news. "What are you trying to steal, exactly?"

Coran looked up at me, his eyes hardening in warning. "You don't need to know, Miss Yorke."

I rushed over and knelt in front of him. He stiffened, visibly uncomfortable.

"You want someone on the inside, I'm right here!" I hissed, folding my hands together.

"No, I'm going to get you out of here—"

"Why? I'm exactly where you need me!" I pleaded.

I'd felt so hopeless since being captured. I had no goal except to survive and keep my friends alive. The prospect of doing something for the kingdom gave me hope. It dragged me out of the endless darkness I was trapped in.

"I could never ask you to get close to a man like Maksim," Coran said, shaking his head in disgust.

"You aren't asking me. I am insisting. You said I've been dubbed *Princess of the South.*" I rose to my feet. "This is my first command: tell me what you're looking for. Let me help."

Coran stared at me with such grief in his eyes that I knew he was already mourning me. Mourning what I'd have to do. But I'd worn him down, and he was clearly desperate.

He sighed. "It's a new elixir. But it's been concentrated. Dried into a powder."

Rynne came closer. "What does it do?"

"If inhaled..." he trailed off. I urged him on. "If inhaled, it causes severe hallucinations. Bad enough to drive a person mad for days. Our plan is to steal his entire stock of this powdered elixir and release them in the palace. If our sources are correct, they have enough to take everyone out of commission in one fell swoop. Maksim, all of his new Skylords..."

Kiera gasped and backed away, as if Coran himself was the poison.

"We would get you out first, obviously," he said through a grimace.

"I can do it," I said. "I'll figure out where it is."

The captain still looked deeply uncomfortable with the idea, but didn't fight it. "Even if you don't, the distraction you'd provide could be helpful." He cringed at his own words.

The smallest hint of a victorious smile twitched at my cheek. "It's settled, then. I'm staying."

Coran pursed his lips anxiously, but something sparked in his eyes.

*Hope.*

A hint of doubt tugged at the back of my mind, and I took a step closer to Coran. "You can still bring Rynne and Kiera back with you, right?"

Coran lifted his chin, and a muscle ticked in his jaw. The room fell deathly still.

"If any of you disappear from this room, that will raise red flags to Maksim and his guards," Coran said softly. "There would be no believable explanation."

Kiera's face fell. She shook her head and buried her face in her hands. "I know I don't have a home to go back to, but I'd rather be anywhere than here. I am so scared." Her voice cracked and sobs rocked her chest. Rynne went to her, climbing on the bed and wrapping an arm around her shoulders.

*She may be full grown, but fifteen is still a child in most ways.*

"Don't worry, Kiera," I said. "Their focus will be on me, not you."

*I'll make whatever deal I have to.*

From the corner of my eye I saw Rynne and Coran both bow their heads. Whether it was out of pity or respect, I didn't know.

## Chapter Eleven

# The Lesson Long Remembered

When Coran left, it was almost dawn. Rather than go back to sleep, Rynne, Kiera, and I fell into wistful conversation. I tried to keep my stories innocuous, but Kiera and Rynne consistently brought our discussions in much different directions.

Rynne interrogated me about my engagement to Arturian, yearning for every detail. She was predictably disappointed when there was very little to tell.

"I just don't understand why you didn't seize that opportunity," Rynne said as she gently pulled a brush through Kiera's hair. "Arturian Exley could've torn my bodice any day."

I shot her a pointed glare, then gestured to Kiera, who was blushing furiously. Rynne mouthed an apology but a giggle still escaped her mouth.

"That was never in the cards for us," I said, taking a sip of water.

"Why not?" Kiera asked.

I pondered her question, unsure about how much I should reveal to them. "He's very... closed off. Formal. Besides, his heart was spoken for before we even got engaged."

Rynne gasped and dropped the hair brush. "Excuse me?"

I cursed my loose tongue. "I shouldn't have said anything, it's not my business."

"Eliandre!" Rynne groaned. "You can't toss that information in my lap and refuse to elaborate!"

A rare smile graced Kiera's lips. "And here I thought Friese would have enough drama for a lifetime after Prince Harley returned from the dead with a wife."

I almost choked on a gulp of water. Their eyes both shot to me.

Rynne threw her hands up. "You know things about *that*, too? Echna's breath! Who is she? Who are these mystery women who are stealing away our most eligible Skylords?"

I didn't have the nerve to tell them it was the same woman. Francie had enough people trying to kill her. I wasn't going to add Rynne to the list.

"It really doesn't matter," I said through a cough.

Rynne rolled her eyes. "I guess you wouldn't care. Your lover can fly. What are windblades to *that*?"

A subtle but dreamy sigh came from Kiera's lips. "How magical."

An unexpected wave of melancholy fell over me.

*I might never see him again.*

“He really is,” I whispered, looking down at my empty water glass. “Magical.”

The room was quiet for a moment, except for the faint sounds of Rynne braiding Kiera's hair.

“Don’t lose hope.”

I looked up at Rynne, who was staring at me earnestly. Her deep eyes glistened with sincerity.

“Believe it, Eliandre. He'll come back for you. For all of us.” She cocked her head knowingly. “He's a windwalker. If that isn't a sign, I don’t know what is.”

I smiled and nodded, but couldn't shake the dejection poisoning my heart. Kiera and Rynne kept chatting, but I stayed quiet. I had nothing to say.

A few hours later, a banging erupted against our bedroom door. We all shot up from our chairs but the door was already opening, revealing a familiar Trenican guard in the doorway.

“Get dressed,” Lukyan said, his eyes showing none of the pity he’d displayed the other night. He lifted his arms, presenting a sleek gown the color of molten silver. “He requires your presence.”

Rynne placed a hand protectively on my shoulder. “Surely he can’t expect her to play the harp again?” she asked, glaring at Lukyan in an impressive display of indignation.

“No. He does not.”

"Then what does he need me for?" I asked as I took tentative steps closer. "I still have time."

*One more day.*

Lukyan handed me the dress and gave me a stern look. One that said, *stop asking questions. You'll find out.*

The silver dress was more modest than the white one I'd worn previously, but the style made me question whether that was a good thing. The back was tastefully low, not exposing too much skin. There was no slit over the thigh, and it showed none of my chest. The high neckline, however, consisted of a row of silver chains, fastening tightly around my neck like a collar. It squeezed my throat—a constant reminder of how Maksim had gripped my throat at his party.

The dress sent a clear message.

My light hair fell long and unbound to my waist. I was unwilling to do any more to my appearance than was required of me. I already felt like Maksim's doll—something to be dressed up and played with.

*You can do this. Get close. Find the powdered elixir. Free the kingdom.*

Lukyan said nothing as he led me out of my room. We walked past the library, the study, then the throne room. The palace was quiet and the halls were empty. It seemed that the partygoers had finally retired.

My stomach dropped as Lukyan turned to the staircase in the ballroom.

"Where are we going?" I asked.

Lukyan climbed the first step, but paused. "To his rooms."

I clenched my fists at my sides.

*How far are you willing to go, Eliandre? To save your friends? To save Friese?*

My escort turned around and offered his hand. When I hesitated, he tilted his head forward expectantly. Thick blond braids fell against his jaw as he waited for me.

"Do you know what kind of meeting this is?" I asked, my voice hardly a whisper.

He pushed his hand closer. "The kind that is not optional. I'd rather not drag you upstairs, but I will if I have to."

I scowled at him, but took his hand anyway. I could've run away with Coran and escaped into the night. But I stayed.

*Think of Friese. Think of your friends.*

*And try not to think of Levick.*

Lukyan escorted me into the Royal Chambers' sitting room, then left me alone with nothing but a subtle nod in my direction. I pursed my lips and perched myself upon a plush black velvet settee.

It was a grand room, larger than my father's chambers at the Yorke mansion. I shifted on the settee, uncomfortable upon noticing my surroundings. The chambers were decorated entirely in black and red, giving the room an air of sultry romance.

Streams of mid-morning sunlight flooded through the windows, covering me in their warm embrace. I closed my eyes and tried to find comfort in them.

*It isn't that sort of summoning. Wicked deeds are best done at night.*

The doors to Maksim's bedroom creaked, and my pulse jumped in anticipation. He stepped out and ran his fingers through his long hair. His eyes found mine immediately.

"Ah, good morning."

I said nothing as I fought against the mortified blush creeping up my neck. He was wearing nothing but trousers. I did my best to keep my stare locked firmly on his face, but the scars on his alabaster chest kept catching my eye.

He fell casually onto the couch across from me—uncomfortably close. "How did you sleep?"

"As well as you intended, I'm sure." I lifted my fingers, partially concealed by the metal gloves and peppered with spots of dried blood. They hadn't scabbed over yet.

A crooked smile pulled at his lips as he examined my hands. "A lesson hard taught is a lesson long remembered."

I did my best to sit up straight, breathe slowly, and keep an air of calm. But I could still feel his hands around my throat... ghosting over my thighs. Locking me in chains of gold. My neck ached from where he'd yanked my hair.

"Excellency!" a feminine voice called from his bedroom. "Come back to bed!"

A beautiful brunette stumbled from the bedroom, clad in a lazily-fastened red silk robe. Her heavy-lidded eyes hardened as soon as she saw me.

"Get dressed, Aurienne," Maksim said, not even turning to look at her. "You know the way out."

Color drained from the girl's face. The hate in her eyes might've made me flinch, but the violence of the last few months had changed me. Jealous glares were nothing to swords and windblades.

I could feel Maksim's measuring stare assess me, even as I looked back at Aurienne. She lingered in the doorway for a moment, then retreated inside.

My eyes remained on the closed doors, and silence fell over us for a long moment. After mentally gathering myself, I looked back at Maksim.

"Why am I here?"

His brows furrowed a bit, feigning a pout. "*Ess*. That's no way to speak to a man who's just rejected a turn in the sheets in favor of your tantalizing company."

I bit my tongue, forcing down the multitude of hateful comments threatening to break free.

*Get close, Eliandre. This is your chance.*

Using my years of formal etiquette training, I schooled my features into those of a content and compliant subject. "My apologies... Your Excellency." The words were acidic on my tongue.

A spark glinted in Maksim's eyes. "It seems your *lesson* wasn't wasted." He poured himself a glass of water from the decanter on the end table. "Do you know Princess Eadlin?"

The question caught me off guard. "I have met her, yes." She and I had become very close, but he was the last person to whom I'd reveal such information.

"She was to be my wife." He took a long gulp from his glass. "I've known her since she was seven and I, six."

I couldn't keep my head from tilting in confusion. His words were bitter, but he didn't seem the least bit lovesick. If anything, he seemed immune to it.

"But unfortunately the draw of the eldest son was too strong."

*Wait... Victas?*

I did the math in my head, but Maksim beat me to it.

"Nine years older, too. Isn't it funny how women are always drawn to power?" He scoffed. "And the fool was too stubborn or too blind to act on it."

I stayed silent, knowing any response to such a story could evoke his ire.

"All this to say," he started again, "I find myself with a conundrum. Would you like to hear it?"

I nodded. "Of course."

"Eadlin was my means of pacifying the Friesian populace. Her popularity and name alone would have helped quell much of the dissatisfaction among the loyalists. But as you know, she is gone. I am now in need of a unifying figure." He leaned forward in his seat, resting his elbows on his knees. "I've recently been made aware of some interesting rumors. Ones that claim you were the windwalker's lover. Adored among the southerners."

The blood drained from my face.

His mouth twitched in a satisfied grin. "I am going to name you as my advisor, and you will publicly accept it."

I blinked, not knowing what to say. Of anything I could've expected, *advisor* was the least of them.

*Wait.*

*He needs me.*

"No marriages for Rynne and Kiera. Take that off the table, and I'll consider it."

He flashed me an amused smile, then leaned back on the sofa. "I think you're getting ahead of yourself, little gull. Not just anyone is permitted to serve in the court of a Toresav. You must be tested, first."

"That's amusing, considering you've just admitted you need me. I'll take no tests."

"Make no mistake. I need you, but I am not desperate. The tests are not optional."

"Then my answer is no."

"Fine. Your friends' weddings are tomorrow, followed shortly by your cousin's execution."

I completely deflated.

"If you pass all three tests, your cousin will live, and I will bar any Trenicans from touching your friends. I will even extend that courtesy to you."

My unease must've shown on my face. Maksim lifted his chin, looking at me with knowing eyes. "I've already driven away half a dozen of your suitors. My soldiers are great in physical strength, but weak in self-control. They lurk these halls, searching for you."

*Dear, Echna. That's why Lukyan almost attacked Yla on our way to the revel.*

I ran over my options in my head, but they weren't good.

*Advisor. Isn't this what you're trying to do? Get closer to him?*

"These tests—what are they?" I asked.

He leveled a skeptical stare at me. "This is not a negotiation. You must choose. Accept, or let your friends face the consequences."

It wasn't a choice. I wouldn't sacrifice them, and Maksim knew it.

"I accept," I said through a tense jaw.

Maksim's face twisted in wicked delight. "Wonderful."

The bedroom doors creaked again. Aurienne slipped out, clad in what was clearly her dress from the previous night. She made her way out of the sitting room, glaring at me until she shut the doors behind her.

"Jealousy is such an ugly emotion, wouldn't you agree?" Maksim asked as he rose from his seat.

I followed suit, hoping our meeting was over. "Ugly, but entirely misplaced. My position is hardly enviable."

Maksim reached down and filled an empty glass with water, then presented it to me. "Don't speak too soon, Eliandre."

Something thrummed through my bones at the way he said my name. I smothered my unease and looked down at the glass in his hands. "Do you expect me to drink that?"

"I'm handing it to you, aren't I?"

I bit back a scoff. "No thank you. I'd rather not hallucinate for hours."

He stepped closer until he leaned over me. "It's water. Your skills are needed today."

My eyes narrowed on him, but I took the glass. "What do you mean?"

"Before your first test begins, you and your friends will be put to use in the palace. Miss Wemberley and Miss Bruckton will work in the kitchens."

I breathed a sigh of relief. "I think we could make ourselves useful there—"

"Not you. Only them. You will spend today instructing me and my men." He turned and walked to his bedroom doors. "Change and meet us in the fields behind the palace."

I pressed my eyes shut and internally groaned. "That wasn't a part of our agreement—"

"It is, now. Get out." He smirked. "Unless you'd like to show me any *other* skills."

Hatred burned through my veins, but I remained silent as I left.

*It doesn't matter. You'll find the powdered elixirs and stop them before they can use the training, anyway.*

## Chapter Twelve

# When Death is a Mercy

I followed Lukyan back to my bedroom, observing him closely for the first time. His back was straight and his shoulders rigid as he walked—a hallmark of military discipline. He seemed to be older than the other guards, most of whom looked my age. Most of the older Trenican men were Skylords. My brow furrowed at the peculiarity of it.

"Will you be joining the training?" I asked as he led me down the staircase into the ballroom. Morning sunlight glowed through the distant windows, casting light on the shaved side of Lukyan's head. I'd never seen such a strange hairstyle, least of all on a Trenican man.

"I will be present at the training, in case His Excellency steps out," he said, his voice coarse and gravelly.

I clenched my jaw, frustrated. "What I meant to ask was, will I be training you?"

He shot an annoyed look over his shoulder. "No. What you meant to ask was, *are you a Skylord*?"

"Fine," I panted, quickening my pace to keep up. "Are you a Skylord?"

"No. I am not."

He said nothing else, but curiosity picked at me.

"Why not?"

Lukyan suddenly turned left into a hallway, and I almost ran into his shoulder. I attempted to sidestep out of his way, but tripped on his heel.

*Echna above, why?*

I'd almost hit the floor when a pair of steady hands grabbed my upper arms, stabilizing me. Lukyan stared at me like I was his largest source of stress.

"*Ess*, are your feet backwards?" he hissed in Vynesic. "It's like you want to hurt yourself."

He righted me and looked me over. Once he was sure I had no new injuries, he promptly turned around and continued silently down the hall.

When we got back to my bedroom, Rynne and Kiera were already dressed in kitchen uniforms. They seemed nervous, but relieved they were only tasked with kitchen duties. We'd barely exchanged greetings before their guard beckoned them out.

Upon rummaging through the dressing room, I'd only managed to find a single pair of trousers. They were pure white and form-fitting. The color and style were far too eye-catching for my taste, but everything else in the dressing room was either nightgowns or sultry dresses. I slipped the trousers on and pulled a white long-sleeved blouse over my head, tucking it in.

*I might as well be a shining beacon.*

After weaving a hasty braid in my hair, I stepped out to meet Lukyan in the hallway.

My heart rate spiked. He was towering over a man I'd never seen before, and berating him in Vynesic. His words rolled together in a thick, continuous rumble. He spoke so quickly and with such growling affectation that I could hardly understand his gory threats.

Lukyan glanced over at me, but quickly turned back to face the stranger.

"She is off-limits. Get out," he said, punctuating it with a shove.

The man stumbled and fell backwards, his eyes wide and jaw agape. He stared at me, but Lukyan stepped between us, blocking his view.

With a menacing growl, my guard leaned forward and said, "I will dig your eyes out of your skull if you look at her again."

The man on the floor gathered his senses and ran away, tripping halfway down the hall.

Lukyan swore and shook his head. I considered making a comment, but thought better of it. He was hardly in a conversational mood. So instead I remained silent as he led me out of the palace.

The sunlight hit me as soon as we stepped through the grand doors leading to the courtyard. Friesian springtime was in full bloom. The distant rustle of wind against leaves harmonized with sparrow songs. The vast rolling hills were greener than I'd ever seen them.

I closed my eyes and lifted my face to the sun.

*You are not a prisoner here. You are a spy tasked with dismantling this horrific rule.*

A pair of white doves flew overhead, catching my eye. I'd never seen birds so beautiful.

*What would it be like to simply fly away from this place?*

I thought of Levick, and my heart ached. His time in the north could very well be indefinite. He could get lost, injured, or captured. A fresh wave of longing crashed over me, and I fought the overwhelming urge to simply run away and chase after him.

*No. Levick would want me to protect Rynne and Kiera. He'd want me to fight for our kingdom.*

A pained warble rang through the air, and one of the doves began falling from the sky. I took a few steps further into the courtyard, tracking the bird's fall.

*What is that?*

I squinted, only to see that the bird had lost part of his wing. I took off at a sprint towards the edge of the courtyard, my heart hammering in my chest.

*No, no, no.*

Lukyan swore and chased after me, but I was already descending the steps to the grass.

My slippered feet padded against the moist ground as I approached the fallen bird. He squirmed and cooed, trying to get back in the air, but one of his wings was partially missing. He flapped it desperately, sending flecks of blood flying around him. I fell to my knees.

"How?" I whispered under my breath.

I caught a glimpse of Lukyan from the corner of my eye, but he didn't get closer.

I shot him a glare. "Who did this?"

He said nothing but his eyes darted across the field, behind me.

A dozen Trenican generals were gathered together, a jarring blur of bright red against a green landscape, like a bloodstain. At their front stood Maksim, arms crossed and eyes boring into me. His mouth twitched in a challenging smile.

My blood boiled, and I felt Isolon's pure power surge through my sore, gloved fingertips.

Their crimson uniforms blurred with the red edging my vision, blinding me to anything except my unadulterated hate.

"Blackhearted animals," I hissed under my breath. I shot to my feet, preparing to lunge for them, but a firm hand gripped my shoulder.

"They are taunting you," Lukyan whispered. "You are unarmed, and all of those men are Skylords."

I spun around and tried to pry his hand away, but he grabbed my arms in an unshakeable grip. His dark blue eyes were hard and serious as death. "They will kill you, and they will kill your friends."

Against my better judgment, I looked over at Maksim. A blond braid fell against his cheek as he tilted his head at me. Malevolence sparked in his eyes.

Lukyan was right. They were taunting me.

I dropped to my knees beside the flailing bird. I ran a finger over its soft feathers, disregarding the fresh blood staining my skin.

Lukyan crouched beside me. "There is nothing to be done—"

He hadn't even finished his sentence before I snapped the bird's neck, ending its misery.

The training passed in a blur. We remained outside all day, breaking briefly for lunch. I showed each man a suitable throwing stance and technique, which they then practiced by throwing at wooden targets across the field. Almost all of my corrections were met with a suggestive comment, laugh, or scoff. The only person who seemed to take my instruction seriously was Maksim.

"Show me again," he commanded.

It was getting late, and the sun was sinking towards the tree line. But I straightened up and showed him a proper throwing form.

"How did you make it so broad? When you killed my men in the throne room?" he asked, his brows furrowed in frustration. His aim was poor, but to my dismay, it was improving. He seemed dead set on broadening his windblade like mine. The ramifications would be devastating.

"I don't make Isolon do that—it's always been that way."

He scowled at my answer. "Come here."

I hesitantly complied, and he reached for my hand. My skin prickled at his touch. He ran his icy fingers over mine, studying the bloody calluses as if they could reveal their secrets to him.

"You killed the bird," he said, still staring at my hand.

"It was a mercy." I tried not to picture it. "Was it you who harmed it?" I asked, almost hoping he wouldn't answer. I didn't need more reasons to hate him.

"Does it matter?"

"If it was you, then your aim is fine and you don't need my training." I tried to pull my hand away, but he held it tight.

"Then it wasn't me."

I looked up at him, and his cold eyes were set on mine. His light brows barely showed against his skin, but they were angled and sharp. There was a slight ridge on his nose, adding to his severe visage. For the first time, I noticed that Maksim might've been handsome if not for the perfidy he exuded so heavily.

*What made him like this? So hateful and scheming.*

Something flickering in his eyes sent a fresh chill up my spine. He loosened his grip, and I snatched my hand away.

A distant rumble mercifully redirected my attention, and I looked to the skies. Just over the distant treetops, dense clouds were forming in the east.

Maksim hummed softly. "The sea is giving us a gift. What perfect timing."

I glanced over at him, but he'd already begun walking towards the courtyard. "You're dismissed."

He paused on the stairs and turned around. "I forgot to mention—your braid is quite becoming. It's good to see you embracing your culture."

I recoiled at the words.

"Sleep well, little gull."

## *Chapter Thirteen*

# Spices

That night, Rynne, Kiera, and I sat beside our hearth. I tried not to think about Maksim's comment on my braid. On my *culture.*

*I am not one of them.*

My light hair and features were certainly rare in Friese, but not completely unheard of. My father had dark hair and typically Friesian features. I assumed I got my looks from my mother, who—while not as light as mine—had flaxen hair and blue eyes.

*She was Friesian. I am Friesian.*

I put the thoughts out of my mind and forced myself to eat some of my dinner. It was another night of poorly seasoned chicken stew, and I struggled to stomach it. I'd told Rynne and Kiera about my deal with Maksim and my upcoming tests, but omitted everything to do with their threatened nuptials.

*There's no need to scare them. I have it under control.*

Rynne poked around her bowl with a spoon. "Do you think bad taste runs in their blood? Or is this just another punishment?" she asked through a grimace.

"You're working in the kitchens," I said after swallowing a bland piece of chicken. "Can't you add something to it?"

Rynne shook her head "They don't let me near their precious stew."

Kiera groaned in disgust as she finished chewing her last spoonful. "There's no excuse for it," she grumbled. "If they needed decent seasonings, I'd have told them to check my mother's kitchen. She had them imported from Corlaea and treasured them so much that she arranged them in alphabetical order."

Rynne snorted a laugh.

"It was the strangest thing," Kiera continued. "She never cooked—we had a chef. But every month or so, she'd go down to the kitchen and make sure her spices were arranged alphabetically."

A fond smile grew over Kiera's features, and I thought she must be the human embodiment of sunlight. I'd not seen her truly smile before.

*Such a lovely smile, robbed by cruelty.*

Rynne burst into more laughter. "I'm sorry, Kiera, but your mother sounds like a lunatic."

I froze for a moment and glanced between them, worried Kiera would take offense. But her smile grew, and she started laughing as well. Even in spite of my despondency, I found myself chuckling along.

"I guess I can't talk though," Rynne said breathlessly. Her cheeks were flushed and her sapphire eyes alight. "My mother isn't mad, but she pushed me on any eligible man at every social event. I love her dearly but it was quite embarrassing."

My ears perked up at the tense in which she spoke. "Is your mother alive, Rynne?"

Her lip twitched. "As far as I know, yes." She set down her stew and began running her fingers over her flame-red curls. "My father, however, is not."

I bowed my head in respect, but wasn't surprised. He'd been a Skylord, and the Trenicans took nearly all of Friese's windblades.

"I know who killed him," Rynne said suddenly. "I know who has Aleria, our windblade."

Kiera and I both stared at her in shock. Kiera finally spoke up after the tension became unbearable. "Who?"

"Jori Volkov."

The name came out of Rynne's mouth so fast that I almost missed it. But I heard, and recognized it.

It must've showed on my face, as Rynne cocked her head at me. "You know the name?"

"He was one of the men I trained today," I said, recalling his face. He was smaller than most of the other generals, but that didn't mean very much. Height, strength, and relative youth were something they all had in common.

The mood in the room grew heavier, weighing us down. Gone was the lighthearted laughter and smiling. I knew Rynne probably wasn't judging me for training her father's murderer—she knew my cousin's life was being threatened. But the knowledge obviously still vexed her.

We resumed a tense sort of small talk after a few minutes, but it wasn't the same.

My bedroom was entirely too large. I decided so on my twelfth birthday after I spent the night alone, reading on my sofa. I had no friends. The other high-born children were always kind to me, but I saw them so rarely that no connections were ever formed between us. My parents kept me busy with music, studying, and etiquette. There was always something more important to do than being social. So another birthday came and went, and I spent it alone except for the company of my parents.

They loved me dearly. Even in my frustration, I could see that. They were very invested in my education, interests, and even my hobbies. Every Friday we spent the entire evening playing games together until our throats were sore from laughter and our bellies full of bread and cheese. They adored me, and I, them. But there were times when I felt like a caged animal, desperate for someone to walk by and smile.

It was on one of those suffocating nights that I overheard singing coming from downstairs.

*The ballroom, maybe?*

I slid out of bed and pulled a robe over my shoulders. Upon opening my door, the singing came more clearly. It was Mother, and it sounded like she was in the ballroom. I smiled to myself.

*Always caught up in your whimsy, Mother.*

I slipped out of my room and crept down the hallway to the staircase. Trilling laughter echoed through the mansion, broadening my smile. I'd made it down the stairs when I began to notice the lyrics of my mother's dreamy song.

*"Vor te vas, vor te vas, tolost es tia tu versey."*

I frowned, trying to place it. It was another language, but I couldn't tell which. Leaning around the open door frame, I watched my father twirl my mother in a circle. She wore a simple chiffon dress of dove gray, and Father wore a loose button-down shirt.

"I love this song," my father said as he swayed with her. She leaned her face against his chest, pausing her song.

"I just told you I love it, and you stop? How very wifely of you." I barely heard his last words, as he'd mumbled them into her blonde hair.

She pulled away to look into his eyes. Her own shone with an anxiety that set me on edge. "I think I'll do it. I'll teach her."

"I'm glad," Father said, running the pad of his thumb over Mother's cheek. "But what changed? You always swore you wouldn't teach her Vynesic."

"We share a continent," she said, shrugging. "And also..." she trailed off, her anxiety seeming to multiply. "My energy isn't what it used to be. This might be my last chance."

Father pulled her head back to his chest, pressing his dark stubbled chin against her hair. "Your energy will come back, Elspeth. I know it."

The dream dissolved into darkness, leaving me shaking and haunted. I had no time to ponder it before Coran appeared at our window again. We let him in, and I relayed all of my progress and the advisor agreement with Maksim. He listened with quiet consideration, asking very few questions.

"You're being careful, right?" he asked, then glanced over at Rynne and Kiera who sat together on the bed. "All of you?"

They nodded, and I mirrored them. "The first test is probably soon. After that, I'll have a better understanding of what the others will look like."

"What happens if you fail?" Kiera asked.

A cool breeze blew in from the window, and I pulled my silk robe tighter. "I don't know," I whispered. Amid all of Maksim's threats, I hadn't thought to ask.

"It won't matter," Rynne said, nodding to me. "She won't fail."

Coran said his goodbyes and snuck out, but the conversation haunted me until I fell asleep.

## *Chapter Fourteen*

# Now and in the Afterlife

Splitting.

Splitting, throbbing pain.

*Where am I?*

The last thing I remembered was falling asleep beside Rynne and Kiera. Working through my memories made my brain feel as if it might burst through my skull.

*What happened?*

Wind ripped at my skin, my dress. I shivered against it—I was still in my silk nightgown.

I fought against the heaviness in my eyelids and pushed them open. Lukyan was leaning over me, an empty blackness behind him. My senses roused from their slumber, and I realized he was carrying me. He had one arm under my legs and the other under my shoulders. He held me tightly against him as he walked.

A drowsy groan escaped my lips, and his eyes flickered to me.

"Good evening, Elucia."

*What does that even mean? Why do you keep calling me that?*

My lethargic mouth refused to form my questions.

"Your first test is upon us," he whispered. He didn't move his head or look down as he spoke, as if he didn't want to be seen looking at me. "We are almost there. I hope your pain eases soon."

A dulled panic hammered on the edge of my subconscious, but my exhaustion kept it buried.

I narrowed my drowsy eyes at Lukyan. "Where..." The word came out like a nonsensical moan.

His eyes briefly flashed to mine. "The tests. Their purpose is not what you think."

A fresh throbbing pounded through my head, and I shut my eyes.

*What did he give me?*

Deep rumbling echoed through the air. The storm was almost over us.

*Why are we outside? What kind of test is this?*

I was filled with fresh panic as the sounds and spray of sea water reached me. Lukyan hunched over and lowered me down into shallow, chilly water. An icy jolt shot through my system.

"What did you give me? What are—" I started, but my words were cut off as my back fell against a large rock.

Lukyan grabbed my hands and began wrapping thick cord around them, binding them flatly together.

"No," I begged, my voice a hoarse whisper through my ragged, panicked breathing. "Please."

He met my eyes for a brief moment, and I could've sworn there was pity in his gaze. But he quickly looked away and continued on his task, tenacious as ever.

Waves splashed around my body and soaked through my nightgown. Looking up, I could barely see the sea cliffs' dark silhouettes against the clouds. We were at the northern shore. My fatigue dissipated, replaced by burgeoning terror.

"What are you doing?" I asked, heaving myself onto my knees in the water.

Lukyan was behind the boulder, tying my rope to something on the ground.

"Lukyan," I croaked just before stumbling in the water.

He appeared in front of me, soaked hair plastered around his haunted face. With a forceful yank, he tugged me to the other side of the boulder until I could no longer see the beach.

"I wish I could bear this for you, Elucia. But you have an opportunity that is available to no one else."

My brows furrowed at his nonsensical words. "What do you mean? What are you doing?"

To my shock, he put a hand on my cheek and touched his forehead to mine. "Hold fast."

With that, he darted out from behind the boulder. I tried to follow, but something caught my hands. I yanked, but Lukyan had tied me to something.

*I'm trapped here.*

Lightning flashed in the clouds above, illuminating the shore. A confident silhouette grew closer. Maksim was walking into the shallows, towards me. His white-blond hair whipped and brushed against his face in the wind.

"What is this?" I cried out, my words lost to the wind. My bindings dug into my hands—Lukyan had tied them too tight. My fingers were already tingling.

Maksim's eyes shamelessly ran over me as he got closer. My white silk nightgown stuck to me like wet paper, and I cursed him for only supplying white sleep clothes.

"Moisture becomes you, little gull," he said, stopping in front of me. I glared at him.

"What kind of survival test is this?" I asked through chattering teeth. "This is an execution."

A crooked smile pulled at his serpentine lips. "This test is not about survival. It is about reasoning and interpretation."

I squinted through the sea spray. "What do you mean—"

He pressed his finger to my lips. "Shut your mouth and listen."

> *"It shapes and it forms. It's given for free. It's with you always, but remains mystery. Warm like the sun, you have only one. When all falls apart, to it you will run. You take it for granted, one day you will see. Its existence is dull. Its loss, agony."*

"A riddle?" My muddled mind tried to make sense of it, but I was still drowsy from whatever Lukyan had given me earlier.

Lighting flashed in the sky above us, briefly revealing Maksim's sinister grin. "If you can solve my mystery, you'll pass the test. Lukyan will unfasten you from the anchor and bring you back to me."

Terror gripped me, and I yanked at my bindings again. “I’m tied to an *anchor*?”

“Don’t fret, you're a good swimmer. Although this storm seems ravenous.” His eyes darkened, and he leaned closer. “Perhaps it will devour you before I will.”

He suddenly reached out, yanking me by the hair on the back of my head. I screamed and pulled away, but he’d already pressed cold glass to my lips and dumped its contents into my mouth.

“No,” I hissed through my coughing. I tried to spit out whatever he’d given me, but I’d already swallowed it.

Maksim slipped the vial back into his pocket. “This elixir is a unique blend. I don’t think I’ve ever tried it.” His voice dropped to a low whisper. “And I doubt I ever will.”

Then, he changed. His presence. His aura.

His pale skin glowed, even under the shrouded moonlight. Platinum strands brushed against his sharp jaw, and I wondered what it would feel like to run my finger over it.

A strong wave crashed into me from behind, and I stumbled directly into Maksim. He caught me in his arms, but didn’t release me. Instead, he ran his cold hands over my waist and tightened his grip. My senses lit up at the contact.

*No.*

*I hate him. I hate him. I hate him.*

Black tendrils of night twisted around my neck, tilting my face up to his. Ice and bones danced through Maksim’s dead eyes. He was so completely revolting. So insidious and empty. But my body melted into him anyway.

*I need him. Right now.*

He leaned in close and whispered in my ear. "A potent elixir, don't you think?"

He reeked of rot and decay, but my skin burned at how close he was. I wanted every inch of his cold skin against mine. Sense and reason abandoned me completely.

*Come closer. Touch me.*

I pressed myself against him and slid my bound hands over his shirt.

*Maksim...*

"I hope you find the answer, little gull," he murmured, his lips brushing my ear.

I clawed at his shirt. Pulling it up, untucking it. My hands moved frantically. Desperately.

"Because your death would be such a waste of a windblade."

He shoved me away, sending me falling into the tumultuous waves. The water crashed over me, enveloping me in its frigid embrace. But no amount of water could wash away my shame.

I sank deeper into the water, and wished to drown.

I was falling.

Slipping beneath the surface.

Lost in the bliss of the moment. The perfection.

Springtime Friesian austoria flowers covered the ends of every pew, and thousands of pink petals lay over the aisle. Magnificent stained glass windows illuminated the throne room in warm, coral light. Each of the three panes depicted stories of love and heartbreak in vivid color.

In the pane on the left was a beautiful woman with dark blonde hair, wearing a glistening golden gown. She danced in the arms of a shadow. He was nothing more than an ink blot in the shape of a man, holding her in hands of pure nothingness. I narrowed my eyes, trying to make sense of the mind-bending vision, but eventually gave up.

On the right side of the stained glass was a singular man, his face and body pieced together in a jarring dichotomy. One side of his body was clothed in a stiff uniform, highlighted in bright red and black. The other side was made up of smaller, vivid blue panes of glass. The red side of his face wore a pained grimace, while the blue side was at peace. The eye was closed, almost as if he were sleeping.

I finally directed my attention to the center of the stained glass, and my mouth fell open. A magnificent man hovered twenty feet above the rolling treetops. He held a fair woman in his arms, and they were locked in an amorous embrace. Nausea churned in my stomach as I studied it further. Her arms were coated in blood up to her elbows. She'd entwined her fingers in his hair, smearing blood through the light brown strands and over his cheeks.

"No second thoughts, I hope?"

I spun around and almost tripped. Eadlin Ainsworth stood behind me, a hand on her hip and a smirk on her face.

"Eadlin. What are you doing here?" I asked, though I had little grasp on where *here* was. I didn't even know *when* it was.

The breathtaking princess just laughed at me and brushed a strand of silky raven hair over her shoulder. "I know it's a long way, but I'd never miss this. You know that."

She took my hand and led me further into the room. To my surprise, the pews were entirely full. And every single person was standing up, looking at me. My stomach dropped, and I looked down.

Panels of shining white silk hugged my body. The dress bore no straps, and was structured with elaborate boning covered only by sheer, snug fabric. It then flowed from the waist, trailing behind me in a reflective, unblemished train.

*This is a wedding dress.*

I lifted my eyes to the vacant throne at the end of the aisle.

*I'm getting married.*

There, beside the throne, stood Levick Roale. My windwalker, my love. He wore a sage green suit with fine golden buttons, and a cravat the color of burlap. He'd even combed his hair aside, showcasing his boyishly handsome face. He smiled at me, and I thought I might cry.

He nodded softly, beckoning me forward.

"Are we walking or not, Eliandre?" Eadlin asked. "As fun as this is, undressing someone with your eyes is not *nearly* as fun as the other method."

A blush burned over my face, and I shot her a glare. She winked, and we began walking. Every step sent a new wave of blissful excitement over me.

Eadlin stopped me beside the throne and gave my hand to Levick. He took it in his own, staring deeply into my eyes.

"I can't wait to marry you, Eliandre Yorke," he whispered. "You are the greatest thing that's ever happened to me."

I fought the tears welling in my eyes. "I love you, Levick."

"Your smile is a beacon of perfection... your laughter is like the song of a sparrow." He smiled at me earnestly. "To hold your hand is to know companionship and tenderness. Each of your fingers were perfectly made to fit mine."

I was freely crying, but didn't care. I was marrying the most courageous and selfless man on the continent.

He continued, "I get lost in my imaginings of our future. Having children, going on adventures." His smile grew more serious. His next words were quiet—meant only for me. "Even just tonight. Knowing you so completely." My blush returned, but he wasn't finished. "Carrying you into our room. Kissing you, touching you. Tearing off your dress. Tearing off your *skin*."

My smile disappeared.

*Did he just say—*

"Devouring you, bit by bit. Taking each piece and dismantling it so completely that your closest friends wouldn't recognize what's left," Levick said, his earnest expression transforming into something hideous and wrong. I stepped backwards, but he held tightly to my hand.

"Levick, what are you doing?" I cried out. "Let me go!"

A sinister laugh escaped his lips, and my blood ran cold. His previously sun-kissed complexion began fading until it was pallid and white. His hair followed suit, turning white and growing down over his neck until it was past his shoulders. I tried to pull away again, but he held tighter and yanked me closer.

"I'll take you apart, Eliandre Yorke. I'll shatter you into perfect, razor-sharp shards." He slid a hand up my neck and forced me to meet his eyes. They shone a pale, milky blue. "Then, I will rearrange you exactly as you were meant to be."

Terror flooded my veins as Maksim leaned closer. Bloody saliva dripped from the corner of his mouth and ran in pink streams down his neck.

"Get away from me," I begged, feeling tears slide over my trembling cheeks. "Give him back. I want him back."

Maksim's smile grew. "There is no going back." He exhaled softly, his grip on the back of my neck tightening. "You will scream for me now, and in the afterlife."

His jaw stretched out, unhinging and expanding until it was the size of a shark's mouth. Terror clawed up my throat like bile. Rows of blood-stained teeth glistened and dripped foul-smelling liquid onto my dress, staining it. I screamed and thrashed against him, but his grip didn't budge. It was hopeless. I was powerless.

Maksim lunged forward and swallowed me whole.

## Chapter Fifteen

# The Answer

I heaved for air, my chest contorting in impotent spasms.

*I'm dead. He devoured me. It's over.*

But sensation flooded my body like the prick of a thousand needles.

My face broke free from the tumultuous waters, only to immediately be pelted by rain.

*Where am I? What's happening?*

I thrashed in the water, and my feet managed to find stability on the sandy seafloor. Something tugged at my hands, keeping me from drifting further out. Memories came back to me in flashes. Lukyan tying me to an anchor. Maksim's riddle, his poison. His breath on my neck as I leaned into him, desperate for his touch. Revulsion churned in my stomach.

His promises spoken with forked tongue replayed in my mind.

*"If you can solve my mystery, you'll pass the test. Lukyan will unfasten you from the anchor and bring you back to me."*

I had to solve the riddle to escape. The tide was rising and the storm was intensifying. Lightning flashed, revealing endless cresting whitecaps crashing against each other like a sea of brawlers in a portside pub. They pummeled against me, spraying water over my face and into my eyes. I could hardly see.

There was no way I'd solve the riddle while under constant assault from the waves. To make matters worse, the tide was rising. It wouldn't be long before I'd have to tread water. My muddled mind raced, searching for a reprieve.

A new bolt of lightning struck the cliffs, and my desperate eyes landed on the boulder nearby. My bindings tugged at me from that direction.

*The rock Lukyan sat me against.*

It was tall and jagged, but the tide was rising to it.

*I could reach it, now. I could climb it and escape these waters.*

My feet dug into the sand, pushing me towards the boulder. My bound hands were useless to keep me balanced and above water. The constant beating and swaying of the sea kept knocking me off my feet, sending me flailing until I could find my footing again.

All the while, horrific visions danced in my periphery, contorting into creatures of insidious death.

*It's the elixir muddying your mind. It's not real. Keep going.*

I was trembling and exhausted by the time I reached the boulder. My fingers scraped against it as I tried to hold on, but the powerful current kept pushing me away. I ran my hands over it and dug my fingers into any angled notch I could find. Barnacles and broken edges dug into my skin.

*Echna help me, please.*

Using every ounce of strength in my body, I heaved myself up and climbed. With my hands bound, I had to lurch up and find a new handhold with every step. When I was finally nearing the top, I reached both hands out and tried to grab onto the edge, but it was too rounded. My fingers slipped over slick rock, and I plummeted back into the water.

I was so tired. Between swimming and climbing, I hadn't stopped moving from the moment I was left in the sea. My legs trembled uncontrollably and my hands ached from overuse. For a brief moment, I considered simply giving in. Letting the sea take me to its depths, where I could forget about everything. The kingdom. The war. My friends. But I couldn't do it. Not when so many people counted on me. Not when I had a life to live... people to love.

So I scaled the boulder again, lungs burning and legs shaking. Wind whipped my hair around my face and rain streamed into my eyes, mixing with the tears. But I refused to stop. I was heaving my shaking body over the rock's top edge when I heard him.

"You shouldn't be out here."

I squinted against the darkness and the elements, only to see my father standing on the center of the boulder. He had his hands casually shoved in the pockets of his trousers, which were somehow completely dry despite the wind and rain. His entire body was dry and spotless, right down to the silver streaks of hair by his temples.

Though I knew that the elixir was responsible—that my father wasn't truly standing in the middle of a summer storm and scolding me—I still felt a pang of guilt at his words. As if I'd chosen to sit upon a rock in the Broad Sea as the tide rose around me.

"I can't do this anymore," I whispered.

*There was something I needed to figure out. Or solve?*

Pain pulsed into my forehead, and I bent down and pressed it against the cold rock.

Father strode over casually, as if he were walking through his study. "What is it? Perhaps I can help you."

I looked up at him, and grief threatened to send me back to the depths. He looked exactly as he had when he was alive, before he got sick. Thick brown brows sat over gray eyes, kind and compassionate as ever.

"You can't help me with this." I pressed my eyes closed and attempted to recall Maksim's riddle.

Father crouched beside me. *"It shapes and it forms, it's given for free..."*

I jerked my head up. "How do you know that?"

He gave me a knowing smile, then continued. *"It's with you always, but remains mystery. Warm like the sun—"*

"You have only one," I whispered along, remembering some of it.

*"When all falls apart, to it you will run. You take it for granted, one day you will see. Its existence is dull. Its loss, agony."* Father finished his recitation and backed away.

I groaned, clawing at the damp rock under me. "What does it mean? If it's so important, why would anyone take it for granted?"

"That is for you to decide. I'm only here to keep you safe."

The frustrations of my last few days reached a tipping point, and I exploded. "*Keep me safe*? That ship's sailed!"

If he was surprised by my outburst, it didn't show.

"All you ever tried to do was keep me safe! From scorn, from risk, from *people*. But all you did was isolate me! Then I finally got away from that—from the suffocating safety—only to be locked away again." My voice cracked. "I lived most of my life as a prisoner, and now I'll die as one."

From the corner of my eye, I watched my father shake his head. "You're not going to die here."

"On a rock in the sea or suffocated in Maksim's grip, what difference does it make?" I mumbled, bitterness filling me.

"Think of your mother, Eliandre. She wouldn't want you to give up."

"She's dead," I growled. "And so are you."

I knew he was right. Mother fought her sickness until the very end. She never gave up, and she would be ashamed of my behavior.

"You cloistered me from childhood. You kept me so distant from other people that you and Mother were my only attachments." I looked up at him, meeting his mournful gaze. "When I lost Mother... when I lost *you*, I had nothing else. No one else."

"Is that still true?" he asked.

I bit my cheek, hating how he still managed to rebuke me, even from the dead. "No. It's not."

"Then you must live. Don't take your friends for granted."

Fresh tears trickled from my eyes, warm against my cold cheeks.

I was about to curl onto my side when something in his words struck me. "Say that again."

Father cocked his head, sending a strand of gray hair over his ear. "Don't take your friends for granted."

My brows furrowed, and I fought against the elixir's slowing effects.

*"You take it for granted... one day you will see."*

I sat up, leaning back on my knees.

*"Its existence is dull, its loss agony."*

The answer came to me like a shout through the night. Unrestrained, victorious laughter tore from my throat.

*That's it. That's it.*

I heaved myself up to my feet. "I found it, Father—"

But he was gone. It was like he was never even there.

My lip twitched at his departure, but I turned to the shore. I could hardly see land through the sheets of torrential rain, but I lifted my hands and shouted.

"Lukyan!" I cried out. "I know it! I know the answer!"

There was no reply. I couldn't even see him on the beach. From what I could tell, it was completely empty.

Nevertheless, I shouted the answer repeatedly. I tried my best to wave my arms, but with them being bound, the movement almost sent me toppling into the sea yet again.

I screamed the riddle and its answer repeatedly until my throat was raw and hoarse. I doubted I was even making any noise anymore.

*Lukyan left. He abandoned me here.*

Slinking dread began creeping out of the steadfast vault in which I'd locked it. My throat tightened as I thought of Maksim's promise.

*He said Lukyan would save me if I got the answer right. What if it's wrong?*

I shook the thought away. The answer was correct. Of that, I was completely sure.

*Maybe this was simply an execution. He taunted me with a chance at survival, only to snatch it away.*

Hot tears burned in the corners of my eyes before being streaked away by rain.

*It's every bit as cruel as I know him to be.*

But the tide was rising, and I couldn't let him win. I'd solved his riddle. I'd deduced the answer.

*I am going to live.*

It wouldn't be long before the water covered the boulder I stood upon. Once that happened, I was as good as dead. I couldn't tread water in such conditions. Not for long. But my hands were bound flat against each other and tied to an anchor at the bottom of the sea.

The wind picked up, wrapping my hair around my face. The clouds above began to flicker with yellow light. I thought it was lightning, but it was too consistent.

*The elixir...*

The effects were worsening again.

Fist-size stars descended from the heavens and joined in the torrent, twisting around me. I could feel the heat radiating from them as they got closer.

*Focus. You have to live.*

I closed my eyes and recalled Francie's windblade lessons back at the Exley estate.

*"A windblade's power originates in the arms, channels in the palms, and is directed by the fingers. The position of your fingers determines the angle of your strike."*

An idea came to me, and my bound fingers danced against each other. But the stars wrapped tighter as they spun around me, and their heat burned my skin.

I screamed into the night. I screamed until I was breathless. The heat crawled up my body, spreading from my ribs, my shoulders, my neck.

My throat tightened as I realized what I had to do. My windblade was notoriously broad. If I failed...

But I was desperate. Anything would be better than burning alive by the stars. Or drowning in the Broad Sea.

I gritted my teeth and blocked out the searing of my skin. The melting of my bones.

*A windblade's power originates from the hand. From the palm.*

I gave my bindings one last tug, in case some miracle occurred and they simply slipped off. But they remained as tight as ever.

*Winds, save me. Echna, bless me. Or may my soul find rest in the breeze.*

I released Isolon from my palm, puncturing my left hand clean through.

There was a hole in my hand. Blood poured from my left palm, running down my arm and over my ruined silk nightgown. I fell to my knees as my mouth stretched open in silent gasps of agony. My voice was gone—I had nothing left. I clutched my mangled hand to my breast and wondered if it had been worth it. If I should've let myself drown. At least then I'd be spared of the excruciating pain.

*Why? Why did I tell them to leave without me?*

My palm had a bloody hole in it, but my bindings fell loose. Just as I'd hoped, Isolon had cut straight through my hand and into the rope around it. Though I held my injured hand stiffly against me, I stretched my right and relished in the freedom.

Waves began cresting the top of the rock on which I stood. The cold water ran over my feet and washed away the streams of blood flowing over them. I didn't have much time.

Searing agony tore at me. I tried to see the shore, but it was nothing but a vague, dark line through the rain. I hated the thought of jumping headfirst back into the waters that almost killed me, but if I didn't, my pain would have been for nothing.

After taking a deep, trembling breath, I leapt into the sea.

I'd forgotten how easy it was to swim when one's hands weren't tied together. I moved in quick, jerky bursts as my vision blurred at the edges and pain ate at my sanity.

*Is that the pain? Or the blood loss?*

I didn't know, but I completely disregarded it. My pain, my panic, my despair—I put everything out like a doused flame. There was nothing to do but swim and keep my head above the water.

A wind-muffled shout echoed in the distance, but not from the shore. I straightened in the water and scanned my immediate vicinity, but I couldn't see through the storm.

"Elucia!"

My heart almost stopped at the word.

*That word... where do I know it?*

I was tempted to swim towards the voice, in the hopes that whoever it was could help me. But a faint whisper in the back of my mind reminded me of the elixir I was fed.

*Don't trust it. It's not real.*

So I swam on, kicking harder than ever. My feet brushed the sandy seafloor, and my tears of pain almost transformed into tears of relief. The shore was in full view now, and no one was there. Not a single soul.

*An execution.*

I emerged from the Broad Sea like a shaking, horrifying specter—dressed in white and covered in blood. Raging winds threatened to knock me over, but my feet stomped through the wet sand with determination.

*I passed your test, bastard. Face me.*

"Stop!"

I swiveled around at the voice, only to see Lukyan's distant silhouette running out of the sea after me. At least, I assumed it was him. Rain trickled into my eyes, obscuring my vision.

*He's coming to finish the job. Maksim's backup plan.*

I turned back around and broke into a sprint. He called after me, but I ignored him and disappeared into the storm.

Old wooden planks dug splinters into my raw feet as I ran across a bridge. I was in the north side port sector, and had taken multiple side streets and back alleys to disguise my route. The streets were empty and silent, except for the elixir-induced jeering echoing through my ears. The voices laughed and mocked incessantly. I blocked them out like I had everything else.

The rest of my trek to the palace went by in a stupefied haze. My thoughts were vague and disjointed, but I never slowed. I knew it was only a matter of time before Lukyan caught up with me.

The palace came into view, and a fresh determination surged through my bones. Trenican gate guards stopped me, their faces paling as they noticed my condition.

"Do you need attention—" one started, but I cut him off.

"I'm going to His Excellency's quarters. He's expecting me."

*Likely, not.*

The guards exchanged a look but let me through, one of them following along.

He trailed me closely as I went in the doors, up the stairs and down the halls. My bare feet—scraped from rough stones—left bloody footprints on the freshly-waxed floors.

After a few hazy minutes, I made it to Maksim's rooms. To my surprise, the guard made no attempt to stop me as I burst through the sitting room, then through his bedchamber doors.

I shouted into the darkness. "*A mother*."

A lazy form rolled over in the exquisite red canopy bed. He mumbled some incomprehensible Vynesic words.

Finally, Maksim sat up and swung his legs over the side.

"The answer to your winds-forsaken riddle," I hissed through numb lips. "*It's warm like the sun, you have only one. When all falls apart, to it you will run*. The answer is *a mother*."

Commotion rang out behind me. I didn't turn around as Lukyan slid to a stop beside me, panting.

"Your Excellency," he said. "She—"

"She's in my bedroom, Lukyan. I can see that." Maksim threw back the covers and walked closer, examining me. Blessedly, he wore trousers.

"I can remove her," Lukyan said, clearly eager to repair his blunder.

Maksim's eyes were locked on my bloody hand, but he spoke to Lukyan. "No. Leave us."

Previously, the idea of being alone with Maksim in his bedchamber terrified me. But I'd just survived being poisoned, almost drowning, and puncturing my own hand with my windblade. There was no more room in my heart for fear.

Lukyan hesitated for a moment, and I could feel his eyes on me. But Maksim cleared his throat in annoyance, and his servant heeded him.

As soon as the doors were shut, Maksim closed the distance between us. He took my injured hand in his own and studied it. I didn't back up. I didn't pull away.

"Is this how you escaped your bindings?" he murmured, examining the wound. The bleeding had slowed, but I could feel the blood loss affecting me.

I ignored his question.

"The answer to the riddle," I whispered, my voice dying again. "Was I right?"

He hummed thoughtfully. Something shifted in his gaze as he stared at my hand. If I didn't know better, I'd have thought something softened in those hateful ice-blue eyes.

"Yes."

He dropped my hand and backed away.

"Bathe. You smell disgusting."

# Chapter Sixteen

# Aftermath

I emerged from Maksim's chambers and immediately collapsed in the hallway. My exhaustion, blood loss, and exposure finally caught up with me. I couldn't see clearly—all I registered was the nicks and dips in the floor under my fingers.

*All of that, just to faint in the hall?*

Muffled footsteps grew louder, and a pair of muscular arms scooped me up from the floor. I knew it was Lukyan despite my visual impairment. He was always there. Except when I needed him.

He cradled me close to his chest, his touch so tender for a man who'd left me to die. But I was frigidly cold, and the burning pain in my hand was returning. I leaned my cheek against him and let the reprieve of darkness envelop me.

I woke encased in blissful warmth. Memories rushed back to me. Seawater in my lungs, insatiable flames searing my skin, pain blooming in my hand. Despite being certain of the events' occurrence, I felt no residual pain. I tried to move, but my limbs refused to respond to my commands.

My eyelids were too enormously heavy to open, but muffled shouting reached my ears.

"Get out!" Rynne hissed. "I already told you, she wouldn't want you here!"

"Let me stay until she wakes up," Lukyan pleaded.

*Lukyan?*

My lethargic mind struggled to make sense of it.

Rynne voiced my own curiosity. "Why do you care? Aren't you the one who drugged her and snatched her from her bed?"

"*Ess, trusevya*," he swore softly.

I finally managed to force my eyelids open, but saw only a faint silhouette of a man. He stood a horse-length away, his posture tense and restless. After lifting my head, I realized I was in a bathtub sitting behind an opaque dressing partition. Rynne stood at the edge of the partition, an indignant hand on her hip.

"She's in the bath, for Echna's sake," Rynne said, making a shooing motion with her hands. "Did Maksim demand that you stay in here?"

Lukyan shook his head, less in denial and more in exasperation. "The numbing elixir will wear off soon. Please... find me when she wakes."

He left before Rynne could respond. She turned to look at me, and nearly leapt in surprise.

"You're awake!" She rushed to me but hesitated, looking back at the door.

"No," I croaked. "I don't want him here."

She nodded and came over, pulling a dark wooden chair beside the tub. "Strange that he even wanted to..." she trailed off, leveling an inquisitive look at me. "Do you know why?"

I swallowed, wincing at the sharp pain in my throat. "No."

An icy chill ran over my body. Despite the warm water, I shivered and crossed my hands over my chest. Pain shot through my left hand, and I yelped in alarm.

Rynne reached for me, gently taking my hand and pulling it away from the water. "You have to keep it dry."

In my lethargy, I hadn't noticed my left hand was covered in bandages and had been resting at the edge of the tub.

I nodded at Rynne. "You're right. Where is Kiera?" I asked, my voice barely audible. It seemed all the screams and saltwater had taken their toll.

"She's working. In the kitchens."

Anxiety flashed in her green eyes. Her fiery curls were piled atop her head in an uncharacteristically messy arrangement. Her fingers, formerly soft and manicured, bore burns and cuts along her knuckles.

*She's not been left unscathed, either.*

"Can I wash your hair?" she asked, her fingers twitching anxiously in her lap. "I don't want to invade your space, but your hair is..." she trailed off, cringing. "I'll just say this: I've never seen so much blood and seaweed in the same place."

I winced and reached up with my right hand, feeling the strands. My fingers ran over coarse grains of sand and multiple patches of slimy substances. My stomach churned, but I took a deep breath.

"Yes please, Rynne."

A relieved chuckle escaped her lips. "Good. Your hair is too beautiful to rot in sludge."

She slid over and began working her fingers into my hair. "What happened out there, anyway?"

I could've sunk into the water at the relaxing touch. She rubbed soap into my hair and began massaging my scalp.

"It was Maksim's first test. A riddle."

Rynne scoffed. "A *riddle*? You have a hole in your palm and countless cuts and bruises."

"I was left out in the storm."

Her fingers paused their movements.

"He had me tied to an anchor in the sea," I muttered, trembling as I recalled it.

She huffed but began scrubbing again. "All to be his *advisor*? Seems unreasonable."

I furrowed my brows as something came back to me. It was Lukyan... something he'd said just before dropping me in the water.

*"The tests. Their purpose is not what you think."*

I shook my head. "He enjoys it. Watching me suffer."

Rynne was quiet for a moment as she rinsed my hair out. Her fingers brushed my forehead, and she froze.

"Eliandre, how are you feeling?" she asked tentatively.

A new chill ran over me at her question. "Cold, I suppose."

She hummed softly and resumed her scrubbing. She said no more, but I could sense her anxiety. Instead of pondering the dread coiling in my stomach, I let my lethargy drag me blissfully back to sleep.

Consciousness visited me sporadically, like a fickle friend. One moment, I'd wake to scenes of incomparable bliss. The next, I'd watch in horror as everything was devoured by razor-toothed maws dripping bile and blood.

I don't know when I was moved or who dressed me. Everything was hot, burning me alive. The stars from the boulder in the sea returned, hovering over me in a silent taunt. Their inescapable light blinded my weary eyes. My sheets tangled around my legs, restricting my movement. Their texture was so rough and scratchy that I was sure they were leaving rashes over my skin.

"Why are you squirming around so much?"

I turned over, following the voice. A breathtaking man lay on his side next to me, his head propped on his hand. His mousy hair was perfectly mussed, like someone had just run their fingers through it.

"Levick," I whispered. My voice was a sad, strangled thing. "You came back for me."

His green eyes glinted in amusement. "What do you mean, El?" He slid closer and reached out, running his fingers over my sticky hair. "I never left. You know I'd never leave you."

My heart raced as he leaned over me. His lips brushed the skin under my ear. "Remember what you promised me?"

I shook my head, unable to remember *anything* while he was so close.

But he moved over and climbed on top of me. His breath was hot against my ear. "You promised that we'd never split up. That we'd stay together." The words came out bitter and hateful.

I tried to move, but couldn't. I was paralyzed under him. With every passing second his skin grew hotter and heavier.

"Levick, get off of me," I said, but my words were nothing but a faint echo.

He began glowing bright yellow like the sun. My skin burned everywhere we touched. He was turning into one of *them*. The killing stars.

"You broke your promise. It's your fault," he growled.

I opened my mouth to scream, but heat flooded into it, burning my tongue.

His face twisted in contempt. "How am I supposed to look at you?"

Then, he combusted.

## *Chapter Seventeen*

# The Insider

"Miss Yorke!" someone shouted.

There was something cold on my forehead.

*No, not only there.*

Ice-cold wetness covered me from head to toe. My hand ached, and a groan escaped my dry lips.

"Please, Eliandre. Wake up."

Something flinched in my mind.

I forced my eyes open. Coran Trust stood beside my bed, leaning close. His dark hair was unkempt, and his shirt was open at the collar, as if he'd been tugging at it anxiously. Rynne was beside him, a cautious hand resting on his shoulder. They both looked exhausted. Behind them stood Kiera, who looked like she wanted to come closer but was frozen in trepidation.

"How do you feel?" Rynne asked.

A metal glove had been returned to my right hand, and it pinched my skin as I tried to scoot up. My left hand remained unshackled, but thoroughly unusable.

"Let me help."

I jerked around at the familiar voice, sending a dizzy ache through my head.

Lukyan appeared by my head, imposing and severe as ever, and slid his hands around my shoulders. I winced and stared at him in shock, but he still lifted me up and rested me gently against my pillows. My stare darted from him to Coran, then back again.

My eyes scanned all four of them, waiting for an explanation as to why Maksim's favored guard was in the same room as a Friesian soldier. "Coran, what's going on?"

Rynne took my hand, distracting me. "You've been sick for a while, Eliandre. Three weeks."

An anxious pit opened in my gut.

*Three weeks?*

"Your hand was infected," Kiera chimed in from across the room. "We were scared. There was a time when we thought you wouldn't recover." She whispered the last words as she nervously fidgeted with her dress.

I looked back to Coran. "How does that explain this?" I gestured weakly to Lukyan.

Coran glanced over at him, then back to me. "Remember when I told you about my sources on the inside?"

My thoughts swam through my mind, fighting to break the surface. They hardly managed to tread water. The words couldn't be true.

"You're working together?"

Lukyan nodded softly, his heavy blond braids sliding over his shirt as he moved.

"Well, not exactly," Coran said. "Lukyan has connections with someone in Trenica. Someone who doesn't want their kingdom spread between two places. Technically, I am working for him."

I looked to Rynne, as if she could provide more context or explanation. She simply nodded at me, looking between me and Lukyan.

Finally, the truth fully sunk in. He was supposed to be my ally.

Furious anger shot through my heart. I spun around to Lukyan, pinning him with the most hateful look I could muster.

"You left me out there!" My strained voice cracked. "You were on my side, and you *left me out there to die*!"

To my surprise, deep regret shone in Lukyan's ocean eyes. "I tried. When the storm picked up, I looked for you. But you were gone."

I let out a disbelieving scoff. "You are the one who tied me up and left me in a hurricane."

Coran cut in. "To go against Maksim's orders and show you favor would've given him away. Maksim already suspects treachery among his generals."

"And he has an unusual... fixation on you," Lukyan said through a tense jaw. "I'm the only man he allows near you, and it's out of necessity."

My lip curled up at the insinuation. "Wait. You think Maksim—"

"He's obsessed with you," Rynne said.

I almost laughed. "He's ridiculed, tortured, and poisoned me."

"Have you heard of the northern frost tiger?" Lukyan asked abruptly.

I met his deep blue stare, confused. "I suppose I knew there are tigers up there—"

He interrupted me. "Once a frost tiger scents his prey, he'll paw, bite and chase until his victim is too exhausted or injured to fight back. But instead of taking advantage and finishing the job, the frost tiger releases his quarry to recover until it's well again. Only to attack again and repeat the cycle."

Kiera made a sound of discomfort. "Wouldn't it just be hungry forever? When does it stop?"

Lukyan was quiet for a long moment, not looking away from me. He opened his mouth, as if he wanted to say something, but hesitated.

"It stops when its prey is hopeless. When the spirit is broken," he finally whispered.

After an unnerving moment of silence, Rynne spoke up. "I'll never visit your homeland, Lukyan. I thought only your men were insatiable savages. It seems the animals are, too."

Despite the insult, Lukyan gave no defense.

Coran leaned closer to me, a look of tender concern in his vivid blue eyes. "How is your hand?"

I tried to flex my left hand, but winced when I was met with a jolt of pain surging through my fingers. I shook my head at him.

Kiera made a sound of disappointment from across the room. "You can't throw your windblade with it?"

"I can't throw my windblade at all," I grumbled, pushing further up onto the pillows. Lukyan moved to help me but I waved him off. "The only reason I'm doing these awful tests is to gain his trust. To find that store of powdered elixirs and use it against them. To use my windblade would be to sabotage my progress, and make all of this," I motioned to my bandages, "for nothing. I'm committed. I'll finish the tests and find his elixir stores."

Coran nodded in appreciation.

Rynne raised a thoughtful eyebrow, but it morphed into a cringe.

I shot her an imploring look. "What?"

She sighed deeply. "There is a quicker way to get closer to Maksim. Have you considered it?"

Kiera picked up on it before anyone else, and turned away in disgust. Coran and Lukyan figured it out a split second later.

Lukyan's hand shot for me. He gripped my arm gently, as if the contact brought him comfort. "No," he breathed.

I gave him a confused look, but he didn't move his hand.

Coran turned on Rynne in shock. "Absolutely not!"

"It wouldn't work. Even if I could stomach it," I said, shaking my head.

*Definitely couldn't.*

But the memory of our interaction in the sea came to my mind. When he'd given me that awful combination of elixirs. In those brief minutes, I'd wanted him more than anything else in the world. I would've let him rip my dress off right there in the sea, a storm raging over us. The memory surged into the forefront of my mind, and I had to swallow the bile rising in my throat.

"Sleeping with Maksim wouldn't get me anywhere. He has women rotating through his bedsheets constantly, and I guarantee he doesn't trust them any more than he trusts me. Disgust aside, it's a bad idea. Besides," I said, looking away from their intense stares. "I already love someone. I'd sooner die than have someone else." I fidgeted with the bandage on my left hand.

Coran gave me a knowing look. "I'm sure the Caelator is fine."

I nodded, but anxiety still ate at me. If I'd been sick in bed for three weeks, that meant Levick had been gone for almost two months. Though I worried for my friends, I knew we couldn't wait around for them to return and free us.

"Will you show me around the palace?" I asked Lukyan, who'd been staring at my injured hand. "We should begin our search for the elixirs. The sooner we find them, the sooner we can get out of here."

He pressed his lips into a thin line. "I've already searched most of the palace. As for the places I've not searched—Maksim keeps them private. Though I am close with the Toresavs, the youngest prince is very cautious about who he allows into his confidence."

I suppressed a frustrated sigh. If Maksim was our only lead to his elixir's location, my only tenable course of action was to earn his trust. Crates of powdered hallucinogens were too dangerous to be left in the hands of a man like Maksim. He'd use them against Levick as soon as he returned from the north.

*But if we could use the elixirs against Maksim and his Skylords...*

I straightened up and faced Lukyan, filled with a fresh urgency. "When is my next test?"

He worked his jaw and leaned back in his chair. "Soon. Maksim is eager to push you through the last two tests quickly. There have been multiple uprisings in the south and he's feeling the pressure to announce his uniting figure," he finished, motioning to me.

Coran rubbed his eyes. "*Uprisings*." He huffed a disbelieving chuckle. "It's a bloodbath down there. We retook the Exley mansion a few days ago. The war isn't over."

My eyes darted to him. "You're holding the mansion? Even against Maksim's Skylords?"

"Before he left, the king taught the Red Legion strategies to injure and resist Skylords. We've not managed to kill any of them yet, but I'm hoping it will happen soon. Maksim's numbers are overwhelming and it's an uphill battle, but I have hope that we will hold the mansion until the king returns."

The news sent my head spinning.

"All that aside," Coran said, redirecting his attention to Lukyan. "If Maksim is so desperate for a *uniting advisor* figure, why not announce it now? Why put her through these tests? It seems unnecessary."

Lukyan hummed thoughtfully, then took a deep breath. "In some small Trenican subcultures, the tests are... significant. Some men see them as an invaluable measure of worthiness."

Rynne laughed and brushed a stray curl behind her ear. "Quite an assessment for the meager role of *symbolic advisor*."

"Do you know what it is?" I asked Lukyan. "The next test?"

He shook his head. "I am sorry, but no."

I deflated.

He stood suddenly, stretching his joints. "You should leave, Captain. I have to inform Maksim that she's woken up. He asks about her often. If I delay, he'll find out."

I stifled a groan. I was far from ready for another challenge. My body ached from being bedridden for so long, and I couldn't fully move my injured hand. Though the infection had subsided, it was a complete puncture through my palm. Barring a miracle, my hand would never be the same.

*I might never play the harp again.*

Grief weighed heavily on my chest.

Rynne shot to her feet and took a step towards Lukyan. "Can you delay the next test? Give her some time to recuperate before it starts?"

His stoic gaze returned to me, lingering. There was undeniable concern in his eyes.

*Hopefully feeling guilty for tying me up and stranding me in the sea.*

He looked back to Rynne and gave her a subtle nod. "I will do my best, but I make no guarantees. He'd find it suspicious if I seemed worried for her."

Nevertheless, she thanked him before he slipped out into the hallway.

Coran left soon after. He placed a quick kiss on Rynne's hand just before climbing out the window. I noticed the pink flush creeping up her neck, but said nothing.

I spent the next four days relearning how to move. Rynne and Kiera would support my arms as I paced around the room, calibrating my balance. The process was incredibly frustrating.

I'd grown weaker since my capture. The regular training and exercise afforded to me at the Exley estate had turned me into an athlete, but it was fading away. Rising from a kneel made my thighs burn, and standing too fast blackened my vision. I missed the days I could sprint for a quarter mile without slowing. When I'd fly through the air on Levick's wind gusts, somersaulting and twisting under the sun. But I was back to a life of stifling walls and idleness.

*It's temporary. Hold fast.*

Just when I began to hope they'd forgotten about my unshackled left hand, an unknown guard came by and encased it once again in the cursed metal glove. I doubted I'd be able to throw my windblade because of my injury, but the returning confinement was still discouraging.

Maksim never came to visit me. The relief of his absence was almost as palpable as my concern for Lukyan's. He hadn't been to my room since our meeting with Coran. Other guards had come to bring Rynne and Kiera to and from their kitchen duties, but never gave an explanation for the change.

"They'll be here any minute," Rynne said as she slid her stockings up her legs. "I just hope they didn't work Kiera as hard as they did yesterday. She's strong for her age, but I can see it in her eyes. She's one impassioned scolding away from a broken spirit."

I nodded my agreement. Kiera had been assigned the morning shifts in the kitchen, which were very work intensive. She returned every afternoon with new burns on her fingers and arms.

"I'll make sure she's okay," I said as I helped Rynne with her dress.

A heavy knock sounded on the door. I rushed to answer it but it swung open before I got there. Rynne huffed in offense but kept her complaints to herself.

A heavy-set guard walked in, entitled as a nobleman. He was new. "Let's go, wench," he rumbled at Rynne.

I watched her jaw tick as she bit her cheek. She nodded and followed him to the door. He turned to follow her, but I called out for him.

The guard jerked his head around and gave me an annoyed stare.

"The guards," I started, taking a tentative step closer. "Why do they keep getting reassigned?"

The burly guard narrowed his eyes at me. "What's it matter to you?"

I immediately regretted asking. "Nothing. It doesn't matter."

He scoffed and led Rynne out, slamming the door behind him.

Kiera was late. I waited in our room, pacing and fidgeting with my hair.

*They've usually brought her back by now, right after Rynne leaves.*

Worry ate at me.

*What if she made a mistake they deemed unforgivable? What if they have her locked away somewhere?*

My overactive imagination kept showing me all of the different ways she could be trapped, suffering, and hurting.

To busy myself, I changed from sleep clothes for the first time in weeks. But upon entering my dressing room and opening my wardrobe, I noticed my clothes had been moved. My preferred dresses were all missing, replaced by gowns of varying indecency. One looked as if it was made of nothing but interwoven red silk ribbons, and the one beside it was little more than a set of black undergarments with strips of black tulle flowing from the waist. My stomach turned.

*The maids came in here while I was sick... to curate my wardrobe.*

One of the dresses was significantly more modest than the others, but I bristled at the idea of wearing it again. It was the white silk gown made of two pieces, connecting over the navel with a golden diamond shape.

I groaned, but took it out and put it on. The alternatives were not an option.

As I ran my brush through my hair, snagging on the numerous tangles, a whisper of an idea came to me. I eyed the door handle. They always locked the door when they left. Without exception.

*Did I hear it click, though?*

I rose from my seat and walked to the door, my steps soft and light.

*Doesn't hurt to try.*

My hand slid over the cold, silver handle.

*They'll see it turn from the other side. If someone is standing guard out there...*

I would be punished. But the thought of Kiera being held somewhere, suffering for something trivial, was too distressing.

I abandoned caution and pulled the handle down. To my great surprise, the mechanism clicked. My lips parted, and the breath left my lungs. The guard had forgotten to lock the door.

My mind raced at the opportunity in front of me. I didn't know my way around the palace, but I knew Friesian architecture well enough to figure out where the kitchens were. But to do it unnoticed? I was one of the very few blonde women in the palace. I'd be spotted immediately.

My eyes darted around my room, landing on a light lavender sash hanging over the canopy bed.

*That could work.*

I raced over and leapt on the bed. The sash easily came loose from the canopy frame, falling to the floor in a dusty heap. After shaking it out, I sat in front of my vanity and wrapped it around my head and hair, letting the excess fall over the floor. It would seem like a daring fashion statement, but my hair color was completely hidden.

Just as I was rising to my feet, my eyes caught on the glaringly obvious metal gloves encasing my palms. I gritted my teeth in frustration.

*I have to cover these.*

I rushed to the dressing room and rummaged through drawers, my fingertips brushing against soft silk and dreamy chiffon until finally landing on a pair of thick, velvet gloves. They were a deep amethyst color, perfect for hiding undesired shapes and textures underneath. I slipped them over my metal gloves and tugged until they reached my elbows. If someone looked closely, they would notice that the fabric didn't slide all the way down to my knuckles, leaving me with what appeared to be webbed fingers. I'd have to be fast and unremarkable.

If I was questioned, I'd pretend to be one of the many Friesian women warming the beds of the Trenican generals. The lie was equally as undesirable as it was unavoidable.

*You can do this, Eliandre. Think of Kiera.*

I took a deep breath, then slipped out the bedroom that had been my prison for a month.

# Chapter Eighteen

# An Impulsive Absconding

It was late in the afternoon and the palace was bustling with activity. It wouldn't be long before the soldiers and generals gathered together for one of their nightly revels.

The finely waxed floors of the upstairs hallway chilled my slippered feet. Exquisite paintings lined the walls. The palace was so inundated with priceless art that many pieces were relegated to hanging in hallways where viewing them properly was nearly impossible.

The Ainsworths had fallen into excess in the last ten years of Lesynna's reign. She constantly engaged in political games with the other High Skylords, calling in debts and spending lavishly to assert herself. Prince Harley was notorious for throwing wild, debaucherous court parties where no attendee was left untouched by lover or drink. I had to acknowledge that even Princess Eadlin, someone who'd become a close friend of mine, was not immune to the siren song of expensive fabrics and imported perfumes. Their lifestyle showed in the decor and ambiance of the Friesian palace. Though much of their finery was burned after Arturian took the throne, the art was mercifully spared.

The hallway grew brighter, illuminated by the afternoon sun shining in the ballroom windows downstairs. I was getting close to the central area of the palace. I made sure my sash was still secured around my hair, then turned out of the hallway.

I let my velvet gloved fingers glide down the staircase's marble railing as I descended, observing the groups of people moving to and from other areas in the palace. Most were soldiers removing their gear and making their way down the eastern hall. I wondered if that was where their armory was.

A few men looked in my direction as they passed me on their way up the staircase. Thankfully, with the sultry dress I wore, their eyes never lingered on my face. A few of them made half-serious propositions for me to join them and help ease their stress. I giggled appropriately and kindly declined.

Part of me briefly considered attempting to search for Maksim's powdered elixir, but we still had no leads on its location. The palace was enormous—without a chaperone, I'd get caught before I even got close.

*That can wait. Kiera needs you now.*

I weaved through soldiers and fawning Friesian women, padding through the downstairs hallways. A narrow corridor branched off of the wide hall. I glanced around to make sure no one was watching, then ducked down the corridor.

My instincts were right. It was a servant's hall. I prayed it would lead to the kitchen, and that I was close. Just before following a tight bend to the left, something rammed into me, slamming me into the wall.

I opened my mouth to scream, but a large hand was already over it, silencing me.

"What do you think you're doing?" Lukyan hissed, pressing me tighter to the wall. His deep blue eyes were ringed and haunted.

I could've sobbed from the relief.

"I'm looking for Kiera!" I hissed through his fingers as I struggled against him.

He didn't budge. Instead, he leaned down, pinning me with the gravity of his stare. "You're lucky it was I who found you and not someone else! How did you escape your room?" He retracted his hand from my mouth.

I almost told him about the guard forgetting to lock my door, but hesitated. If he knew about it, he'd ensure it didn't happen again.

"Where have you been? It's been *days*!" I whispered.

Lukyan rolled his head around and groaned. "You can't be here. I'm taking you back to your room."

"No!" I said, jerking my hand away from his searching grip. "I'm not going back to that room just to wait around and hope my friend isn't dead. Just for you to drop me off and disappear again with no explanation."

He was quiet for a minute, clearly debating whether to simply toss me over his shoulder.

"It's not that simple," he murmured.

"You were supposed to be helping us, but you disappeared."

His jaw twitched. "Let me bring you to your room, and I'll explain everything that's happened. I'll even try to find Kiera afterwards. But I can't explain anything here. It isn't safe."

Though I hated the idea of going back to that room, I nodded.

He grabbed my sash and pulled it up over my nose and mouth. "*Ess*, Elucia. It's like you want to get caught."

My eyes shot daggers at him, but I still followed him down the hallway and prayed that his answers wouldn't crush me.

Lukyan followed me closely as we walked back through the palace. Even with my hair, nose, and mouth covered by my sash, a bold Trenican soldier stepped in front of us just before we reached the stairs. He made a casual Vynesic greeting to me and Lukyan, only to shortly follow it up by crossing the distance between us and slurring a proposition at me.

Lukyan nearly growled at the man. "No, Petrov. Find someone else."

The stranger reached out and slid a finger over the excess fabric of my sash. "Why?"

I acted out of instinct. I slipped my arm through Lukyan's, then ran my free hand over his chest. He went ramrod straight at the contact.

"I'm sorry," I began, smiling bashfully at the man Lukyan called Petrov. "We already have plans. And in case you didn't know, Lukyan doesn't share."

Lukyan didn't move a muscle, and I bit back a laugh at his clear discomfort. The soldier looked back and forth between us, suspicious.

"Good to see you've finally let yourself loosen up," he grumbled to Lukyan before stalking off.

As soon as Petrov was out of sight, I put some distance between myself and my tense guard. The separation seemed to calm him.

*Don't touch him like that. Noted.*

I almost made a comment about it, but he'd already taken my hand and began leading me up the stairs. My atrophied legs ached at the incline, but Lukyan didn't let me slow. His pace didn't let up until we stopped in front of my door.

He slipped his hand over the handle, but turned on me before opening it.

"Promise me, Elucia," he whispered, his earnestness catching me off guard. "No more sneaking out. It will get you killed." He brought my hand up between us and held it in his own, almost like a prayer.

"How else will we find the elixirs?" I asked, slipping my sash off so it hung over my shoulders.

Lukyan shook his head, frustrated. "I've told you, they're not just lying around in a bedroom somewhere. The only way to find them is through Maksim, and his circle of trust is shrinking. That's why you're completing the tests."

My skin prickled in annoyance. "Fine. Where is Kiera?"

Footsteps sounded nearby before he could respond.

"How interesting."

The blood drained from Lukyan's face. I almost wanted to hold his head still, as if I could stop the nightmare from unfolding if I could keep him from seeing it.

But he turned away and met his master's eyes. "Your Excellency, I was just returning Miss Yorke from the library."

I hadn't seen Maksim in weeks, since I barged into his room after I passed his first test. He was dressed entirely in black, contrasting starkly with his luminously pale skin and hair. The sight of him sent an anxious jolt through my system.

His brow twitched with doubt. Though Lukyan had dropped my hand, Maksim's pale eyes lingered on it, as though it betrayed evidence of a crime. Something hateful glinted in his irises, but it quickly disappeared.

"You are not her guard anymore, and I've given no indication that she is allowed from her room," Maksim said, his tone careful and gauging.

*Not my guard anymore?*

Maksim took a step closer to us, and Lukyan shifted his weight in front of me.

Maksim tracked the movement, his lips twitching at the corners.

My stomach dropped.

"My apologies, Excellency," Lukyan began, bowing his head deferentially.

An uncomfortable silence settled over us. Maksim narrowed his eyes on Lukyan, a clear warning in them. Lukyan heeded it and stepped back, away from me. The loss of his presence beside me made me feel so vulnerable. Exposed.

Maksim approached, and it took my every ounce of courage not to back away. He was tall—though not as tall as Lukyan—and looked down his ridged nose at me. His eyes traveled further, lazily roving over every curve and exposed inch of skin. I gritted my teeth but remained still.

His eyes flickered up, looking over my shoulder at Lukyan. Then, without looking away, he slid his hand over my waist and tugged me closer until we were nearly touching. He still didn't look away from Lukyan, even as he leaned in close to my ear.

"Quite serendipitous meeting you here, little gull. I was just coming to see you." His words were soft, but not quiet.

I hated how close Maksim was. I hated how he was tracing his fingers over my skin and whispering to me like a lover. It made me sick. But I held fast. I only hoped Lukyan's expression was as stoic as it had been when we first met—before I learned he was my ally.

"What do you need?" I asked, willing my voice not to break.

His lips pulled up at the corner, and malevolent purpose filled his eyes. My throat tightened as he spread his fingers over my waist, then began tightening them. He continued to stare at Lukyan as his nails pressed into me.

It was a test. Maksim was waiting for Lukyan to flinch, or expose any level of concern for me.

I tried desperately not to squirm, but his fingernails were sharp, and they dug into my skin like knives.

*Don't flinch, Lukyan. Don't move a muscle.*

I bowed my head, unwilling to reveal my discomfort to Maksim. He'd enjoy it too much.

A long minute went by before a dark chuckle escaped his lips. "Coldhearted, indeed."

I stifled a sigh of relief.

Maksim's fingers relented, but he leaned close to my ear again. "It's time for your next test."

He drew back, his eyes flashing to my lips. I didn't have time to react before he shoved his fingers into the hair on the back of my head, gripped it tightly, then kissed me hard on the mouth.

Maksim was kissing me. I tried to pull away, but he shoved me into my closed bedroom door, boxing me in.

*No, no, no. This isn't real.*

I hadn't kissed anyone besides Levick.

*Levick.*

Maksim's right hand remained firmly in my hair, and the other slid around my back, pulling me tighter against him. His mouth was jealous and unrelenting against mine, like it still wasn't enough. Like he was desperate for satisfaction. Despair filled my heart, bubbling over.

*Like he wants to devour me.*

But just as a tear began sliding down my cheek, darkness crept into my vision. Unnatural lethargy weighed on my bones, stealing away my energy to fight back.

*He drugged me... how?*

My body relaxed and my arms slid off Maksim's chest. He pulled away, giving me a relief from his assault. His eyes searched mine for a moment, but mine drifted down to his lips, reddened and slightly swollen.

*Animal. Sick, disgusting animal.*

"Don't fret, little gull. I was only sharing something with you," he whispered, running a finger over my cheek.

He took my chin in his fingers and leaned down again. I had no strength to fight back—I was barely standing up. His lips pressed against mine, gentle and soft. He caressed my cheekbone with his thumb as he slid his hand over my face. The kiss was so tender... so subtly amorous. I hated it more than the violent kiss he'd just given me.

*At least that one was a true reflection of him. This is just a pretty lie.*

A fresh wave of exhaustion sent my knees buckling, but Maksim easily bent down and swept me into his arms. A quiet, panicked groan escaped my mouth.

I glimpsed Lukyan from the corner of my eye, his face twisted in distress. He looked like he was one step from blowing his cover and attacking his viceroy. But Maksim didn't take me into my room—he turned and presented me to Lukyan.

"Put her in the carriage and blindfold her," he commanded.

Maksim handed me off to Lukyan, who nodded dutifully at his leader. But as soon as Maksim turned around, I felt Lukyan's arms tighten around me. The last thing I felt was his breath in my hair as he leaned in and whispered. "I am sorry, Elucia. I am so sorry."

# Chapter Nineteen

# Dropped

I didn't remember the carriage ride. I woke up on the cold stone ground, drenched in pain and darkness. My arms ached and burned. I tried to sit up, but my hands—while free of the metal gloves—were bound behind my back. I searched my memories, but only recalled the feeling of Maksim's lips against mine. I fought the urge to retch. The poison elixir must've been on his lips. Trenican royals often inoculated themselves to commonly used poisons, which explained why he hadn't been affected by it.

"Time to wake up."

I flinched away at the voice, even though it sounded distant.

Though I'd expected sunlight, I was met with a full moon. It shone down on my surroundings, casting everything in a cold, blue light. I was lying in a ravine, near the 'U' shaped end. Made of narrow and sweeping canyons of stone, it seemed to be void of vegetation. A soft trickling reached my ears, telling me there was water nearby.

*Where are we?*

My eyes eventually landed on Maksim, who stood on the edge of the ravine, high above me. He wore a bright red coat to guard against the night's chill, and his hair was smooth and combed aside.

"I hope you slept well," he called down. My eyes caught on a silhouette behind him.

*Lukyan.*

He displayed no emotion as he stood behind Maksim, watching me closely.

I heard a groan come from nearby, and I rolled over. To my complete and utter dismay, Kiera was lying on the ground beside me.

"No," I hissed, twisting around until I could sit up on my knees. "These tests were only supposed to be for me!"

Maksim's smile was so bright that I could see the moonlight reflecting off of his teeth. But before he could speak, a new, jarring noise erupted.

It was a chorus of snarls, barks, and the snapping of teeth against metal. My heart started racing as I followed the sound. There, below Maksim at the base of the ravine, was a cage filled with half a dozen ravenous dogs. They were enormous—much larger than any dogs I'd ever seen in Friese. Their fur was thick and matted, and looked to be a mottled gray color.

"Do you like them?" Maksim called down. "We brought them all the way from Trenica. They were quite disappointed to have missed out on the invasion, but I knew I'd find a way to make it up to them."

Kiera finally stirred awake. She swiveled around at the noise, only to cry out in terror upon seeing the feral animals. "Where am I?" she screamed, scrambling closer to me. Her hands were free of bindings, unlike mine.

*No windblade, no threat.*

"You are in the Wastes," Maksim said with a patronizing wave of his hand. "That large swath of useless and unnavigable land that keeps our nations apart. Although I suppose I can't call it useless anymore," he finished with a chuckle.

I bit down an insult.

"The tests are only for me, Maksim!" I shouted. He cocked his head as I said his name. "No matter what you have planned for me, get Kiera out of here!"

The hateful man just stared down at me and laughed. "Your test is simple. Survive."

The dogs growled and pawed at their cage. There was a wire affixed to the cage door, and Maksim held the other end.

*As soon as he pulls that wire, the cage will open. We'll be done for.*

Maksim interrupted my spiraling thoughts. "Escape the dogs and find your way back to Friese. When you return, this test will be considered passed."

Kiera began crying beside me.

"What about her?" I asked. "What's her role in all of this?"

"No role. That was just for fun."

A strangled cry escaped my lungs. "Maksim, please! I'll do anything, just get her out! She doesn't need to be a part of this!"

His pale eyes danced in excitement. "Really? *Anything*?"

Nausea churned in my stomach, but I nodded.

"That's good to know. But alas, this test has already been written."

I tore my eyes from Maksim and began scouring the ravine wall, searching for any reasonable slopes or footholds.

"Ah, good girl," Maksim said. "That's what I want to see. Your mind at work, your survival instincts."

Kiera helped me to my feet and began tugging at the bindings on my wrists.

"You have five minutes—after which Lukyan will release my dogs. You should get started." Maksim turned to walk away, but aimed one last sneer at me. "I hope you fly fast, little gull."

He handed the wire to Lukyan, then walked off without a backwards glance.

Lukyan stared down at me apologetically. He didn't say it out loud, but I barely saw him mouth, "I'm sorry." I simply nodded, releasing him from his guilt.

"We need to start moving," I said to Kiera, whose shaking hands were still fumbling with my bindings.

She shook her head frantically. "You can't run with your hands behind your back!"

I was about to prove her wrong when a muffled thump sounded nearby. I scanned the ground only to find a hefty hunting knife to my left, the blade buried in a patch of dirt. Kiera spotted it just after me, and rushed for it.

My eyes met Lukyan's, and I could've sworn there was glassiness in his. Despite his recent aloofness, it was clear to whom his loyalty lay.

*Thank you, friend.*

Kiera came over and started sawing at my bindings. Whatever materials they were made of, they refused to come free.

"Hurry up," I hissed.

"It's a strong cord," Kiera cried. "It's going to take a while!"

We didn't have long before the dogs were loosed on us. I'd hoped I could kill them all with my windblade while they were still in the cage, but there was no time.

I pulled away from Kiera. "We have to go now."

Her eyes were conflicted, but she nodded.

I turned and looked up at Lukyan one last time, then took off down the ravine.

Never before had I run with such panic heaving in my lungs. Such desperation coursing through my veins. Pinprick jolts of pain shot through my feet with every step as they slammed against the cold, unforgiving stone. My dress tugged and restrained my legs, and I silently cursed Maksim for the thousandth time for culling my wardrobe.

"Hurry up," Kiera called back to me.

With my hands bound, I was barely keeping up. But it wouldn't be long before Lukyan released Maksim's bloodthirsty dogs from their cage.

We followed dizzying twists and turns deeper into the ravine. My eyes scanned the walls for a ledge or suitable footholds, but the further we ran, the steeper the walls became.

*Please don't let us die here. After everything we've survived.*

A loud banging sound echoed through the ravine, and my stomach dropped. I looked at Kiera, and all the color had drained from her sun-kissed face. Her pitch-black hair hung in tangles around her eyes, which were far too young to hold such harrowed fear.

"The dogs," she whispered breathlessly.

I nodded. "He's let them out."

With newly invigorated fear, I resumed sprinting through the narrow chasm, Kiera holding my arm.

"We can't outrun them!" she said through rapid pants.

I knew that. I could already hear the barks and snarls growing closer. Hopelessness crept in on me, leadening my steps. Just before it paralyzed me completely, my eyes caught on a dark impression on the ravine's wall ahead. A small bud of hope grew in my heart. I spotted an outcropping of rocks below the dark spot, and the bud began to bloom.

*We won't die here.*

"This way!"

Kiera followed behind me as we made a bee-line to the shadowy spot on the wall. Water splashed over my feet as we ran across a shallow stream, then slid to a stop beside the wall.

"Look, up there," I whispered.

Kiera followed my stare and gasped. "A cave!"

"I can't climb with my hands bound behind my back," I panted, turning to present my bindings to her.

She pulled out Lukyan's knife and began sawing at them again.

"If they won't budge," I whispered. "Just go up without me."

"No!" Kiera said through a choked sob.

After what felt like an eternity, I felt my bindings slip down slightly. They'd loosened, but I wasn't free.

The snarling got closer.

A wild idea formed in my mind, giving me a precious shred of hope.

"Go!" I said, backing away from Kiera. "I'll be alright!"

She looked at me like I'd lost my mind, but I held firm. She turned and began scaling the wall.

I rubbed my arms together, shimmying the bindings to the side. They didn't need to be completely loose, only enough for me to turn my palm and twitch my fingers.

"Please, Echna," I whispered to the starry sky. "No blood this time."

I released Isolon from my right hand, directly into the taut edge of my bindings.

To my relief, they fell free.

I scrambled to the wall and began climbing after Kiera.

She had trouble spotting ridges and outcroppings in the darkness. Nevertheless, I urged her upward. She'd made it ten feet off the ground before the snarls got unnervingly loud.

"Eliandre! They're getting closer!"

I couldn't see them around the bend, but I knew she was right. It would be any second, now.

"Go!" I said with a wave of my arm.

She turned back to the wall and climbed faster. I'd only made it five feet from the ravine floor when the dogs made it over to us.

I screamed as they jumped and nipped at my feet. Kiera cried out for me, but continued to scramble up the wall. My left hand was still weak and mostly unusable since piercing it with my windblade. It wasn't strong enough to hold me to the wall while I threw my windblade with my right hand—I'd slip and fall. I also worried that the movement involved with throwing my windblade would upset my precarious balance.

"I'm at the ledge!" Kiera yelled as she started heaving herself over.

A relieved smile twitched at the corners of my lips, but it was short lived.

I felt the breath on my skin before the teeth. Pain tore through my leg as one of the dogs bit into my ankle. I screamed and tried to shake him off, but he bit down harder and whipped his head back and forth. His teeth tore through muscle and ground against bone.

*Echna above, save me from this.*

Abandoning caution, I reached back with my right hand and flung my windblade at the dog. A strangled yelp escaped his jaws and he let go, falling to the ground in two pieces. But I didn't have time to celebrate—my grip on the wall was slipping.

I swore to myself, but blocked out the pain and clung to the wall. The remaining five dogs were jumping and biting at me, coming close enough that their spittle flecked over my feet.

"Come on!" Kiera yelled as she extended a hand to me. She'd pulled herself into the cave while I fought off the dog.

I grabbed on and let her help me over the edge. My ankle tore and split with pain, but I didn't stop.

Tears of shocked relief streamed from my eyes as I slid over the cave floor. Kiera pulled me close, squeezing me against her.

"You're alive," she whispered. "We're alive."

I peered over the edge, determined to kill the rest of the dogs while we had the height advantage, but they'd retreated down the ravine once I was out of their biting range.

For the moment, we were safe. Kiera scooted back to lean against the side of the cave entrance, and I followed. My heartbeat pounded in my ears like thunder. But the effects of the adrenaline weren't indefinite. Red hot pain bloomed from my mangled ankle, and my left hand ached from overuse.

"Let me see it," Kiera whispered. I let her pull my ankle on to her lap, but it was too dark to see it clearly. I only knew what I felt. Excruciating pain, and the warmth of blood trickling over my skin.

I made to rotate my ankle, but Kiera yelped at me. "No! You shouldn't be moving it, right?"

She meant well, but I assured her it was fine. Gingerly, I rotated my ankle in a circle. Though the movement pulled at my torn skin, my range of motion was intact.

"It's not broken." I sighed in relief, and let my head fall against Kiera's shoulder.

I stared out over the ravine, bathed in moonlight. I'd never been in the Wastes—no one I knew had ever dared such a venture. It was known to be full of dangerous animals and winding, unnavigable canyons.

*One of which I am now trapped in.*

"How far from Friese do you think we are?" Kiera asked.

My body trembled in the chill, and I hoped it was caused by the feeling of the night air against my bare skin, rather than from blood loss.

"I don't know," I whispered.

"What do we do next? How will we even find out where we are?"

My throat tightened at the onslaught of questions. I'd just been mauled by a ravenous dog and had nearly fallen to my death. I wasn't ready to face our imminent future.

"I have to go down to the stream and clean this," I said, shifting my ankle. "But not yet. The dogs are too close. After that, our first priority will be finding a way out of these canyons. There's no sense of direction down here."

"Maybe if we stay up here for a day or two, the dogs will forget about us."

I sighed deeply, reluctant to dash her hopes. "There's no food or water here. Our only hope is to escape the ravine before we grow too weak."

*And before my ankle kills me.*

Kiera didn't respond, but I felt her disappointment.

I leaned forward and turned to look at her. The moonlight didn't quite reach her from the edge of the cave, but it was obvious that she was fighting fresh tears.

A bitter, poisonous feeling spread through my body. I'd never hated Maksim more than at that moment. Not when he drugged me and chained me to a harp, making me play for over ten hours. Not when he left me anchored in the sea during a summer storm. Not even when he forced his lips onto mine, stealing away the affection I'd only ever shared with Levick, the man I loved.

*His birthday passed... he's eighteen now.*

I'd slept through it, crying and thrashing in a burning fever.

"You have to stay with me," I whispered to Kiera. "We're a team. Never split. Promise me?"

Kiera snuggled closer to me. "I promise, Eliandre."

## *Chapter Twenty*

# THE DOGS

I paced back and forth in my bedroom, trying to make sense of what I'd just seen downstairs. My mother, Elspeth Yorke, had been embracing a man. A man who was not my father. My stomach turned at the memory. I'd only seen the back of his head as he wrapped his arms around her, his blond hair brushing against her head. The embrace had been long—suspiciously so. It was the kind of embrace reserved for family and lovers.

*Lovers.*

At thirteen years old, the idea of my mother loving someone other than my father was anathema. As far as I knew, my parents had a very loving relationship. They talked, flirted, and spent every free moment together. Their arguments—while rare—were always sorted out with rational and understanding discourse. I'd never seen my father so much as glance at another woman, let alone hug one as intimately as my mother hugged the stranger in our entryway.

I seethed.

*How could she do this to him? To us?*

Her behavior had been strange lately. She'd retreat upstairs and nap for hours, which was very unusual for her.

*Could that have something to do with this?*

I didn't know what to do. Surely, my father didn't know about it. I was in an impossible situation. Tell my father and shatter their marriage, or keep my mother's secret? My mouth twisted into a grimace. To make matters worse, my private harp recital was starting in an hour. My instructor was already downstairs, preparing.

Swallowing my indecision, I forced myself to power through.

The recital was a disaster. My eyes kept catching on my parents, sitting together and watching me intently. Mother had her fingers intertwined with Father's. The small display of affection usually escaped my notice, but now it burned bright in the corner of my vision, like a funeral pyre.

*How can she hold his hand like that? After what she's done?*

While my harp instructor's face showed only disappointment at my underwhelming performance, my parents knew better. Their faces transformed from blindsided confusion to sincere concern. I wished they didn't know me so well.

Afterwards, my father led me into his study. He leaned against his ebony desk and leveled a worried look at me. "What happened in there, Eliandre? You've been practicing incessantly."

I fidgeted with my nails, not knowing what to do. I was already imagining the devastation on his face when I told him the truth. But keeping to myself was clearly not an option.

*An ugly truth is better than a pretty lie.*

"I saw Mother with a man. Earlier today," I said, my words flowing out of me like water from a broken dam.

Father's stubbled jaw twitched, and he crossed his arms over his chest. "Where?"

My throat tightened, but I forced myself to continue. "Here in the house. They were... hugging goodbye."

A flash of understanding gleamed in Father's eyes.

*He already knows? No, that wouldn't make sense. They were huddled so close at the recital.*

I wished he would say something. But he looked away, towards the rays of setting sunlight shining through the window.

"Father?" I asked, taking a few steps closer. His eyes were darting around but looking at nothing, as if he were trying to work out a complicated equation in his head.

Finally, he met my eyes again. "I know."

My stomach dropped at the confession, and my mouth fell open. "You know? But why—"

"It's not what you think. Your mother isn't being unfaithful."

My brows scrunched up. It made no sense. Though I hadn't seen his face, the stranger was much taller than my mother and very clearly a grown man. Their hug had lasted far too long for it to have been a simple social kindness.

"You know who he is?" I asked.

Father took a deep breath and rolled his shoulders. Mother and Father always wore their finest formal attire to my recitals, even though it was only us in attendance. He lived much of his life in stiff and dignified suits, but he suddenly seemed uncomfortable in it.

"Yes. I know him. He is someone your mother knew a long time ago. Before she met me."

I shook my head, confused. My mother was a few years older than my father. She lived a significant amount of her adulthood before she met him, but they never talked about it. Whenever I asked, she'd always say things like, *what happened before I had my family doesn't matter. My life started with you.*

"You're not worried at all? You don't find it strange that she was hugging him?"

His brows ticked up ever-so-slightly. He was a very patient man, but that patience was clearly being tested. "No. I'm not worried, Eliandre. Your mother loves me very much, and I would never doubt her loyalty to me."

I looked down at my callused fingers.

Warm arms wrapped around me, holding me tight. I rested my head against my father's chest and took a deep breath. He had a way of always knowing when I needed a hug.

"We're not going anywhere," he whispered, patting my hair gently.

But the dream ended, and my parents were dead again.

I woke to searing pain burning up my leg. My back and tailbone ached from sleeping on the hard stone ground. Nevertheless, I knew the tears falling down my cheeks weren't brought on by my injuries.

Seeing my parents again, even in a dream, was more painful than any physical wound.

I opened my eyes and scanned the ravine below. Warm sunlight streamed over the ridges and cascaded down onto the trickling stream at the bottom. As far as I could tell, the dogs were still gone.

*Good. One less thing to kill us.*

Kiera was breathing softly next to me, her arm still hanging over my shoulders. Her attire, while much more sensible than mine, was nothing more than a brown linen shift dress with a belt slung around her waist.

"Kiera," I whispered, nudging her.

She stirred and looked around, then flinched away from the ledge. "Great oceans," she muttered.

I smiled at the Corlaean swear.

*I'll bet she picked it up from her mother.*

"I need to go clean my ankle," I said, gesturing to the stream. "You can stay here. I'll be quick."

She shot me a look of incredulity. "You can barely walk with an ankle like that, let alone climb down from here. I'm coming to help you."

I hated needing her help. Though she was only three years younger than me, fifteen felt so much younger than eighteen. It was I who should've been helping her, not vice versa.

But my pride didn't outweigh my sense, and I nodded in agreement.

Climbing down from the cave felt infinitely more precarious than climbing up. We'd had a pack of hungry dogs biting at us, so the height had previously seemed like more of a blessing than a curse. But as we climbed down, we had only the distant stone ground and the body of a decapitated dog to look at.

Though we had a few near-slips, we reached the bottom of the ravine without new injury or making loud noises. The last thing we wanted to do was alert the dogs of our descent. I had my windblade, but if they split up and ran at me, I couldn't kill all of them at once.

Kiera wrapped her arm around my back and helped me get closer to the stream. The water was clear and didn't show any evidence of growth or vegetation. I hoped that was a sign it wouldn't give me an infection.

"Careful," Kiera muttered as we got closer.

She helped me sit down beside the water, then settled next to me. I reached in and let the water flow over my fingers. It was cool and refreshing against my skin.

Gritting my teeth, I began scooping the water over my ankle. Though it stung, I could tell the wound was no longer actively bleeding. I washed away all of the blood and grime until the water ran clean.

No bones were broken, but the idea of walking on it made me nervous. I had no idea how far we were from Friese. There was no way to find out until we climbed out of the ravine.

"This won't be easy," I whispered, not meaning to say it aloud.

Kiera reached over and took my hand. Hers were still wet from washing in the stream. "We'll make it out of here."

I looked up at her, and she was smiling at me. It wasn't a broad smile, and its sincerity was dubious, but she was trying. I nodded, forcing a smile of my own.

"I think I see a ledge over there," she said, pointing across the ravine. "I'm going to go check it out."

"I'll go with you." I started to rise, but my legs buckled.

"No, you stay here and drink some of that water. I'll be fine. It's only fifteen or twenty horse-lengths away."

It didn't sit right with me, but she was right. It was fairly close by, and I could see the outcropping she referred to. It seemed promising, so I agreed.

While she investigated the wall, I made myself a binding for my foot. I tore a strip of silk from the bottom hem of my dress and began wrapping it around my ankle, thanking Echna that my father insisted I get a basic medical education.

*I'd have died multiple times over if not for you, Father. Some of my friends, too.*

I looped the fabric around and tied it tightly. It was makeshift work but better than leaving the wound exposed to the elements.

Hairs stood up on the back of my neck. The sound of claws against stone echoed through the ravine. I jerked my head up, only to see my greatest fear coming true. The five remaining dogs were racing towards Kiera, closing the gap in long strides.

"Kiera!" I screamed across the canyon.

She spun around, and her face went pale. The dogs were nearly upon her.

I launched my windblade at them with my good hand, but I stumbled and fell to the unforgiving ground.

*No!*

Kiera was trying to climb the ravine wall, but one of her footholds broke, and she fell backwards.

*No! This isn't happening. You have to stand up. You have to throw.*

I heaved myself to my feet just in time to send my windblade through three of the ravenous dogs, splitting their bodies apart and spraying blood over the rocky wall. But the other dogs were too close. They leapt upon my friend and tackled her to the ground.

I cried out for her, but the only response I received was blood curdling screams and the sickening sounds of flesh being torn from bone.

## *Chapter Twenty-One*

# Obscene Unfairness of Life

Life wasn't fair.

It was a simple fact—one I'd known for years. Though the phrase commonly graced the lips of disappointed parents and exasperated teachers, I never needed anyone to tell me. While my peers drank, waltzed, and seduced their way through parties, I studied. I practiced. I trained for wifehood.

Then, my father died. Shortly thereafter I was spurned by my fiancé, kidnapped, then thrown into a horrific war. A war we lost. I was a prisoner again, only this time, my captor was not a kind, compassionate leader. He was a bloody stain on the throne of Friese. A torturer of mind and soul. A man I hated more than anyone else.

But when put into perspective, every ounce of pain I'd experienced in my life was nothing. The glass roof of my library caving in and slicing into my back... Isolon piercing straight through my left hand.

I'd rather live through it all again if it would prevent the sight in front of me. The mangled girl lying motionless on the ground. Her blood-smeared limbs, twisted in unnatural angles.

The last two dogs lay beside me, lifeless and dissected. The vengeance was empty.

I crawled past them and stopped beside Kiera's body. It was so young and beautiful—reflecting the kindness she had inside. Her dark eyes stared into the blue sky, and for a moment, I pretended she was simply watching the clouds. Waiting for peculiar shapes or patterns. But my eyes drifted to her throat, which had been ripped completely open.

I tried to find comfort in the fact that her death was quicker than it could've been. She had stopped moving before I'd even finished killing the dogs. But the thought brought me no solace, and a strangled cry escaped my throat.

"Why?" I shouted into the air.

The universe made no response, which came as no shock. I was completely alone, now. My foes were dead along with my friend. There was no one to defeat. No one to protect.

*And no purpose in anything.*

I don't know how long I cried over Kiera—only that by the time my tears ran dry, the sun stood at the center of the sky.

*She would want you to survive.*

I knew it was true, but I was riddled with guilt by simply being alive.

*You should be the dead one. These tests were yours, not hers.*

My fingers curled into a fist, bunching Kiera's shift dress into my fingers. I would find justice for her death, and the only way to do that was to survive. So I gathered myself up and pulled Lukyan's knife from Kiera's belt. I laid a soft kiss upon her brow, then turned to face the future.

It wasn't easy to walk away from Kiera's body. I couldn't shake the feeling that I was abandoning her, even though I knew better. There was nowhere to bury her at the bottom of a rocky ravine, and I'd never be able to carry her out. With my injured ankle and aching left hand, I doubted my ability to get myself out, let alone to escape with the added weight of a corpse slung over my shoulder.

So I walked along the ravine wall, carrying the thin bag I'd made from dress scraps and trying to ignore my numerous aches and pains. I followed a slight incline and hoped desperately that it would lead to a viable route to the surface. Thankfully the stream was running along my inclined path, making it easy to stop for water. The afternoon sun shone unencumbered by clouds. I tried to walk in the shadows cast by the cavernous walls, but the heat radiated from the stone ground until I was sweating.

*Hold fast, Eliandre. For Kiera. For Rynne and Coran. For Levick and all of your friends in the north. Even for Lukyan.*

Despite the power given to me by my windblade, the weight of Lukyan's hunting knife in my hand gave me comfort. It was my last connection with civilization.

Carrion birds circled overhead, watching my wavering steps with interest. Their looming shadows spurred me forward, but I could feel my strength waning with the setting sun.

"Hold fast..." I muttered. "Hold fast."

Eventually my strength left me, and I collapsed against the ravine wall. I only hoped nothing would attack me in the night.

I woke to a soft, tickling sensation on my arm. Something was touching me.

Panic surged in my veins, and my eyes shot open. There, not six inches from my arm, was an enormous vulture. Its thick feathers were the color of sandy rocks flecked with lines of white, and its long neck and head were covered only in thin wisps of feathering. It was completely revolting.

Its long black tail feathers brushed against my arm as it searched around. It was rifling through my makeshift bag.

"No," I groaned, surging forward and swatting at the bird. But he'd already eaten half of the bag's contents, and seemed dead-set on finishing it. I tried to yank the bag away, but he had the other side in his bloodied beak.

"Let go, you winds-forsaken scavenger!"

The vulture began clawing at me. I was holding the bag with my good hand, and still couldn't throw with my left. Gritting my teeth, I grabbed Lukyan's knife from the ground and slashed at the bird. He squawked and jumped away, but not before I cut a few inches from the feathers on his wing.

I breathed a sigh of relief when he finally gave up and retreated. But that relief was smothered when I watched the injured bird barely get three feet in the air before crashing back down. He hopped and jumped, but always ended up back on the ground.

Frustration and guilt gnawed at me.

*He was only trying to find food. Trying to survive. Isn't that what you're trying to do?*

With deep reluctance, I walked closer to the bird. He looked over and snapped his beak at me, but it was half-hearted.

"I'm sorry," I mumbled. "Looks like you're stuck down here with me."

He simply looked at me, his beady eyes unblinking and unsure.

I knew I couldn't leave the poor bird alone after stealing away his gift of flight, so I began walking along the wall, searching for a way to make amends. Every few minutes I'd hear him jump and fall, talons scraping over the rocky ground. Thankfully it wasn't long before I came across a scurrying rat trying to squirm under a pile of rocks. I threw my windblade and sliced it in half.

"I'm sorry for cutting up your wing," I whispered as I crept closer to the injured vulture. He was exhausted from his incessant attempts at flying away. "You were only trying to have a snack, and I understand that." It briefly occurred to me that I'd likely lost my mind, but I kept on. "But this particular snack," I lifted my bag, "is off limits. I need it."

The creature perked up as I raised my other hand. I held the dead rat in my fingers, hanging in two bloody pieces. "I know this won't make up for it, but it'll stop the hunger for a little while." I tossed the rat at the bird, and to my shock, he snapped one of the pieces in his beak.

A smile spread over my chapped lips as he greedily swallowed my offering. "I'll bet that tastes a lot better than what you stole from my bag." My nose wrinkled up in disgust. "Maybe that's what I'll call you."

When I eventually resumed my trek through the ravine, the clicking sounds of talons followed along.

"Stick with me, Bollock. Maybe I'll manage to keep you alive."

*It's more than I can say for Kiera.*

I followed the stream for miles, stopping every so often to hydrate or cool off. I could feel the sun burning my shoulders and the part in my hair, but I had no way to cover myself. It occurred to me that I could've stripped Kiera and taken her dress, but the mere thought of it had my stomach twisting. I'd rather burn to ash.

Bollock followed along, venturing closer and closer as we walked. Any small and unlucky wildlife that crossed my path became his meal, with help from my windblade. His pace was slowing—unused to walking rather than flying—but I didn't let him fall too far behind.

The sun was setting on my second full day in the Wastes when it occurred to me that I hadn't eaten anything since being stranded. My consistent hydration and intermittent horrifying memories kept my stomach perpetually nauseous.

But the path was, in fact, rising, and vegetation was becoming more common. I'd even happened upon a bush covered in berries, and managed to eat my fill before my body insisted I stop. I was rinsing berry juice from my fingers when Bollock began squawking and jumping beside the ravine wall.

*Rabid thing.*

"Need me to kill something for you, scavenger?" I asked as I walked over to investigate.

But it wasn't the prospect of dinner that had the bird riled up—it was the echoed sound of waves coming from a fork in the canyon. My mouth fell open.

*Waves! If we find the sea... we find south. We find Friese.*

I nearly leapt for joy. "Winds bless you," I huffed, lunging for the unsuspecting vulture. He flinched away, but was obviously too exhausted to truly fight back. I hoisted him from the ground and spun him around.

"You don't deserve the disparagement your species receives," I laughed. He snapped at me, but I smacked his face away. He couldn't dull my excitement. We might survive.

*We.*

Then, reality hit me. I was celebrating with a carrion bird instead of my friend. The girl who'd never make it out of the ravine. My excitement evaporated.

I placed Bollock back on the ground, then took a step back. The sun had long since fallen behind the shadow of the ravine's edge. It would be fully dark soon.

"You should get some water," I muttered as I limped away to the ravine wall. I said nothing more as I slid to the ground and watched the sky fade, joining my spirits.

I woke before the sun rose. Bollock was beside me, sleeping in what might've been the most unsettling position I'd ever seen. He was standing upright, but his head was hanging between his talons. His beak barely touched the ground, creating the illusion of fervent prayer.

*Creepy, macabre creature.*

But my lips still twitched up at the corners.

Eventually I woke him and we began our trek up the fork in the ravine. To my great excitement, the slope became steep as we walked. Bollock began falling behind, but graciously allowed me to carry him in my trembling arms. The sky widened above us as we slowly emerged from the hell we'd been trapped in for days.

"We are going to live," I whispered, my chapped lips brushing against his feathers. They smelled of festering flesh. "I won't let you die."

The image of Kiera's ripped throat burned in my mind, pushing me closer to the edge. Through all of the death, hunger, and sunlight, I knew I was approaching insanity. A large part of my jumbled brain wondered how much of it was real.

*Is the slope really getting steeper? Are we truly emerging?*

I held tight to Bollock, as if the scrape of his talons against my forearms could reassure me of my sanity.

"You'd tell me if I was crazy, right?" I asked.

He looked at me, and I could've sworn his eyes rolled.

*I've truly lost it.*

But the slope ended, and I gazed upon the most beautiful thing I'd ever seen in my eighteen years of life.

The horizon.

Tears flooded down my cheeks, and I fell to my knees in the sparse grass. To my left were cliffs overlooking the Broad Sea, gloriously crowned in countless whitecaps crashing against each other. Straight ahead was the horizon, painted with a faint blot of green. The color I feared I'd never see again.

I lifted my eyes to the cloudless sky and let the sun seep through my eyelids. I'd done it. I'd escaped the ravine. And I wished I'd died alongside Kiera.

I opened my mouth and shrieked into the heavens.

As I collapsed onto the ground, the last thing I saw before closing my eyes was the vague shape of a horse in the distance. I didn't care.

## *Chapter Twenty-Two*

# Rose

The sea always brought me comfort. There was something about standing face-to-face with an unconquerable force that grounded me. My parents didn't bring me out very often, but when they did, I extended the excursion for as long as possible.

Mother held my hand tightly as we walked along the beach, but I tugged harder the closer we got to the water. "Come on, Mama!" I shouted, my voice a chipper bell tolling over the water.

"Slow down, El," she said, shuffling to keep up. In truth, she didn't have to try very hard. My six-year-old legs gave no real threat of outpacing her.

I finally reached the fluctuating waterline and crouched down, trying to catch the tiny clams before they burrowed themselves back under the sand. Every new splash of water brought a fresh wave of vibrantly colored clams rolling by. The moment the water retreated again, the little creatures reached out an arm and dragged themselves back under to safety.

"Look, Mama!" I said, showing off my handful of light purple bivalves. "For you."

She smiled softly down on me as she gathered the clams in her hands. "I'm honored. My favorite color, too!"

I smiled back, immensely pleased that my efforts were appreciated. But my smile faded as Mother crouched down in the sand and released the clams into a shallow wave.

I turned on her, tears pricking my eyes at the insult. "I picked them out for you!"

Ever-patient, my mother took both of my hands in hers. "I loved them, Eliandre. It was so kind of you. But those clams will die if we hold onto them forever."

She picked me up, and I wrapped my arms around her neck.

"You have such a thoughtful heart, Elucia," she whispered into my windswept hair.

I pulled away, confused. "What does that mean? Elucia?"

She smiled and tucked a strand of my platinum hair behind my ear. "Some people have more than one name. Your first name is Eliandre," she said, pausing for a moment to squeeze me tighter. "Your second name is Rose. Which, in my language, is *Elucia*."

My young mind briefly pondered the unusual nature of her words.

*We only have one language in Friese.*

The allure of life pulled me away, and I leapt from her arms to splash in the shallows again.

*Rose.*

*Rose.*

*Rose.*

"Elucia."

It was my name. How had I forgotten it?

Something gently shook me by the shoulders, and my eyes shot open.

Kneeling above me was a tall and wiry Trenican man, sweating and panicked. Messy braids hung over one side of his head, and the other side was shaved clean.

"You!" I hissed, my eyes widening on him. I squirmed away but pain bloomed in my ankle, and I stopped with a gasp. "How? How did you know?"

Lukyan looked as if he wanted to reach for me, but fell back on his knees upon hearing my words.

I tried to move further away, but my back met with a thick canvas. We were in a tent, faintly illuminated by the light of the setting sun.

"What do you mean?" Lukyan asked, his hands outstretched in a peace offering.

My eyes narrowed on him. "*Elucia*?"

"It means *rose*. A common Vynesic word."

I scoffed at him, not believing the excuse. "But why did you call me that? Where did you hear it?"

His chest fell and his eyes softened, conceding. "It is your name."

My heart leapt into my throat.

*Who is this man? How does he know me?*

I couldn't help but recall the memory of my mother hugging a stranger in our entryway. My stomach churned at the possible implications. I'd always had fairer features than were considered normal in Friese.

"Are you—" I started, my voice breaking. "My father?"

Lukyan's light brows rose in offense. "*Ess*, how old do you think I am?"

He had a point. He was likely not even thirty.

"Then who are you? How do you know that name?" I asked. My head was spinning. It didn't make sense.

He looked down, flexing his knuckles. "I was there. When Mother gave you that name."

My heart stopped.

*Mother.*

"You aren't saying—"

"I am," he said, meeting my eyes.

It began falling together. The protective behavior he'd displayed towards me. The way he stiffened when I pretended to be his paramour. His whispered words of mourning after Maksim forced his kiss on me.

*"I am so sorry, Elucia."*

The truth became so obvious that I couldn't believe I hadn't noticed it yet. Mother married late in life. She was thirty-three when she married Father, and thirty-five when she had me. Lukyan was probably ten years older than me, and that would've made her twenty-five at the time. My mother truly did have an entire life before she married Father and had me.

She had a *son*.

The air left my lungs in a massive rush, leaving me doubled over and gasping. Without hesitation, Lukyan rushed to my side and enveloped me in his arms. He pulled me close and rested his hand on my head, petting it gently.

It might've been the shock of the discovery, or it might've been the undeniable bond I suddenly felt with him. It could've even been the trauma of the last few weeks finally breaking me. But I curled up in my older brother's arms and cried.

Lukyan held me until the sun went down, leaving us in darkness. I clung to him, still in disbelief. I'd never had a sibling. Despite my cousin Louis's existence, my father's death had left me feeling abandoned. But I wasn't alone... I had a brother. A Trenican one, at that.

*All of those whispered rumors. Maksim's comments about my true culture. They were right. Mother was Trenican.*

*I am Trenican.*

The thought led me to a question. I finally shifted away from Lukyan, leaning against the central tent pole. "Who was he? Your father?"

Lukyan worked his jaw, as though he knew I'd ask it.

"Mother married him young. Twenty, I believe. I was born a few years later, in Grevalst. He died before I could know him."

The answer only created more questions. "But why did she leave for Friese? And why didn't she bring you with her?"

*Why did my mother deprive me of my only brother?*

"A man in the royal family had shown interest in her. He was relentless in his pursuit. My father's body hadn't even frozen over by the time this man was knocking on our door." His lip curled up in disdain as he said it.

"Was he not a viable option for her?"

Lukyan laughed bitterly. "No. The man is an animal. Just like his son."

My stomach dropped. "His son?"

"Maksim."

I gasped. "The king of Trenica was pursuing Mother? Wasn't he married already?"

Lukyan nodded. "Yes. He wasn't looking for a wife." He gave me a dark look, and I grimaced. "She knew him well enough to know better. So she escaped the kingdom and went south."

My mouth twitched downward. "But why didn't she bring you with her?"

"She did, at first. But my father came from a long line of distinguished royal Trenican guards, and they didn't like the idea of me growing up Friesian. So I spent my time split between my uncle's house in Grevalst, and my mother's house in Friese. Though Mother had to keep my existence a secret from the Friesian court, it wasn't all bad. I was there the day you were born." He paused, a soft smile tugging at his lips. "I got to hold you. You were so small... and loud. You spit up on me."

Though I was fighting tears, I couldn't help but laugh.

"Things changed though, after you were born," he continued, his eyes growing somber. "I reached the age where more was expected of me in Grevalst. The royal guard is competitive, and I couldn't compete if I spent half of my years in Friese. That, coupled with the suspicions of Mother's true nationality, limited my options. I went years without going to Friese, until the last time. I'd just gotten promoted, and had been awarded leave. It wasn't until I got to Friese that I learned Mother had kept my existence from you."

I was fully crying, now. The betrayal from the person I'd most trusted was a twisting knife in my back.

"I confronted her about it. I wanted to know you, and I wanted you to know me. But there were rumors circulating about you, about your parentage. Disgusting slander against Mother and her fidelity to Nestor. She didn't want you to question where you belonged, so she deemed it safer to keep you in the dark. I hated it, but couldn't find it in myself to fight it. She'd already gotten sick and knew she didn't have much time. So I tried to respect her wishes, and said goodbye for the last time. Though I was sick with grief, I did my best to forget. I knew that if I thought about you too much, I'd give in and find you. But that wasn't what she wanted. So I committed myself to my work, and eventually transitioned from guard duties to work that was more... clandestine."

I nodded knowingly. "Who is it? Your secret employer?"

Something ticked in his jaw. "I'm sorry, Sister, but that knowledge is of no benefit to you. It would only put you in more danger."

I frowned, but nodded.

"I'd resisted the urge to visit you for years," Lukyan said, looking down at his hands. "But I was assigned to Maksim when I heard about the plan to take Friese. I immediately thought of you, and knew I couldn't stay behind. I volunteered to join the occupation and try to sabotage it from the inside. Thankfully, my true master agreed. It wasn't long before I formed a connection with Captain Trust, and we've been working together ever since. But you can imagine my shock," he said, pausing and looking up at me, "to see my baby sister paraded out and degraded in front of Maksim."

The guilt in his eyes brought fresh tears to my own.

"It's not your fault—"

"I should've abandoned the soldiers and gone to find you immediately after we landed."

I shook my head, firm. "No, absolutely not. I would've taken one look at your uniform and killed you before a single word escaped your mouth. I am so glad you didn't do that."

He huffed his disagreement, looking away again. "After seeing you like that, I'd never felt like such a failure. Your survival has been due to your own strength and wit. I have been utterly insufficient."

I crawled closer and took his hand in mine, but he didn't look at me. "If you had stepped in, Maksim would've deduced our alliance. Our plans. The plot would've been foiled before it ever had a chance."

"Though it may be true," Lukyan said, finally meeting my stare. "It will do nothing to help me sleep at night. Brothers are their sisters' protectors."

My heart ached for him, but there was nothing to be done about it. Our plan remained unchanged. I needed to find the powdered elixir—it was our only hope of liberating Friese. I wanted to believe Levick, Francie, and Arturian would return soon, but I knew Maksim would use me as leverage over them.

*Best to remove that strategy before he can enact it.*

"I've passed two of the three tests. It's almost over. Once he makes me his advisor, I'll be granted more freedom. I'll find the poison and we'll free the kingdom."

Lukyan nodded, but his eyes were distant. "Elucia... the tests aren't—"

Just then, a hoarse squawk interrupted him, and a black talon slashed through the side of the tent.

"This thing, again," Lukyan groaned. He reached for the tent's flap, but I grabbed his hand.

"Don't hurt him. That's my bird."

Lukyan shot me a confused look, but I crawled past him and opened the tent flap. Bollock bobbed his head upon seeing me, and immediately began nosing around my clothing.

"Useless creature," I grumbled, but ran my fingers over the bird's velvety neck. "I'm glad you didn't leave me."

Lukyan's mare was tied to a heavy log nearby, looking deeply uncomfortable with Bollock's presence.

"Don't touch that thing," Lukyan said, following me out. "It's a filthy scavenger."

I jerked my head around at him. "Excuse you. This is *my* filthy scavenger."

My brother's grimace deepened. His mouth opened and closed, like he didn't know which question to ask first. He settled on a simple "why?"

I sat down on the dry grass. Bollock's talons—previously sharp enough to slice through skin—had been filed down by our trek. They didn't so much as scratch me as I pulled him onto my lap.

"Did you wonder where Kiera was?" I asked, keeping my eyes on my preening bird.

"I made assumptions. I didn't want to ask."

"I couldn't save her," I whispered through a tightening throat. The image of her mangled neck flashed through my mind, and I pulled Bollock a bit closer. "I clipped his wing when he was only trying to feed himself. To survive. I couldn't leave him down there to die. That winds-forsaken ravine took enough already."

Lukyan took a deep breath and nodded. "Does he have a name?"

"Bollock."

My brother sighed and looked to the stars, as if they could provide him some relief. "For stone's sake, Elucia. I don't even want to know why you chose that. Can you change it? Or at least abbreviate it?"

I frowned. "Abbreviate it? How?"

For the first time, Lukyan's eyes settled, unwavering, on the vulture resting on my lap. He cocked his head and ran his fingers over his knuckles.

"Lock."

He sat back, evidently satisfied with his contrivance.

I mulled it over in my head, then said it a few times.

Finally, I met Lukyan's eyes and nodded. "Lock."

Something occurred to me, and I froze. "The bag—the one I was carrying with me! Where is it?"

"In the tent," Lukyan said slowly, waiting for an explanation. I didn't give one. "What's in the bag that's so important?"

I almost opened my mouth and told him, but thought better of it. Before I knew he was my brother, I probably would've shown him. I would've been open and unashamed about my tenuous grasp on reality. But after learning how concerned he was for me—how much he worried about my wellbeing—flaunting my madness seemed unnecessarily cruel. So instead, I deflected.

"It's not that important. I just didn't want to lose it."

He eyed me suspiciously, but didn't question any further. "You should eat something. I have some cured beef in the tent."

To my surprise, my stomach growled at the thought. But Lock shifted on my lap, investigating my hands again. I glanced up at Lukyan, eyes wide and unblinking. I even jutted my lip for good measure.

He tilted his head at me and scoffed. "*Ess*, Sister! I am not sharing our food with an animal that would be satisfied with a rotted corpse!"

I straightened and made a show of scanning our dark surroundings. My gaze returned to my brother, and I twitched my lips.

"It's too bad there aren't any of those nearby. I'm sure Lock would love to fly away and find one, but..." I trailed off, stroking his clipped wing gingerly.

Lukyan's eyes fell shut, and he inhaled deeply. "Already pouting and asking for favors. Remind me why I admitted to being your brother?"

Though he complained, Lukyan was more softhearted than he let on. All three of us sat outside his tent under the moonlight, sharing strips of salty beef.

Over the last few months I'd lost my lover, my kingdom, my freedom, and my friend, Kiera. But for the first time since then, I gained something. I had a brother, staring up at the stars and telling me stories of his homeland. I had an avian freeloader, revolting and disease-carrying as he was.

And maybe, just maybe... I had hope.

## *Chapter Twenty-Three*

# Trek

For the first time in weeks, it felt safe to fall asleep. Even at the palace, I slept with the knowledge that Maksim and his generals could steal me from my bed at any moment and I could do nothing about it. I thought of Rynne, alone and scared, and sent a silent prayer for her safety.

*I'm coming back.*

"How long is the walk?" I asked Lukyan as we crawled out of the tent. I quickly found Lock, who'd been cruelly barred from joining us in the tent, and gave him a soft stroke over the neck.

"A little over a day," Lukyan said, his voice straining as he stretched.

My jaw fell open. "More than a day? How could it have taken that long for Maksim to get us out here?"

I'd been asleep at the time, knocked out by whatever drug Maksim had dusted over his lips.

Lukyan began saddling his dusty brown mare, periodically pausing to scratch her shoulders. My eyes caught on the hunting knife he'd strapped to his saddle. It was unexpectedly painful to return it, but keeping it obviously wasn't an option.

"I'm sure you figured this out by now, but when Maksim... kissed you," Lukyan's voice took on an edge, "his mouth was coated with powdered memorexum. An elixir of forgetting. It can also simply knock someone unconscious, if delivered in a potent dose."

Maksim's kiss played over my senses. He'd been so aggressive, so persistent. I'd assumed it was driven by lust, but he'd made sure I tasted every inch of his tongue and lips. He wasn't overcome with lust, he was simply being a thorough poisoner. Nevertheless, the memory sent my stomach roiling with nausea.

Lukyan continued speaking, mercifully distracting me. "Such a dose would've sedated him, too, if not for the inoculation the royal family undergoes."

New concern flooded me, and my eyes darted to Lukyan. "Does he know you're here?"

He dusted his hands off and began disassembling the tent. "Yes. I was preparing to sneak out and damn the consequences when Maksim summoned me." His brows furrowed, pausing for a moment. "It was a peculiar conversation."

I set Lock down and went to help roll the tent. I waited for Lukyan to elaborate, but he seemed lost in thought. The sound of crashing waves filled the silence, beating against rocks down below.

Finally, I spoke up. "What do you mean?"

My brother hummed softly, pushing his long braids over his shoulder. "I went into his room and found him alone, pacing back and forth. He asked me to go and look for you—to make sure you were still alive."

My lips parted in confusion. "These tests have been death sentences. What does he care if I die?"

Lukyan strapped the last of his things to his horse. "He was pacing," he said, then shook his head in frustration. "I've known Maksim Toresav since he was a child, and I've never seen him pace."

An unnerved pit opened in my gut. As much as I hated Maksim, I'd taken a certain comfort in his consistency. Always vicious. Always confident. If there was a crueler option, he would take it.

"You think something is wrong with him?" I asked as I crouched down. Lock hopped onto my shoulder, eager for a free ride.

*Selfish thing.*

But I presented him with a strip of beef anyway.

Lukyan beckoned me over to his horse. "I have suspicions, but I hope I'm wrong. Now get on, you need to ride."

"I can walk."

He gave me a doubtful look. "You've walked enough, don't you think? How are you even standing on that ankle?"

"It's not that bad." It ached, but didn't bleed or show any signs of infection.

*Yet.*

I tried to walk around Lukyan, but he stepped in front of me. "I had to leave you down there, not knowing if you'd live or die. I've had to watch him test and torture you while I stood by and did nothing. Please. Let me take care of you."

My heart softened at his words, his expression. His deep blue eyes glistened with unfallen tears of guilt.

I bowed my head, conceding. "I'll ride."

He smiled, but it was quickly followed by a grimace. "You'll have to drop the bird, though."

I brushed Lock's feathers protectively. "He can ride on the horse's rump."

"The moment those talons touch her, she'll throw both of you."

I pursed my lips and looked up at Lukyan in a wide, pleading stare. My eyes darted to his shoulder, then back to his face.

He groaned. "Absolutely not. You may have lost your mind out here, but I have not. I am not carrying a carrion bird through the Wastes."

Four hours later I dismounted, needing to stretch my legs. I hadn't ridden in quite some time, and my body was not conditioned for it. Additionally, I could tell my ankle was stiffening and needed to be exercised.

The grass had become more lush as we got closer to Friese. I flexed my toes in the soft green blades, enjoying how much nicer it felt than the hard stone ground of the ravine.

I walked over to Lukyan and took Lock from his arms. He shoved the bird to me with all the gentleness of a bull, grumbling in disgust.

"He can hear you," I said, running a gentle finger over Lock's neck. He stretched and preened.

Lukyan looked at me like he was doubtful of my hold on reality. "Good."

I scanned the distance and caught a glimpse of the tallest spire of Friese's palace, jutting out above the tree line. It was too far to see, but I knew the trees had started blooming. Springtime in Friese was unmatched in beauty. A chilly breeze blew over me, giving me goosebumps. The pressure was dropping.

*Another storm is coming.*

Thick gray clouds hung over the sea, far in the eastern distance.

Lukyan caught my gaze, then glanced over the water. "We'll make it back in time."

I nodded, but quickened my steps. After the last time I'd been trapped outside during a summer storm, I wasn't keen on repeating it.

Though I was relieved to see Friese growing over the horizon, I couldn't deny the somber tug backwards, into the wilderness. The reminder that I'd left someone behind. I held Lock tighter.

My mind drifted to my other friend—the one whose life I could still protect.

I walked closer to Lukyan. "How was Rynne doing before you left? Without me and... Kiera." The name was physically painful to say.

He huffed in amusement. "She panicked at first. She was worried for you, and was too scared to sleep in that room by herself."

I made a soft sound of disappointment.

"Oh, don't worry," Lukyan said, flashing me a sly grin. "She didn't endure that fate for very long."

My jaw dropped and I sped up, stopping in front of him. "What do you mean?"

My mind played through all of the terrible things Lukyan could've meant, but I couldn't reconcile them with the facetious smile on his face.

"Relax, Elucia. As far as I know, she is fine. Just not as lonely as before."

I shoved him in the shoulder. "Out with it, for Echna's sake!"

The gleam in his dark blue eyes told me he was having far too much fun torturing me by his omissions.

"Fine," he laughed. "I caught her with Captain Trust."

My eyes shot open wide. "What do you mean *with*?"

He rolled his eyes, as if he now deemed himself too important to be relaying such sordid details. "They were clothed. But very much in bed together."

An embarrassingly loud and enthusiastic gasp escaped my mouth, making Lock flinch. He ruffled his feathers and sent a cloud of dust into my lungs, which in turn sent me into a fit of coughing.

Lukyan laughed at me through a smug grin.

I glared at him, but was too overwhelmed by fresh gossip and foul dust to do much else. I'd noticed Rynne's flustered blushing around Coran, but hadn't thought anything real would come of it.

Once I managed to clear my lungs, I laughed along, too. "After everything that's happened, people are still finding love."

Lukyan scoffed and gave me a condescending pat on the shoulder. "I don't think it was *love* they were finding. If so, then Maksim's revels are the most loving occasions the world has ever seen."

I gagged at the thought, but morbid curiosity crept into my mind. I glanced over at my brother, who was still shaking his head and chuckling.

*Does he... participate in them? No. I don't want to know.*

Even the thought of it made my nose scrunch and my lip curl up.

Lukyan glanced over and read my expression easily. His features soon mirrored mine.

"I know what you're thinking. For stone's sake," he muttered. "No. I don't join the orgies."

I groaned, hating hearing the words but somehow relieved by them.

"Good," I said, stroking Lock's dirty feathers. "I'd hate to lose you to whatever fatal diseases they're spreading around."

He laughed and shook his head, and despite the revolting topic of conversation, I found myself smiling, too.

By the time we reached the outskirts of Friese, light rain was falling on us. It was a warning of the summer storm brewing off the coast. Though we could no longer see it through the darkness, I felt the unrest in the air.

When we made it to the center of the kingdom, the sun had been down for hours. At Lukyan's estimation, it was likely past midnight. It was surreal to be walking through the pristine streets of northern Friese in a torn and bloodied dress, carrying a vulture on my shoulder. I wondered what Levick would think if he saw me. The thought brought me nothing but cold nausea.

The woman he knew was an innocent and protected heiress. Newly confident and uniquely powerful. Though I felt immense satisfaction at having bested Maksim's absurd challenges, the feeling was distinctly less dignified than that of being powerful. It was smugness. Spitefulness.

In my rational mind, I knew Levick was kind and caring, and wouldn't judge me for doing what I needed to do for the sake of Friese. For my survival. But the irrational, poisonous side of my mind whispered words of insufficiency in my ears.

*He is good. He is pure.*

*You are none of those things. Not anymore.*

*You are not worthy of him, and maybe you never truly were.*

I shook the thoughts away and focused on my immediate surroundings. The homes were towering and grand in northernmost Friese. They loomed over us like beautiful, taunting phantoms, showing me what I could've had. We eventually crossed the street that led to the Yorke mansion, and I paused. Lukyan glanced over at me, but in the darkness, he hadn't discerned our proximity to my home.

"We are almost there," he said, tugging my arm.

*Has my home fallen into disrepair? Or worse... has it been destroyed?*

I shook my head at the notion.

*No. Maybe Louis is there.*

As useless and incompetent as he was, I had to believe he could protect the mansion.

*One challenge at a time, Eliandre.*

I nodded to Lukyan and walked on.

As we got closer to the palace, I passed Lock to Lukyan, who was clearly unhappy with the arrangement.

"He will take good care of you. This is only temporary," I whispered to the disgruntled vulture. I ran a finger over his head, and he pushed up against it. "I'll come and see you soon."

Lukyan gave me a deadpan stare. "He will be in the old stable, just outside the gate. Stop fawning over a bird as if he were your pet."

"Who says he's not?" I asked as I gave Lock one last affectionate stroke over the feathers.

My brother sighed but didn't argue. "You should go to your room to wash and change before seeing him."

I shook my head. "No. I have to deliver this," I said, lifting my makeshift bag. "I'll bathe and rest afterwards."

Lukyan cocked his head at me, but didn't inquire further. He walked me all the way to the palace's front gate, where he commanded the guards to let me in. They were the same guards as the last time I returned to the palace in the middle of the night—wearing a torn dress and looking half-crazed—so they didn't question it.

It was difficult to resist hugging my brother goodbye, but the guards would certainly raise a brow at such behavior. So we exchanged a subtle nod before Lukyan led his horse to the old stable, carrying Lock along.

I walked towards the palace's towering doors, clutching my bag and filled with hate.

## Chapter Twenty-Four

# A Tenuous Grasp

No one attempted to stop me as I stepped through the palace doors, but many people paused in the hallways to gawk and gape at me. They made no efforts to lower their voices as they whispered,

*"Disgusting."*

*"What is she holding?"*

*"He should kill her and be done with it."*

They leaned against the walls and looked down their powdered noses at me. Even their scanty attire reeked of intoxicated indulgence. Their golden tasseled dresses reflected candlelight like lures meant to lead people to their deaths. Glittering finery with none of the legacy.

Despite my undeniably privileged upbringing, I'd never thought myself as part of the royal class. I was happily in love with an orphan from the slums who didn't appreciate high society. When push came to shove, jewels and gold were nothing to loyal sincerity.

So I ignored them and their sneering, and instead focused on the feeling of cold marble under my aching feet. The wrinkling of my silk scrap bag in my aching left hand. The dust gathered on sweeping lines of silver filigree along the walls and picture frames. It was a beautiful palace, rotting from within.

*He's killing this place.*

*He's killing Friese.*

The sounds of riotous celebration echoed through the halls. Even in the small hours of the morning, their debauchery continued unimpeded. I made it to the doors of Maksim's ballroom of indulgence, but stopped short.

My dress hung off of me in shredded white tatters, marred with dust and blood stains. My ankle remained wrapped in a bloody piece of silk, and my hair fell over my back in dirty tangles. I looked like I'd emerged from hell itself.

*So I have.*

I gritted my teeth, leaned forward, and shoved the doors open.

Shouting and laughing filled my ears, but they weren't directed at me. In fact, the revelers hardly seemed to notice the doors opening. They instead were fixated on a duel taking place in the center of the room. Except for a handful of overeager couples along the periphery, everyone seemed completely invested in the central conflict.

I rolled my eyes at their jeering and began pushing through. I was so tired. My legs trembled, pleading for rest. My left hand ached and barely held up the bag I'd brought all the way back from the ravine. But I'd deliver my gift. Even if it killed me.

Drunken partygoers glared and scoffed as I passed them, uncaring whether I hit their shoulders, backs, or faces. But as soon as they recognized me, they stilled.

*That's right. You know who I am. The girl who should be dead.*

Word of my return hadn't quite made it through the masses by the time I made it to the center of the room. I shoved past a couple of gaping women only to step into a dueling ring. A tall, angry soldier swung his sword with the fury of a thousand ravenous bears. His form—though slowed by inebriation—was stellar. I almost averted my eyes from the final arc of his swing, sure that his opponent would fall under such an assault.

But across from him was Maksim Toresav, standing tall and holding firm. His eyes were crazed and bloodshot, and his hair fell over his face in disheveled blond strands. His loose white shirt slipped from his shoulder as he raised his sword in defense.

The weapons met in a deafening ring, locking the men in a test of strength. But Maksim's eyes caught on mine, and his entire countenance shifted. He flicked his sword to the right, easily tossing off his assaulter, then threw the weapon to the ground.

The room was as still as a cemetery. No one dared to speak. No one deigned to breathe.

Maksim's chest heaved from exertion, but his eyes scanned me frantically. He looked as if he'd seen a ghost.

"You really didn't think I'd survive that last one, did you?" I asked, taking a few steps closer.

His stare fell upon my unbound and uninjured right hand, and a warning of caution shone in his eyes. "I made no bets either way, little gull."

His voice, raw and rasping, scraped against my eardrums like talons over soft flesh.

He looked over my appearance once again. "Did Lukyan find you?" he asked.

I almost answered, but paused upon noticing the slight twitch in his lips. It was a test.

*I've had enough of those.*

"I made it back. I passed your test."

I crossed the space between us. With every step closer, the tension in the room grew thicker. It was like the crowd were all holding a collective breath, waiting for everything to combust.

"I even brought you a gift," I said as I stopped a few feet away.

Maksim looked down at my feet. His jaw ticked, as if he were disappointed that I stopped so soon.

"Well?" he asked, raising an entitled brow. "Is it in that filthy bag?"

I felt something snap in my brain as he looked down his nose at me. The man who sent Kiera to her death. Who dropped us in the wilderness and loosed half a dozen starving dogs on us.

*Sadistic, hateful cur of a man.*

My lips pulled up at the edge, and my eye twitched. "In fact, it is."

In one smooth movement, I seized the dog testicle from my bag and tossed it in the air. Before anyone could react, I leaned forward and threw my windblade through it. Blood sprayed over Maksim and his opponent.

I felt the raw laughter spill from my mouth, unrestrained. For days I'd clung to that gruesome trophy as I'd clung to my sanity. But they'd both exploded in front of me, spilling blood everywhere.

The entire room erupted in gasps and shouting, but I didn't care. Guards lunged for me. I closed my eyes and waited to be knocked down.

"Stop."

Everyone went silent. The voice dripped of pure authority. The kind that could only be created through consecutive generations of entitlement.

Maksim stepped towards me and cocked his head. He hadn't even wiped the blood dripping down his temple.

*He's mad.*

But blood trickled down my cheek, and I didn't wipe it away.

"Was that what I think it was?" Maksim asked, a strange mixture of revulsion and interest playing on his fair features.

Through great effort, I stifled my laughter. "If you thought it was a piece of your dog's most prized body parts, you'd be right."

A chorus of disgusted groans echoed through the ballroom, followed by the rustling of multiple people rushing out.

Maksim's eyes narrowed on me for a split second before he asked, "Only one?"

I nearly gasped at the absurd question, but answered it, nonetheless.

"My vulture ate the other one."

At that, the crowd had enough. They shouted, calling me insane and begging Maksim to have me executed.

But he closed the gap between us and took my hand. I was just unstable enough to tighten my fingers around his and let him lead me from the room.

I ignored the yelling and distress coming from behind us. My eyes remained lazily unfocused on what was ahead. Maksim's loose white shirt, stained and bloody. Enigmatic icy eyes glancing back at me ever so often.

*Where is he taking me?*

*Do I care?*

If he took me to his room, I'd kill him. I'd slice him open and send Friese down with him.

*Please don't.*

I didn't want to abandon my plans and damn my kingdom, but it had become too much. Hatred and vengeance were pushing into the cracks of my broken heart, filling it completely. If he tried to hurt me, I'd forget every rational thought, every shred of leverage, and end him.

But he turned down the hallway towards my bedroom. I expected to feel relief, but I felt nothing.

*I feel nothing because I* am *nothing.*

*A priceless porcelain vase. Desirable until it was shattered and glued back together with the marrow of innocents.*

"I'll have a bath drawn for you," he said, looking back at me again.

I didn't respond.

*Does he want me to thank him?*

*I'd rather be grimy and disgusting forever.*

His thumb twitched over my hand. "Your friend is dead?"

"Yes."

We walked in silence until we reached my door. Maksim stepped in front of the handle and stopped. His pale blue gaze bore into me, dissecting.

"What is it?" I asked, my voice barely audible. My adrenaline was spent, leaving me completely drained.

He tilted his head, looking down at my wrapped ankle.

I took a deep breath and willed patience into my bones. "Maksim."

His eyes snapped up to mine, flaring a bit.

I didn't like his behavior. I thought of Lukyan's words earlier, how Maksim had been pacing and behaving unusually. But I was too exhausted to conjure much concern for it.

*That's a problem for tomorrow.*

The last few days had worn me paper-thin. I hadn't stopped moving since waking in the Wastes. I knew if I didn't rest soon, I'd collapse. The notion of doing that in front of Maksim made me bristle.

"I don't have the energy for more mind games. May I bathe?" I asked, my tone sharpening.

He pulled the key from his pocket and turned around. "I need to see your ankle."

"I have medical training. I'll take care of it," I argued, but he'd already opened the door.

Rynne shot up from one of the plush velvet chairs, her eyes wide with alarm. "Eliandre! You're alive!"

She stepped forward, as if she wanted to embrace me, but Maksim's presence deterred her.

"Go in the dressing room and shut the door," he commanded. "I have to assess Eliandre's injury."

I physically flinched at the sound of my name on his lips.

"Why do I have to leave for that?" Rynne asked.

"Don't make me ask twice."

Rynne inhaled like she was going to argue, but I shook my head at her. He'd demonstrated his ability to hurt people without a second thought. It wasn't worth it.

She looked me up and down, concern written all over her face. But I motioned to the dressing room, and she complied.

As soon as the door latched shut, Maksim led me over to the bed and told me to sit.

I frowned, but perched on the edge. "Can this not be done on a chair?"

"Quiet."

To my surprise, Maksim knelt on the floor in front of me. He lifted my foot, sliding his fingers gently over my calf as he inspected the bandage. I tensed at the contact and flinched back, but his fingers tightened over my leg.

Maksim looked up, his expression stoic. "I'm not going to hurt you."

He pulled at my bandage and let it slip to the floor. He pressed against my bones and joints, checking for breaks, just as I'd done.

*Medically trained, as well.*

I furrowed my brows, more terrified of his gentleness than the cruelty I'd come to expect. "Why not?"

He looked up, his lips parted in confusion. "What?"

I didn't even blink. "Why aren't you hurting me?"

"What kind of question is that?"

"It's all you've done since I was captured. Why the change? Are you simply not in the mood for your usual sadism?"

A malicious darkness flashed in his eyes. "Why do you ask? Do you miss it?" He dragged his thumb over my open gash, making me whimper. "I'm deciding whether you'll need a tonic. Your last infection rendered you useless for nearly a month. Don't let your exhausted delirium loosen your tongue. Now sit still."

I did as he told, and leaned back on my hands. He unfastened his shirt buttons and slipped it from his shoulders, then proceeded to clean some of the blood and grime off my leg. I didn't know why he bothered—I was going to wash it, anyway—but the sight of his fingers so close to my open wound kept my mouth shut. I tried to block out the feeling of his cold skin brushing over mine.

*Another trick. Another mind game.*

"When is the last test?" I asked, slurring my words together. The embossed ceiling was starting to look alive. I desperately needed sleep.

"Don't worry about it right now."

"How could I not? When I could be tossed in a den of angry vipers, or trapped in a building with a dozen Frost Company soldiers hell-bent on stealing my virtue?"

Maksim's fingers paused on the back of my ankle, and I saw him look up from my periphery. "Virtue? You're untouched?"

I regretted the tacit admission immediately. But despite the technical truth in it, my recent experiences left me feeling far from virtuous.

"I suppose I am," I mumbled.

*And I'll remain that way until Levick returns. Or until I die in this wretched palace.*

Maksim hummed thoughtfully, but returned to his ministrations.

When I first was captured, I often worried about my bodily virtue being stolen away. It was something I always valued, and only planned on giving to the man I married. Though it remained intact, I'd never felt dirtier.

I thought of the grotesque spectacle I'd just put on in the ballroom, and a humorless chuckle escaped my lips. "Of what value is an untouched body if the mind has been warped beyond recognition?"

"You mistake mental fortitude for mania," Maksim said, rising from the floor. "You've been strengthened. That is a good thing."

A genuine laugh shook my chest, and I fell back onto the bed. "My mental state is anything but fortitudinous. If that is what you see in me, you might be further gone than I am."

It vaguely occurred to me that I was clad in a dress of scraps and lying on a bed directly in front of the most depraved lech in Friese. But I smelled awful and looked like death... and if he tried something, I'd simply kill him. Responsibilities and repercussions still hadn't worked their way back into my area of concern.

*I need sleep.*

The muffled sound of retreating steps made their way to my ears, then the click of the door handle. I almost didn't hear his parting words.

"It is only the beginning, my dear."

## *Chapter Twenty-Five*

# Desired Neglect

I eventually woke to a fussing Rynne herding me into a hot bath. She didn't ask me anything about the second test, but mentioned that Coran and Lukyan had come by while I was asleep. From the puffy redness in her eyes, I knew Lukyan had told her about Kiera. I appreciated her silence on the subject. If I spoke of it, I'd have to think of it. It would all come back. The screams, the growls. The bones of her neck peeking through exposed blood and muscle.

*Stop thinking about it.*

The metal gloves were never refastened over my fingers, which I'd initially assumed was an oversight. But I thought of the previous night—how I'd wielded my windblade in a ballroom full of Trenicans. I'd thrown it a mere horse-length from Maksim's head.

*I had an opportunity, and didn't take it. He knows I won't hurt him.*

I didn't even want to consider what he was assuming from that new information.

Rynne eventually broke the tense silence, only to tell me that Coran and his resistance had lost the Exley mansion. Maksim's tireless efforts against the southern Friesians were paying off. The news placed yet another weight upon my shoulders.

*They're counting on you, now. You might be their only hope until Levick returns.*

A hot tonic was brought to our room by an unfamiliar guard. He refused to say anything about it other than that it was sent by Maksim. My strange interaction with him made me think it was likely a simple tonic to prevent infection. I wouldn't have risked it, but my ankle ached and throbbed.

The tonic had notes of amber and cinnamon, and went down smoothly. When an hour passed and I didn't have any horrific side-effects, I finally relaxed again.

"So," I muttered as Rynne brought me a towel. "I heard about you and the captain."

She dropped the towel and tripped on it. Despite the somber heaviness in the air, I chuckled.

Rynne huffed as she returned to her feet. "I should've known Lukyan would tell you."

"What does it matter? I'm happy for you. Coran is a good man."

She rolled the towel and gestured for me to lean forward. I did, and she placed it behind my neck.

"You know who else is?" she asked as she guided my head back again. "Lukyan. That was a long way you two traveled together."

I barely stifled my disgusted grimace before it could fully take over my face.

*Lukyan didn't tell her we're siblings.*

I almost said something, but bit my tongue. Lukyan wouldn't keep something like that to himself without a compelling reason. Thankfully, I had an easy and truthful deflection.

"You're very imaginative, Rynne, but I love Levick."

*Despite the fact that he probably wouldn't recognize me anymore.*

Rynne rolled her eyes. "I know a bond when I see one."

*Oh, there's a bond. But not that kind of bond.*

"It's not like that. Besides, we were talking about you."

"There's really not much to say." She flipped her hair over her shoulder.

But eventually my prodding paid off, and she spilled some of the sweet moments she'd had with Coran.

A bittersweet smile grew over my lips as I listened. Their love—whether they'd call it that yet—seemed so pure and uncomplicated. She gushed about the little gifts he'd brought her, and how he held her cheek when he kissed her.

I nodded along enthusiastically, and encouraged her to appreciate every moment they had together.

*You never know when it could end.*

I attempted to sleep for most of the day, but visions of Kiera's final horrified expression haunted me. I still heard her gut-wrenching screams repeating in my mind. She was so young—hardly fifteen. Even her voice had sounded naive. I wished I could recall what her laugh sounded like, but all I remembered were her cries.

Coran and Lukyan came to our room that night. It was difficult to pretend Lukyan was nothing more than my accomplice, but based on the subtle warning looks he'd given me, I knew he didn't want Rynne and Coran to know about our familial relation.

Coran pressed me on my progress, asking if I'd managed to get closer to Maksim. I detailed the strange interaction we'd had after he brought me back to my bedroom. The gentleness, the cryptic words. Coran was very encouraged by it, and took it as a sign I'd soon be allowed into Maksim's confidence. Lukyan, however, seemed deeply unnerved. He refused to look at me for the rest of the night.

*It might be a good thing. Maybe Coran is right, and Maksim's new concern will allow me to make some progress soon.*

I let the thought comfort me. The last few days had brought me no closer to finding his elixirs, and I needed a lifeline.

Five days passed without any tests or visits from Maksim. My meals were delivered by bitter guards who'd scowl as they waited impatiently for me to eat my food—evidently part of Maksim's new and unnerving interest in my recovery.

Lukyan came by to tell me how Lock was doing, then informed me I'd been tasked with kitchen work to replace Kiera.

I chewed on my lip as I straightened my new uniform. Rynne stood behind me, weaving a braid into my hair.

"What about the generals' windblade training? Or my third test?" I wasn't eager to resume them, but the change of plans was making me nervous.

"I don't know. He didn't mention either of those things," Lukyan said.

My brows pulled together, and I told him about the strange behavior the meal guards had been displaying. "Why would Maksim care if I starve? Both of his tests almost killed me."

Lukyan looked away, shaking his head in confusion. "I'm not sure. Maybe to prepare you for the last test. It's hard to say—he's been withdrawn lately."

Rynne scoffed and brushed a red curl over her shoulder. "His revels sound just as lively as ever."

Lukyan shook his head. "He's not attended any of them. Not since El—" he stumbled over my name. "Eliandre returned."

*Good save.*

"Maybe he's sick," Rynne said, a wistful sigh on her lips. "It's about time with all of the strangers he has passing through his sheets."

Lukyan didn't respond, but from the look on his face, he doubted it. I wished I knew what he was thinking.

"Weren't you sacked from Eliandre duty? Are you allowed to be here?" Rynne asked.

My heart dropped at the question—I'd forgotten Lukyan had been reassigned after Maksim caught us in the hallway.

"Yes, before the second test. But after I helped guide her back to Friese, he reinstated me." There was an uncertainty in his voice.

"Did he say why?" I asked.

He shook his head.

I flexed my left hand, then winced at the pain. It was still stiff, despite the weeks of healing. I had an ominous feeling about the injury. Though I hadn't completely severed any bones, something didn't feel right. A vague numbness lingered in my knuckles.

My eyes flickered down to the dark, grotesque scar. It ran vertically down my hand, stopping just before my knuckles.

*One day, my wedding ring will have to share a hand with this abomination.*

*If I survive long enough to get married.*

Rynne finished my braid and pulled me to my feet. Her rusty painted lips were pressed in a firm line as she assessed my uniform and smoothed out various wrinkles.

"I hope you know how to proof dough," she muttered.

I didn't.

The kitchen staff worked me hard. For three weeks I did nothing but eat, sleep, and work. My injured hand was clumsy, and I was subjected to multiple disciplinary tasks because of my poor coordination. As the numbness in my left knuckles endured, I tried to come to terms with my new reality. I only had one hand to wield my windblade, and there was a possibility that would never change.

Lukyan walked me to and from the kitchens. He was quiet on our walks, but always kind. I'd occasionally attempt to uncover whatever was occupying his thoughts, but he'd respectfully deflect or go quiet.

It was obvious that he was concerned for me. I wasn't sleeping well and my appetite had vanished. Despite the guards' insistence that I eat, my clothes hung off my body rather than clinging to it as they used to. Lukyan never explicitly asked about it, but I'd notice the worried twitch of his brow every time I emerged from my dressing room.

I only saw Coran a few times, as Lukyan became my primary point of contact. Seeing Coran became a rarity—his visits to our room usually coincided with my work shifts. I noticed, with some amusement, that Rynne's mood had markedly improved.

Maksim made no contact with me, in person or by message. Lukyan continued to worry about his strange behavior, though he never went into detail. He only claimed Maksim was becoming more and more reclusive, hardly attending or participating in any revels or court meetings. I wanted to be happy about the change—I'd been offered relief from his torturous attentions—but something didn't feel right. I knew nothing of when the final test was taking place, or what it would consist of.

I knew I'd have to approach him at some point. He was my only lead in finding his elixir stores. With every day that passed, our chances of thwarting Maksim's rule dwindled. It was only a matter of time before Levick and the others returned, and airborne poison would be fatal to their attempts at reclamation. If Maksim didn't contact me, I resolved to seek him out soon.

## Chapter Twenty-Six

# An Indecent Appeal

It was late in the night when a deafening pounding echoed through our door. Rynne flinched away under the covers, pulling them up to her chin.

"Who is that?" she whispered. We'd both grown accustomed to Lukyan's polite knocking, and this was entirely different.

I willed my shaking legs to slide over the side of the bed. With tenuous steps, I crossed the room and slid my fingers over the door handle.

"Who is it?" I asked through the door crack.

An unfamiliar voice answered. "His Excellency summons Miss Yorke. She will dress and open this door in five minutes, or I will enter and collect her."

I turned to Rynne, whose face was barely visible in the moonlight streaming through the window. She tilted her head and pursed her lips as if to say, *that's not much of a choice.*

They'd barged into the room before. They'd do it again.

I leaned next to the door. "I'll be just a moment."

There was no time to light candles, so I dressed in the darkness. I had no idea what color my dress was, I only knew it was smooth, silk, and seemed to be more modest than the other attire I'd been provided. I slipped the straps over my shoulders, tied the lace ribbon in the back, and rushed to the door.

"Eliandre!" Rynne whispered. "Please... be safe."

We both knew such a request was out of my hands, but I nodded back to her.

"I will."

My guard was a stocky bull of a man. His hair hung in pale, thinning strands over his crimson-uniformed shoulders.

"Hurry up," he grunted, pushing a meaty hand against my back.

As we walked through the more highly lit areas of the palace, I noticed a flash of bright red below me. I looked down only to see that I'd dressed myself in a gown the exact same color as Trenican guard uniforms. To make matters worse, the thin fabric clung to my withering frame as if it were soaking wet. I almost groaned at my misfortune.

*What kind of silk is this?*

I gritted my teeth and tried not to think about it. I pulled some of my hair in front of my shoulders to partially conceal my body.

"Where are you taking me? Is this the third test?" I asked.

His answer was curt, and invited no further questions. "The revel."

I anxiously chewed on my cheek. I'd had enough reveling to last a lifetime, but followed along on shaking legs.

We entered into Maksim's ballroom of indulgence, and my senses were assaulted with all of the objectionable sights, sounds, and smells of unrestricted debauchery. I tried not to let my eyes linger on them as they danced and swayed to disjointed harmonies.

I expected the guard to push me towards the throne, but I quickly noticed it was empty. He instead guided me to the stone staircase at the back of the room, leading up to the balcony. The crowd thinned the further we went up the stairs—most of them preferring the vague concealment of other dancers to hide their wicked deeds.

The guard led me to a set of arched doors, then stopped. They were inlaid with silver vines, twisting up and around the arch and down the sides. He wasted no time on admiring the beautiful work and instead shoved them open. He urged me to go through alone, then shut the doors behind me without another word.

I frowned at the strange behavior, but stepped onto the moonlit balcony. It was expansive—large enough for a waltz—and was bordered by a tall stone railing. Each baluster along the rail seemed to be carved differently than the next, many depicting crashing waves or beautiful women.

Leaning over that railing was a lone man, dressed in a bright crimson uniform and wearing gloves of pure white. His hair was partially collected in intricate braids over his ears, but the rest fell loose over his back. His body language wasn't that of a man who'd summoned company. He seemed like he wished to be left alone.

*But here I am.*

I spoke his name softly, not wanting to surprise him. "Maksim."

His head turned slightly, but he didn't look at me. "Come here."

The rasp in his voice set me on edge, but I did as he commanded. I stopped beside the railing and leaned against it. He still didn't look at me. He gazed out over Friese, the beautiful kingdom bathed in pale moonlight.

"Is this about the third test?" I asked, risking a glance at him.

His jaw twitched. "Stop thinking about the tests."

*This again? What does he expect?*

I said nothing and waited for some kind of explanation. My eyes scanned the kingdom, pausing on every familiar house and building. Eventually I landed on the sea, and I watched as the faint glimmer of whitecaps crashed against the shore.

From my peripheral vision I saw Maksim turn to face me. I didn't move my gaze from the sea. Something about his energy was deeply unnerving. It wasn't hate or malintent. It was something else, and it terrified me.

"Look at me, Eliandre."

My heart pounded in my chest. When I met his stare, it was like slamming into a brick wall. The moonlight shining in his light irises intensified whatever emotion was swirling inside his black heart.

I swallowed the lump forming in my throat and forced kindness into my tone. "What do you need? It's quite late—"

"I am amending our deal."

My lips parted in surprise, but he continued before I could argue.

"The role of advisor... the title. It's no longer enough," he said, his expression never shifting.

"W-what do you mean?" I stammered.

Maksim took a step closer, but I took a step back.

"Breaking you has been a pleasure I've never known before. I'll not give it up."

I shook my head and gripped the railing. I held on as if it could anchor me, but the tide of Maksim's words drowned me.

"Over the last few weeks, I've had to accept something. Something I'd sworn would never happen to me." He leaned in closer, catching my eyes. "I want you. I need you. No other diversions will suffice anymore."

His words made no sense.

*What is he asking for? Sex? Romance? Love?*

*An eternal prisoner?*

"I don't understand," I muttered.

"I want to keep you. Forever."

"Forever?" My eyes widened in disbelief. "When I am hateful and bitter, cursing your name, what will you do? When you've turned me into a monster as horrific as yourself, and I have no purity left to corrupt, will your hunger be sated?" I scoffed at him. "You will throw me away."

I turned and walked towards the doors, but he followed closely.

"You're not listening. I love you, Eliandre."

My entire body froze, and I turned to face him. He stepped closer until he leaned over me. I tried to move away, but my back met with one of the massive stone statues.

He reached up and threaded his fingers through the hair on the back of my head. "I am enamored with your tears. Besotted with your screams. I yearn for the scrape of your fingernails against my skin, clawing me away, layer by layer."

The words sent an icy chill down my spine. "I don't know what it is you feel for me, Maksim Toresav. But that is not love," I whispered.

His fingers slid over my jaw, and his thumb rested on my chin. "What is love, my dear, if not obsession? What is passion if not a neurotic craze, gripping the mind and heart until reason suffocates? It is a poison that eats us from the inside until our minds are rotted and our souls are burned to ash." He leaned in until his lips brushed my ear and his hair tickled my cheek. "For the first time in my life, I've found myself begging. Let me consume you, Eliandre. Let this love consume us both until we are unrecognizable and indistinguishable from each other."

His words sucked the air from my lungs. Suddenly, all of his strange behavior made sense. The pacing, his absence from revels. The disquieting gentleness when he inspected my injured ankle. He'd become fully obsessed. Shock and terror flooded my system, threatening to rob me of reason and send me running away. But the whisper of strategy was tenacious in my ear, reminding me of my initial goal.

*Get close to Maksim. Find the powdered elixir.*

Another voice told me I was playing with fire, and it would burn me alive. But I smothered that voice until it was silent.

"If not your advisor..." I trailed off, just barely leaning closer to him.

"Wife," he said, his pupils dilating at the word. "Marry me."

It was toxic. Maksim was a corrosive substance that ruined everything he touched. But he'd already touched me, and I was long since ruined.

*Might as well get something out of it.*

"I have conditions."

While most men might've been offended by such a response to a proposal, Maksim's face split into a dark, enthusiastic grin.

*Just another game.*

"I'd expect no less. Name them."

I didn't hesitate. "Protection for Rynne."

He nodded and rolled his eyes, bored with it. "And?"

"No more guards and escorts."

A subtle, amorous smile crept over his lips. "You won't need them. You'll move into the Royal Chambers tomorrow, where you'll be quite safe."

Something told me Maksim's bedroom was the least safe place in Friese.

"That brings me to my last condition," I said, reaching out and sliding delicate fingers over his chest. His eyes darkened at the contact, but I pressed on. It would be a hard sell. "Even if I agree to move into your rooms for the duration of our betrothal, I wish to retain my virtue until after our vows are made."

Maksim tilted his head back, dissatisfied. But the look was quickly replaced by something far more concerning.

"Fine. But I have my own conditions." He moved closer until his body was almost pressed against mine, trapping me between him and the statue. "The wedding takes place one month from today."

My fingers, still resting on his chest, curled into a fist.

*One month. Just one month to find the elixirs and make a plan to steal them. If I fail...*

*A lifetime with Maksim.*

"You stay by my side. You do as I say. But most importantly," he said, sliding a hand over my waist and leaning close to my ear. "Forsake all others. Purge the thought of any other man from your heart. Because you, beloved, are a prize I will not share."

*Prize.*

My stomach turned at the word.

He backed away, only far enough to look me in the eye. "What is your answer?"

I'd let it go on too long. I was in over my head. But from the malicious gleam in his eyes, I knew there was only one acceptable answer. Only one that would permit Rynne's and my survival.

*Forgive me, Levick.*

"Yes."

His lips twitched into a feral smile, and my stomach flipped. Then, to my surprise, he dropped to a knee and reached into his coat pocket. From it he pulled a glistening platinum ring covered in diamonds. It cast reflective stars in peculiar angles, around the inner portion of the ring.

He reached out, his white gloved fingers almost glowing in the moonlight. I presented my trembling left hand.

He pulled my fingers to his lips, leaving a lingering kiss on them. Then, he slid the ring over my finger.

Pain shot through my hand. The razor-sharp prongs cut into my finger as he slid it on. I cried out and tried to yank my hand away, but Maksim held firm to the ring, and it dug further into my finger.

“Maksim, what is this?” I hissed through panicked sobs. Drops of blood ran down my finger and over my hand.

He clicked his tongue as he finished placing the ring. “Now, now, little gull.”

He rose to his feet, took my bloody hand in both of his, then lifted them to hold my face. I felt the warm liquid smear over my cheeks. I trembled and shook against the statue, but there was nowhere to go. No way to escape.

*I've damned myself.*

“I hope you didn't think things would change between us,” he whispered, stroking my cheekbone with his thumb. “Because it is your agony that I am in love with... and I will do anything to have it.”

A chill blew over the balcony, sending his pleasant aroma of spruce and citrus wafting over me.

*Maksim Toresav... a tantalizing terror.*

“You're a sadist,” I whispered.

He slid an arm around my back and one behind my neck. “Only for you, my dear.”

He pulled my lips to his. A mixture of coppery blood and salty tears ran over my tongue. I suppressed my revulsion. I blocked out the screaming guilt and groaning hatred and wrapped my arms around my fiancé's neck.

I kissed him back while indulging in vivid fantasies of his demise.

We were quite a spectacle coming down from the balcony together. Maksim held my hand around his arm, where my jagged diamond ring could be seen. Our faces, mouths and necks were smeared in blood. We looked like a pair of star-crossed ghouls, emerging from the dead to terrorize innocents.

With every step down the marble staircase, I attracted a dozen more gawkers. The soldiers' expressions were firm with smug satisfaction—proud that their leader caught his prey. The women's eyes were darting between my engagement ring and blood-smeared mouth, which matched Maksim's. Their clear jealousy made me want to vomit.

*Masochists. You don't really want this.*

My finger dripped from a handful of stinging cuts. If the ring was pushed towards the tip of my finger, it dug in tighter, almost piercing me anew. To take it off would be to mangle my finger. It was now a part of me. The design was every bit as insidious as its giver's heart.

I couldn't help but notice Maksim's glare linger on some of his generals, almost like a threat. But those looks were tame compared to the gaze he leveled at Lukyan.

He was by the doors of the ballroom, breathing heavily as if he'd just run a long distance. His dark blue eyes were wide with horror as they fixated on the ring on my left hand. I broke into a nervous sweat and tried to catch his eyes with mine. His stare didn't budge.

*Get it together, Lukyan. He's already suspicious.*

I dared a look at Maksim, whose head was tilted in sinister intrigue.

"Interesting," he muttered.

My arm tightened over Maksim's, and I stood on my toes to whisper in his ear. "Didn't you want to enjoy the revel together?"

He tore his stare from Lukyan and looked down at me. I nodded my head towards his throne. His lips twitched, and he led us over.

He sat down and leaned into the jewel encrusted chair, then tugged on my waist. I wasn't surprised when he pulled me down to sit on his lap, but my soul bristled anyway. I could still see Lukyan in the crowd, trying to school his reaction.

Maksim lifted his hand, pinched the tip of his blood-stained glove between his teeth, then slipped it off. Then, as if he knew Lukyan was watching, he slid his hand over my waist and pulled me further onto his lap. I pressed my eyes shut and prayed to Echna for Lukyan to look away. Or for Maksim to practice restraint.

Maksim's fingers languorously traced my hip bone, but to my infinite relief, strayed no further. I could've cried. There were a multitude of things he could do that would technically keep his promise of preserving my virtue, but shred any vestige of dignity I had left.

I felt his heat over my neck as he leaned in close. "Don't worry, beloved. My message has been received. I've no desire to make a whore of my future wife." He brushed a strand of hair behind my ear, letting his icy finger trace the curve of my neck. "Unless I have to."

# *Chapter Twenty-Seven*

# SORDID OPTIMISM

It felt like the night that would never end. Maksim spent most of it sitting on his throne, drinking and running his fingers over me. I'd hoped I'd eventually stop noticing his touch, but I was granted no such respite. He periodically handed me his goblet and told me to drink, and I'd take the smallest possible sip before giving it back.

The first time he offered it, I brought it to my lips but didn't drink any of it. I regretted this dishonesty when he kissed me, and noticed none of the elixir's taste on my tongue. My lip still ached from where he bit me.

So I drank his elixir sip by sip, and with every passing hour, his touch became less revolting. It even began to border on *tempting*.

I knew it was amourelixir. The effect felt similar to when he poisoned me with his potent hallucinogenic blend, then left me anchored in the stormy sea.

*Not before I all but offered myself up to him.*

I gritted my teeth at the memory, but Maksim's laugh distracted me. One of his generals had just made a sly remark in Vynesic, and my betrothed evidently found it amusing. He responded in their thick, growling language, his accent deliciously heavy.

*No!*

My rational mind screamed.

*He's trying to make you rescind your condition. Think of the pain in your left palm and your wedding finger. Your shredded ankle.*

*Kiera.*

Her smile appeared in my mind, dousing my treacherous elixir-induced desires.

I searched the crowds for Lukyan, hoping his presence would ground me. My eyes scanned over the dancers as they waltzed. The women's scanty gowns were a sharp contrast to their partners' full dress uniforms. Only a few of them had begun shedding their thick coats.

Just as I speedily averted my eyes from an overly enthusiastic couple in the back, I found Lukyan on the other side of the room. He was talking to a young Friesian woman who'd rested her hand on his arm. He backed away and bowed his head, appearing to respectfully decline her advances. She walked off in a disappointed blur of green silk.

My brother turned and immediately met my eyes. He then glanced at the door, nodding his head. He wanted me to leave, but I wasn't sure if Maksim would let me out of his sight. He'd escorted me everywhere, even going so far as to wait outside the door while I relieved myself.

I considered simply asking to retire for the night, but I worried he'd bring me to his room.

*The room you'll be sharing with him tomorrow.*

The thought almost sent me into despair, but I gathered myself together. I had one more night in my room. That's what he'd implied.

He dismissed his general—evidently bored of his company—and returned to lazily trailing his fingers over my upper arm.

"Maksim," I whispered, letting myself settle closer against his chest.

He looked over my shoulder at me. "Yes, my dear?" His eyes flickered to the red mark he'd left on my lip.

"It's very late, and I have to move my things tomorrow—"

"You won't lift a finger. It will be done for you."

I pursed my lips, then winced at the pain. "I would like to see Rynne and get some sleep."

His light brows twitched downwards. He looked like he wanted to decline, but soon decided against it.

"I'll walk you to your door."

A string of curses surged through my mind. "Why do I need an escort? Everyone knows I belong to you," I said, raising my blood-crusted and bejeweled left hand.

He took it and ran his thumb over my ring finger. "This is exactly why. Trenican men want what they can't have. Though you'll no longer have escorts during the day, you will never be left unguarded at a revel."

He pushed up on my waist, and I stood from his lap. He stepped up beside me and rested a hand on the small of my back.

"Who could you possibly be safer with?" His pale eyes danced at the question—laughing at his own joke.

*Anyone would be safer.*

I didn't say it. I didn't say anything as he led me out.

The walk upstairs was excruciating. I held my breath as we approached the hallway to my room—terrified he'd pass it and lead me to his. But he turned and brought me down the correct hall, dimly lit by sparse candle sconces.

He stopped in front of my door, but intercepted my hand as I reached for the handle.

"Answer something for me," he said, his voice coated in layers of practiced ambiguity.

His eyes were sharp as ever, despite hours of imbibing. The Toresav family's methods of inoculation and tolerance-building worked well.

I gave him a subtle, if not amiable, smile.

He took a breath as if he was going to speak, but closed his mouth and let his gaze drift from my face down to my shoulders. Deceptively delicate fingers slid over my neck, my collarbone, under my dress strap. I willed my heartbeat to slow.

"Tell me," he began, toying with the thin red silk. "Why does he look at you?"

The color drained from my face. I knew he'd been eyeing Lukyan suspiciously, but hoped my acceptance of our betrothal had quieted his concerns.

"I don't know," I whispered.

He released my dress strap and wove his fingers through a strand of my hair.

"Yet you immediately knew about whom I spoke."

I bit my lip, cursing myself.

*Eliandre, you fool.*

"Lukyan is a valuable asset in my arsenal. Favored by my father, he is an expert tracker and a talented killer. After you stabbed Stepan in the back, I didn't think much of it when Lukyan volunteered to be your guard, despite the role being somewhat wasteful of his skills. But frankly, I loathe his gravity towards you. So tell me truthfully, my dear." He came closer, cornering me against the doorway. "Has he had you?"

I fought the urge to vomit.

*At least he doesn't suspect our relation.*

"No," I whispered.

"Then why does he look at you like that?" Maksim growled, leaning closer. His eyes bored into mine, demanding explanation.

"You sent him to come and find me in the Wastes. He knows I'm valuable to you. That's why he delivered me back to the palace. For you," I said, willing my voice to remain even. One wrong word and I'd surely be punished.

*Lukyan, too.*

Maksim looked unconvinced. Sparks of hatred flickered in his glacial eyes.

I steeled myself, then raised a trembling hand to his face. My fingers slid gently over his bloodstained cheek, cupping it. For an unbearably long moment, he didn't move. Panicked thoughts screamed in my ears, declaring how foolish of a ploy it was. A tyrant like Maksim Toresav wouldn't be swayed by something so trite as a soft caress.

But before I could withdraw my hand in mortification, he leaned into it. I almost cried with relief.

The firm set of his chiseled ivory features slackened—so slightly that the change was almost imperceptible—but I knew his face too well. I despised myself for it.

"I was becoming distracted. Invested," he said, the corner of his mouth brushing my fingers as he spoke. "I regretted even starting the tests. So I left you out there, sure you would die, and I'd be free of it. Of this," he said, sliding his fingers over mine. His jaw twitched and he leaned in closer, almost as if he wanted to embrace me. "When I got back from the Wastes, I began... unraveling. The game you and I play, the dance we share, it's too important."

*He's lost his mind.*

My throat tightened. His words might've sounded romantic if I wasn't covered in wounds of his own making.

"But you survived. You returned to me. And when I watched you cover my ballroom in canine gore, I knew it had been worth it. The tests had worked, and you'd proven your fortitude."

My brows pulled together. "The tests, they—"

"A niche but traditional Trenican marriage custom. Very few practice it anymore, but it's quite effective in selecting and strengthening a future wife. Trenica is a cutthroat kingdom, the Toresavs a cutthroat family. Only strong women survive."

My lips parted, and I fought against the shock threatening to buckle my knees.

The tests were never for an advisorship.

Lukyan's cryptic words before my first test suddenly made sense.

*"The tests. Their purpose is not what you think."*

The betrayal split my heart from the inside. My brother had known what was going to be asked of me, and he chose to keep me in the dark. He let Maksim shape me into his own madness.

*Why?*

Maksim leaned close, but stopped a breath away from my lips. "Goodnight, beloved."

He pressed his lips to mine, treacherous and tender.

*My brother lied to me.*

Heartbreak and self loathing overwhelmed me, dulling my awareness and muddying my judgment until I couldn't see past the moment I was in.

So I ignored my thoughts and caved to my instincts. I slid my fingers over Maksim's neck and pulled him closer. I knew that once he let me go, I'd have to face it all. The pain, the trauma, the death. None of it could make it past the potent taste of amourelixir on Maksim's tongue, or the unyielding pressure of his hands on my hips as he pressed me harder against the wall. I was lost and didn't want to be found.

But when he finally drew away, something new glimmered in his irises. A spark of sordid optimism.

"Ah. I thought I'd imagined it," he whispered, taking my hand from his face.

He studied the bloodied ring he'd put on my finger, a proud smile tugging at his lips. My stomach turned. Though I'd just been drawing him closer, encouraging his enamored attention, the unstoppable reality barreled into me. I was backed into a corner by the youngest prince of Trenica, the usurper of Friese. The man who just admitted he enjoyed my suffering—delighted in it.

"I'll see you tonight." He pressed a soft kiss against my knuckles, then leaned close to my ear. "In your nightmares."

Then, he twisted my ring, digging it into my flesh once again.

Despite the hour, there was already a warm bath waiting for me in my room.

*He must've sent for one before we even left the revel.*

It was the sort of thoughtful gesture that would've made me smile, had I not been clutching my hand and fighting back fresh tears.

"Eliandre? Is that you?" Rynne asked just before I shut the door behind me, blocking out the light from the hall. Fabric rustled and I heard the metallic squeak of an oil lamp. Soon the room was bathed in a soft amber glow.

Rynne gasped at my grisly appearance. I still had bloody handprints on my face, neck, and shoulders. I surely had them all over my dress, but the red fabric hid the evidence of Maksim's more ardent affections.

"What happened to you?" she whispered, slowly crossing the room.

I took a few shaky steps towards the bathtub, then slipped my dress from my shoulders. I didn't care that Rynne was there.

Her presence had hardly registered to me. I was doing everything I could not to vomit.

"Eliandre, talk to me. What's wrong with your hand?" she asked, reaching for it.

But I kept undressing, then stepped into the bathtub. I let myself sink until the water was up to my neck and my hair floated around my shoulders. The bathwater slowly turned pink as the dried blood seeped off my skin.

I winced as Rynne plucked my left hand from the edge of the tub.

Her voice was breathless and haunted as she asked, "What is this?"

My eyes fell shut. "I'm engaged."

Everything hit me at once. With the absence of Maksim's distracting touch and terrifying presence, I had to face the things I endured. The things I'd done. I'd accepted his proposal for the sake of my mission, for the sake of Friese. That mission was what kept me patient and compliant at the revel, and appropriately deferential as he walked me back to my room. But my plans were not on my mind when I'd pulled him closer, or when I let my tongue dance along with his. That was pure weakness. Indulging in folly to hide from reality.

*What if I fail? What if I can't find the powdered elixir, and my wedding day comes unimpeded? My friends will return to poison in the air, and their deaths will be my fault.*

But another, more disquieting thought came to my mind.

*What if I succeed? If we use their own poisons against them, and liberate Friese?*

Silent tears began streaming from my eyes.

*How can I face them, now?*

*How can I face Levick?*

It was the question I'd been avoiding for weeks. The woman Levick fell in love with had been corrupted, distorted into an unstable creature of madness. I still loved him... I loved him so much it hurt. But Maksim's tests had left their marks on me, physically and mentally. The damage was soul-deep. He'd made a monster of me, and there was only one possible match for such an abomination. Another monster.

*I kissed him back.*

*I kissed him back.*

*I kissed him back.*

My throat tightened, choking every last bit of hope I had left. There was only shame, self-loathing, and feral determination.

I'd save Friese. I'd kill Maksim. If the only cost was my sanity, I could accept it. It was already gone, anyway.

## Chapter Twenty-Eight

# CONSEQUENCES

I don't know when my sadness went away. It might've been while Rynne rubbed my back as I fell asleep beside her. She'd whispered words of reassurance into the darkness, as if I could truly believe any of them. But at some point in the night, I stopped thinking about what I'd lost. About the life I could've had. My past and future hovered around me, existent but completely out of focus. I'd run out of tears and my heart was spent. There was only the next immediate step: use my new closeness with Maksim to find his elixir stores.

It was just before dawn when I heard a familiar muffled knock on the door, waking me. I roused from sleep, only to see Coran and Rynne standing from our small sofa. Rynne opened it, revealing my brother. The person who'd known my fate, yet kept it from me.

Flaxen braids hung over his left shoulder, brushing against his shirt. Dark circles ringed his eyes, matching his blue irises. He looked as sleep-deprived as I was. His eyes found mine immediately.

"I—" he began, but faltered upon glancing at Rynne and Coran. They still didn't know we were siblings.

"You're awake," Lukyan said, taking a cautious step closer to my bed. His eyes searched mine, seeing the betrayal in them.

I sat up and threw my legs over the side of the bed. I was wearing a white silk nightgown—the only kind that were supplied in my dressing room. It appeared regrettably like something a bride would wear on her honeymoon. Lukyan and Coran averted their eyes.

Rynne rushed over and slipped a deep blue robe over my shoulders. "You should tell them," she whispered, rubbing a soothing hand over my shoulder. "Tell them what you told me."

I couldn't restrain the scoff that slipped from my lips. I looked at Lukyan. "Why don't *you* tell them?"

Coran's vivid blue eyes darted to Lukyan, confusion written on his face. "You found out already?" he asked. Rynne had clearly informed Coran of my betrothal while I slept.

"I saw. At the revel," Lukyan said to Coran, but his eyes never left mine. He'd caught the accusation in my previous words.

Rynne and Coran glanced back and forth between me and Lukyan, noticing the tension in the air. Rynne tugged on Coran's sleeve, whispering in his ear. He took a deep breath and straightened up.

"Rynne wants me to help her..." he faltered a moment, glancing at Rynne, "choose her gown. For tomorrow."

It was the most obvious ruse I'd ever witnessed, but Lukyan and I both nodded at them. Rynne grabbed an oil lamp and rushed Coran off to the dressing room, closing the door behind them.

Lukyan immediately took a few steps closer, but stopped upon noticing my steely glare.

"Are you alright?" he whispered. "Elucia—"

"Don't call me that!" I hissed, fighting the tears that were threatening to break free. "You knew! You knew the true purpose of his *tests*!"

Lukyan flinched, but didn't step backwards. "I wanted to tell you, but I didn't want you to panic. I thought he'd abandon it. He's only ever expressed disdain at the idea of marriage."

"Not anymore," I said, a rogue tear slipping down my cheek. "I'll share a bed with him tonight, and everything else in *one month*."

My brother clenched his jaw and raised a hand to his forehead. "We'll stop him before then. We'll find the elixirs."

I rolled my eyes, a foreign tang of bitterness on my tongue. "And if we don't, you might become an uncle within the year."

Lukyan groaned at the notion. "No! You won't marry him. He won't touch you—"

"I am moving into his room *today*! Any minute now, a guard will knock on my door to gather my things." I marched towards him, pinning him with my tear-soaked glare. "You knew this would be asked of me. You knew Maksim was eyeing me for a wife, and you didn't tell me."

"I'm sorry," he whispered, his face wrought with regret. "I thought he was just entertaining himself, and we could use that to our advantage."

I felt my brows furrow in disbelief. "I'm just a mindless tool, then."

"No, Sister. I was investigating independently of you. I thought I was close, but that was right before he left you out in the Wastes."

I clenched my fists at my sides. "I was a distraction."

He said nothing, but came closer until he was within arm's reach. "I regret it. I wish I'd just stolen you away and left this continent behind."

Before I could respond, he wrapped his arms around me and held me tight to his chest. "This is the last thing Mother would want for you. For us." He suddenly pushed my shoulders away and leveled a serious look at me. "I have friends in the north. We could be safe there indefinitely."

I gave him a quizzical look. "And leave Friese behind?"

He cocked his head, pleading. "You might be a Skylady, but you're one of us. Please consider it."

I couldn't. Bloodlines aside, Friese was my home. It was Levick's home. And Francie's, Arturian's, Eadlin's, Harley's. Rynne's.

*Kiera's.*

"No," I whispered, shaking my head. "Maksim is already suspicious. Last night he asked—" I stopped myself. It was too disturbing.

Lukyan gave me an inquisitive look, not understanding. I clenched my jaw and powered through my next words. "He asked me if we... slept together."

Lukyan pressed his eyes shut and backed away from me. He looked like he wanted to evaporate from the earth, never to be seen again.

"*Ess*, it's worse than I realized." He shook his shoulders, as if the movement could shake off the revolting thought.

"Nothing can be done. I'll do my best to find the elixir stores, but you can't be my guard anymore. He's too suspicious."

Lukyan shook his head. "We have to keep in contact somehow."

"Rynne," I said, gesturing to the closet door. "I'm sure Maksim will keep her in this room. I'll come by every few days and we'll all meet here to catch up. Rynne is my friend—Maksim won't suspect anything."

"He would suspect me. As far as he knows, I should have no business in this room."

An idea came to me, and my brow twitched. "Tell him you're bedding her."

My brother's lip curled up. "She is with the captain. I couldn't—"

"I'm not asking you to actually sleep with her, Lukyan," I said through an exasperated sigh. "But Maksim would believe it."

His jaw tensed, deep in thought.

"Wait," I began, curiosity crawling through me. "I've never asked. Do you have someone? Back in Trenica?"

His eyes flickered at the prying, but I saw the resignation on his face. "In a sense, yes. I love her, but her situation is... complicated."

I raised my eyebrows in inquiry, but he shook his head.

"I will agree to your plan," Lukyan said, reaching out and taking my hand. "But it can't be made public. Please."

I nodded, squeezing his fingers in mine.

The door to the dressing room clicked open. "Are you two done in there?" Rynne asked, poking her head out. "Get dressed, we're coming out."

Lukyan couldn't stifle his groan at the insinuation.

"For stone's sake, Miss Wemberley!" he said, leaning against the back of our sofa. His pale face was tinged with green. "Eliandre is my sister!"

Thanks to my brother's nauseated outburst, we spent the next hour detailing our background and family lineage. Rynne looked deeply apologetic that she assumed there was anything romantic between us.

"This knowledge can't leave the room," Lukyan said, looking at Coran and Rynne gravely. "Maksim would use it against us in a heartbeat. My employer," Lukyan said, hesitating. "He doesn't know about this, either. I would like to tell him someday, but not through gossip and court rumors. He wouldn't take kindly to such a revelation."

Coran and Rynne both nodded in agreement.

"But, Eliandre," Coran started, giving me a concerned look. "Are you sure you are willing to risk this? One month is not much time."

I pursed my lips. "Yes, Coran. I can get the information out of him. Maksim, he—" I stumbled over the words. "He's claimed he loves me."

Rynne and Coran gasped, and my brother's face completely drained of color.

"You didn't tell me that," Lukyan muttered.

I cocked my head at him. "He asked me to marry him. I thought I'd implied it."

Lukyan shifted on his feet. "Toresav men are different. Wives are for producing heirs. Love—rare though it may be—is reserved for mistresses."

"What does that mean?" Rynne asked, her eyes wide on Lukyan.

My brother ran a hand over his hair and walked over to the fireplace. He spread his fingers over the mantle and leaned against it, staring into the glowing coals. "It means there is no breaking it off." He looked up at me, resolve hardening his features. "He won't give you up. Not for anything. This only ends in death."

Coran and Lukyan didn't stay much longer. The sun was creeping up on the horizon, and it wouldn't be long before a guard would show up to move my things into Maksim's rooms.

Things remained tense with Lukyan, but nevertheless, he hugged me tightly before he left. I resolved not to hold his omission against him. He was among my only remaining family, and times were desperate. I couldn't afford to hold a grudge against him when our situation was so dire.

I averted my gaze when Coran left, but from the corner of my eye, I saw him press a kiss to Rynne's lips just before ducking out the window. A smile crept over my face at her blush, but it didn't reach my eyes. The purity and gentleness of their love further convicted me of the malignant ardour that Maksim felt for me. I tried not to think of Levick, and how distressed he would be when he learned I was betrothed to the most depraved, sadistic man on the continent.

It was almost a relief when I was finally summoned upstairs. Rynne hugged me tightly, whispering encouragement in my ear before letting me go.

The gown I'd chosen trailed behind me as I followed my guard up the stairs. Panels of crimson silk made up the bodice, gathering at my waist and flowing out in shining ripples behind me. The top of the dress rose high and wrapped around my neck, leaving a small portion of my back exposed. I'd been surprised to find it in the dressing room. It was a new addition, and was far more modest than everything else Maksim had provided thus far.

*Now he decides to dress me modestly, after I've sold myself to him. How ironic that I had more dignity when he dressed me as a whore.*

Maksim wasn't in his rooms when the guard left me there. I tried to take advantage of the privacy and search his things for any hint of where he kept his elixirs, but came up empty. I rustled through every cabinet, drawer, and desk, careful to return everything exactly as I'd found it. Maksim might have been bringing me closer, but I wasn't under the delusion that he truly trusted me.

Hours passed, but Maksim didn't come. Servants came and went, bringing gourmet meals and tidying up, but they never stayed long. I'd searched his dressing room and found one side of it already stocked with dresses and slippers. Most were varying shades of red, but some were black or white.

Despite the rows of expensive silk dresses and finely carved boxes of jewels, one dress in particular captured my attention. It stood in the center of the grand dressing room, fitted over a mannequin bust. Unlike most of the other dresses, this one was made up of white velvet so bright that it almost seemed to shimmer, even in low light. Tiny red gemstones dusted the fitted sleeves and the bottom hem, like stardust had been blown over it. I knew immediately what it was.

*My wedding dress.*

I hated it. Hated looking at it, hated knowing it was looming nearby, taunting me with the inevitable countdown to my life sentence. But in those hours of solitude, I kept finding myself standing in front of it. Even after the sun went down, and I had to light candles to see it.

"Eager?"

I spun around at the voice. Maksim stood in the doorway of the dressing room, unrolling the sleeves of his shirt. My heart leapt into my throat.

"Where have you been?" I asked, my voice barely audible from a full day of disuse.

Maksim came closer until he was mere inches away. "Tending to important business." He looked me over, admiring the dress I still wore. "Red is your best color."

"Thank you for the dress," I said, tucking my left hand behind my back. The skin around my ring was still raw and stinging from where he'd twisted it the previous night.

He raised his hand to brush my cheek, but I subconsciously flinched backwards. It was subtle, but he noticed.

"What's wrong?" he asked, slipping his fingers over the back of my neck. "You didn't seem afraid of my touch last night."

The memory filled me with shame, but I forced myself to lean closer.

His lips twitched in a faint smirk. "It's late."

Just those two words sent a chill down my spine. I'd avoided looking at his bed, but I knew what was coming.

*He promised to leave you untouched until the wedding.*

"I should change," I said, motioning at the rows of dresses.

He simply nodded and walked away, closing the doors behind him.

Rapid gasps shook my chest, and it was all I could do not to fall to my knees.

*You will survive this. You agreed to this. You knew what was coming.*

I forced deep breaths into my lungs, chose the least alluring nightgown, and changed. When I came out, Maksim was sitting on the edge of the bed reading a book. The sight was so jarring that my jaw almost fell open. It seemed entirely too normal of an activity for a sadistic murderer to take part in.

He set his book aside and beckoned me over with a casual wave of the hand. I tried not to look at his bare chest or the shocking number of scars peppering his skin. But something caught my eye—something hanging from his neck.

*A key.*

My mind raced, but I tried to mask my eagerness.

*What if it leads to his elixir stores?*

But there was no way to ask him without rousing suspicion—especially on my first night in his room.

I stopped in front of him, but he took my hand and pulled me closer until I was standing between his legs. Fear and shame thrummed in my veins. He reached up, ran his fingers over my cheek until they were threaded in my hair, then pulled me down. The kiss was soft and reserved, absent the hunger he'd shown in the hallway. I returned it only so far as to appease him.

He backed away and pulled over the covers beside him. An invitation.

My legs trembled as I walked around the bed and climbed in, but Maksim had already resumed his reading.

*Maybe he takes the key off when he lies down.*

Eventually Maksim blew out the candle and settled into the bed. I dared a glance over my shoulder, but couldn't see him clearly in the darkness. I gritted my teeth in frustration.

*There's only one way to see if he's wearing it.*

But I couldn't bring myself to go to him. I would have to run my fingers over his neck and chest to know if he was still wearing the key, and he'd surely take such an advance as a signal I was open to rescinding my condition. After that, there would be no backing out without arousing suspicion.

*No. I can't. I'll find another way.*

So I lay still, half terrified Maksim would renege on his promise. Though his earlier behavior was reserved, I was paranoid it would end when the darkness came.

But Maksim kept his distance, and I eventually fell asleep in the bed of my enemy.

# Chapter Twenty-Nine

# Bound in Blood

I woke alone to cold sheets and faint light streaming through the windows. A large part of me thought it might all have been a nightmare—that I hadn't truly shared a bed with Friese's usurper. But my nightgown was made of imported silk, and the bedspread of luxurious red and cream velvet. The furniture was black ebony decorated with silver fixtures. Even the air in the room smelled of expensive cologne, wafting in from nearby.

I turned over in bed only to see Maksim Toresav walk out of the dressing room, shirtless and fastening his black trousers. My body completely froze. Though I'd seen him shirtless before, the sight of him so casually dressing himself seemed almost... vulgar.

His eyes found mine immediately. A sly smile pulled at his lips, and he took his time fastening the last few buttons.

"No one is making you wait, little gull," he said, his gaze heavy on me. He reached back into the dressing room and pulled a black shirt from a shelf. "Just say the word."

My stomach twisted at his casual proposition. He wasn't serious. His smile turned smug as he slipped his shirt over his shoulders and began buttoning.

"Would you like to come help me? Or would you rather keep watching?"

I looked away and silently climbed out of bed, suddenly feeling all too vulnerable there. My feet met the cold floors, centering me. The entire situation felt so painfully intimate. The Trenican usurper of my kingdom—the murderer of Victor Droughton and Kiera Bruckton—stood behind me, unhurriedly dressing for the day.

I began walking around the bed but froze mid-step. I wanted to change, but he stood in front of the dressing room, unmoving.

"May I get dressed?" I asked, risking a glance at him. He was fastening a button over his lean abdomen and cocking his head at me.

He took a few steps closer. "You don't have to ask. This is now your room as well as mine."

I couldn't tell whether he meant his words to be a comfort or a reminder of my inescapable fate. His pale features were like marble—hard and unreadable. I could hardly believe I'd slept beside him all night.

After taking a deep breath, I made to walk past him, straight into the dressing room. He didn't impede, but followed me inside. I turned to see him leaning against the door frame, watching my every move.

"May I get dressed *in private*?" I asked, lightly gesturing to the door.

He ran his fingers through his pale blond hair, giving it the casually sleek look it always had.

"I'll help choose your gown. Today we will publicly announce our engagement."

It took me off-guard, but didn't truly surprise me. My advisorship was originally meant to be a symbolic gesture of peace with the discontented Friesians in the south.

*Of course he'd want a big, public announcement.*

He must've noticed my reaction, as he slowly drew nearer in unwavering steps. His finger and thumb held my chin and lifted it up, until I met his eyes.

"You are questioning my motives," he said without a shred of doubt.

I blinked, not knowing what to say.

*Is he trying to comfort me?*

"No," I muttered, saying anything that might appease him.

He lifted his other hand to slide over my cheek, below my ear. "I saw that look in your eyes. You think I proposed solely for political gain."

It had crossed my mind. The increased unrest in the south certainly made our betrothal a beneficial alliance for him. I shook my head but said nothing.

"Be assured, my dear—an advisory role would be fully sufficient in that respect. I could maintain my freedom, unchained to a wife, and keep the rebels under control." He leaned closer, gently brushing my hair over my shoulder.

"You considered it," I breathed. It was another game, and I had to play it right.

"I did. I tried desperately to accept the idea. But it wasn't right." He looked over my shoulder, briefly scanning the dresses folded up on the shelf behind me. "Once I want something, it isn't good enough to simply have it. Casual possession is insufficient."

My throat tightened, and I thought of Lukyan's words of caution.

*"It means there is no breaking it off. He won't give you up. Not for anything. This only ends in death."*

Maksim pulled a dress down. It unfolded from his hand, the bottom hem falling to the floor in a pile of midnight black silk.

"You are desirable in this court, little gull. My generals... they hunger for you. The prestige of having one of the only Skyladies in existence is unmatched. Not to mention the fact of your previous high-profile connections." His eyes darkened, and his breaths came faster. "Betrothed to the former king. Lover to the windwalker. You must be truly special to merit attention from such powerful men."

Maksim's jaw ticked, and he wrapped the length of the dress around my shoulders like a rope, pulling me closer with it. My heart raced at the contact—at the tension in the air. Jealousy was never a safe emotion when it came to Maksim.

"I could've easily made you my advisor and still enjoyed all of the perks of marriage. My family and court have no rules against sharing beds with servants. But I knew if I left you officially unclaimed, you'd eventually be stolen away and married to whichever of my politically ambitious generals decided to challenge me that month. And *that*, my dear," he hissed, pulling me closer, "would be the ruin of this continent because I would execute every one of my own men to keep you mine. *Only* mine. So no," he said, leaning in until he was whispering in my ear, "an advisorship is not good enough. Not even close."

I was trembling when he finally backed away and handed his chosen dress to me. My eyes were wide and my chest heaved, but Maksim's expression was completely unwavering. He finished his last few buttons, his intense stare never leaving mine.

"Come find me when you're dressed."

He turned and left without another word.

The dress he chose for me was unusual. I spent an embarrassing amount of time figuring out how it was supposed to fit. Eventually I discerned it was meant to be completely strapless. Wide strips of shining black silk wrapped around my ribcage and breasts, then tied at the back. The skirt was long and simple, flowing from my waist in an uninterrupted stream of silk.

The only thing keeping the bodice from falling down was the knot on my back and an impressive set of vertical boning along the panels. It still felt rather precarious, but I was certainly not going to challenge Maksim's selection. Especially not after the tense speech he'd given me.

I emerged from the dressing room to find Maksim reclined on the bed, book in hand. He immediately set it aside and rose to inspect me. He gestured for me to turn for him with a quick twirl of his fingers.

"Very nice," he said, catching my shoulders as I was facing away, stopping me. "Although..." he muttered to himself.

The pressure around my ribcage suddenly lessened. A quiet gasp left my throat—Maksim had untied my bodice. I immediately lifted my arms to hold up the dress, but he was already refastening it.

"Relax, my dear. You should be thanking me." He punctuated his words with an aggressive tug on the silk ribbons, tightening them until I could hardly breathe. "It would've slipped down within the hour. We don't want that, do we?" he asked just before gently gripping my arms and turning me back around to face him. His appraising stare ran over my hair, face, and body.

"Is everything—" I started, my words catching inside my restrained chest. "In order?" I managed to whisper.

His eyes lit up and a satisfied smile pulled at his lips. "Alluring *and* breathtaking. This dress might be my new favorite of yours."

My vision began clouding along the edges, and I wavered on my feet. Maksim caught my waist and laughed. I hated how he reveled in my pain.

"Would you mind loosening it?" I whispered against his shoulder. I highly doubted my ability to walk straight in my current state.

Maksim ran his fingers over my back, pausing above the knot he tied. "If I touch this ribbon again, I'm untying it completely and we will postpone the announcement. I'll let you decide."

My stomach felt like it fell to the floor. I'd rather be suffocated completely. I shook my head and straightened up.

"That's too bad. I'll just have to wait a few weeks," he said through a downright sinister smile.

*Playing games. Always playing games.*

I was so tired.

The carriage ride was mercifully silent and uneventful. I had no idea where we were going, and had no intention of wasting my precious air to ask. It made no difference to me, anyway.

But when Maksim helped me down from the carriage, I wished I'd had a warning.

In front of me lay the Exley mansion, covered in blooming vines and greenery. It was the first home in which I had truly found myself. Where I learned to wield my windblade and strengthened my body. It was also where I fell in love with Levick.

I looked up at Maksim, and I could've sworn I saw a hint of gloating in his eyes.

*He knows.*

I had my first kiss in the Exley mansion.

My eyes darted up to the roof—where I'd stood as I promised to love Levick forever.

"The perfect venue to announce our engagement. Wouldn't you agree?"

I looked back at Maksim, but I wasn't truly seeing him. I only saw the future I could've had. The one I *should've* had.

To announce my engagement to our mortal enemy at the same home where I'd fallen in love with Levick... it was too much.

A lone tear fell over my cheek—I hadn't even noticed I was crying. My chest and throat were so tight, I could hardly breathe.

Maksim made soft sounds of appeasement and tugged me close.

"It's all in the past." He brushed a hand over my hair, his rings snagging on the strands.

It was disguised as heartfelt consoling, but I saw it for what it was. Relishing in his triumph.

He broke away and led me up the steps. The inside of the mansion had been cleaned and decorated for the occasion. Swarms of Trenican soldiers and wealthy Friesian civilians bustled about, chatting and laughing amongst themselves. There was a victorious undercurrent in the air, as if they knew the engagement was coming. The final surrender of Friese.

Maksim dragged me along to meet with various members of his court. They were entirely male, and stared at me as if I were a piece of meat. The conversations were unbearably tense. Maksim kept a tight arm around my waist, as if he thought they'd try to pull me away the moment he let go. I could sense him attempting to walk the line between keeping the peace with his supporters, and wanting to slice their heads off for leering at his fiancée. Ultimately he decided political favor was more important.

There were a handful of Friesian families in attendance. They were the few who quickly surrendered their riches, properties, and daughters as soon as they sensed the tide shifting in the war.

Mortimer Stokes approached to offer his congratulations, followed by his very bitter daughter. Doressa's black curls were pinned up on the top of her head, decorated with lavender purple accents matching her skimpy dress.

"Good to see you, Excellency," Mortimer slurred through inebriated jowls. It was hardly noon and he was already drunk.

Maksim nodded but made no effort to extend a hand or even respond. His eyes scanned over the Stokes' heads, searching for someone else.

"Hello, Eliandre," Doressa said, taking a step closer.

"Doressa," I said with a tactful nod. It was clear she didn't intend to offer sincere congratulations.

Her lips twisted into a nefarious smirk. "Seems you got what you wanted." She giggled and reached up, tugging at the edge of her neckline with silk-gloved fingers. "What did it take?"

My mouth went dry at her poisonous words. Maksim didn't even notice amid his scanning of the crowd.

"Let's not do this, Doressa," I whispered, tugging gently at Maksim's arm.

Her eyes hardened. "It wasn't enough to open your legs to Exley *and* the windwalker, was it? You just have to sleep with *anyone* with a claim to power?"

Maksim's jaw twitched, and I saw his eyes dart to Doressa.

She was too absorbed in her tirade—she didn't even notice the predator she so fatuously roused.

Doressa took another step closer to me, eyes narrowed and lip curled in bitter resentment. She pointed her finger at me. "I'll bet Harley Ainsworth's had you, too. Do you even remember?

Or have you lost track of the men you've seduced for political gain?"

It was too far. *Leagues* too far. Maksim would accept an insult or occasional degrading comment to me. But to suggest I'd been bedded by not one, but three other powerful men was perhaps the worst possible thing to say in front of Maksim Toresav.

For Doressa, it was the last thing she'd say.

Silently, Maksim reached up and threw his windblade through Doressa.

*Echna above!*

The top of Doressa's head slid free from the bottom, falling to the floor as the rest of her body collapsed. Blood spurted and pooled over the marble flooring.

*He killed her. Just like that.*

Screams erupted around the room as people hunched down, searching for the source of the chaos.

*He killed her.*

I couldn't breathe.

Jumbled wailing poured from Mortimer's slack lips. He fell to the floor, his knees splashing in the expanding puddle of blood.

I stumbled away from Maksim, but my vision was failing again. Deep, authoritative voices shouted, demanding cooperation. Red uniforms flocked around the pooling blood, containing the chaos.

My chest was spasming impotently, heaving for air. I was falling.

A shade of black and white lunged for me, catching me just before I crashed to the floor. A low growl rumbled against me, but before I could squirm away from it, everything went black.

## *Chapter Thirty*

# Spectacle

The faint hum of distant chatter roused me from my stupor. A set of gentle fingers massaged my scalp, running through my hair and down my neck.

"Wake up, my dear."

The voice was familiar. The voice of a monster.

"I need you, now. It's time to wake up."

*My monster.*

His fingers worked at the muscles between my neck and shoulders.

I forced my eyes open, only to see a ceiling of ornately gilded tiles sprawled above me.

*The Exley mansion.*

Everything came back to me in a rush of burning panic.

*Doressa.*

I jerked up and turned in my seat. Maksim was sitting behind me, watching me closely as he twirled a dark strip of cloth in his fingers. My head had been resting on his lap.

"What—" I began, but a disquieting chill pricked at my skin, and I felt something sliding down my chest.

I snatched my hands up just before my untied dress slid off and exposed me.

Maksim feigned a pout. "You're very quick."

My eyes darted around, but much of the room was obscured by a partition. It seemed the party was still in full-swing on the other side of the room.

"How long was I—did you—" I stammered, clinging tightly to my dress.

My fiancé furrowed his light brows and leaned away, offended. "Ill-gotten pleasures merit no satisfaction. Trust me in this," he said, suddenly leaning closer. "When I touch you, you will know."

I desperately attempted to glean only the comfort from his words and ignore the dark promise in his undertone.

"Doressa. You—"

"Killed her, yes. And I'd advise you not to mention her to me again. The things she—" His nostrils flared and he looked away.

His pale complexion was slowly reddening. Long fingers gripped the upholstered bench, digging into it. I recognized the look on his face—the anger.

Doressa's mutilated body appeared in my mind. It was jarring—the speed at which she transformed from an impassioned young woman to a lifeless corpse. Maksim had no regard for the lives of those he deemed insignificant. His killings were trivial. I doubted he even remembered many of them.

*A man who has no respect for life other than his own.*

In a desperate attempt to prevent a new outburst, I slid closer to him. I lifted my hand and pressed it lightly against his cheek. Then, as before, he leaned into it. I watched his tension and anger evaporate at my touch. His eyes fell shut, and he raised his hand, holding mine against him.

In a moment of pure shock, I realized I had a tenuous influence over Maksim. It was hardly reliable—he was volatile and unpredictable—but it was certainly more than I'd presumed.

*More than anyone else.*

He opened his eyes and let them linger on me. His stare was guarded, but unwavering. He reached forward and pulled me against him, wrapping his arms around me.

My pulse raced. I kept my left hand clutched over my dress, but the back of the bodice was open.

Maksim pulled me tighter against him until I was nearly on his lap. He ran his fingers over my shoulders, my spine.

"Let go," he whispered in my ear.

My throat constricted. I was pressed so tightly to him that the top of my dress wouldn't fall down unless he pulled away. But it was a risk I was not willing to take.

He gathered my hair in his hand, then slid it around until it was pulled over both of our shoulders and fell on his back.

"Trust me," he said, holding tighter. "Let go."

It was another one of his games. I wondered if he'd ever stop playing with me. But I knew better than to anger him. I released my bodice and wrapped my arms around him, holding tight.

I closed my eyes and let my cheek rest against his black shirt. I felt so powerless in his arms. Completely without choices. It was all intentional.

But he dutifully gathered my dress's broad silk ribbon and began tying it again. My breathing quickened, anticipating another tight binding.

"I will never accept it. You are entirely mine. Anyone who suggests otherwise will be silenced," he murmured against my hair. "They needed to see that."

He was trying to justify himself to me. The notion would've been amusing if the tang of blood wasn't lingering in the air. I nodded against his shoulder.

He finished tying my dress and pulled away. It was secure, but not as constricting as it had been.

"Come. It's time for the announcement."

Maksim led me up the first few stairs in the back of the ballroom, then turned to make his proclamation. It was very obvious that at least half of the attendees already knew of our engagement, but the rest were gleeful with excitement.

Suggestive comments were hurled our way from Maksim's more inebriated generals, and with every new one, he held me tighter to his side. It was obvious he was taking every comment as a subtle sign of desire, even though most were simply vulgar encouragements. He was becoming more possessive.

Drinks were passed around afterwards, and I was once again relegated to following Maksim as he socialized with his sycophants. I made sure to act appropriately demure—speaking only when spoken to.

*This is temporary. Once you find the elixirs, you can forget about everything you had to do to get them.*

Most conversations drifted to the unrest in the southern sector of Friese. Multiple people even expressed their surprise at Maksim choosing the Exley mansion for the engagement announcement. They'd glance back and forth, as if they were waiting for rebels to burst through the doors at any moment. Those comments seemed to amuse Maksim rather than worry him.

"No, Petrov, I am not concerned," Maksim said to one of his generals, his Vynesic rumbling together in a menacing purr. "Their morale is all but gone. I've silenced their rallying cry and stolen their princess."

Petrov chuckled and took a long drink from his goblet. "I still think a public execution would've made more of a statement. Wife is a position of high esteem. An honor. This woman doesn't even look Friesian." He scoffed. "But she's not Trenican, either. Not really."

I stiffened. Petrov didn't know I understood him, or simply didn't care. Maksim held me tighter to his side.

"She knows Vynesic, Petrov. Watch your words."

"Does she?" The boorish soldier hid a laugh. "I think she's in too deep to be running away at the first mention of execution."

My eyes darted to Maksim's, expecting anger at the suggestion his future wife be executed, but he was calm as ever.

A bitter taste filled my mouth. He would kill someone over the mere speculation that I'd been with other men, but had no reaction to the idea of my execution. It was a necessary reminder.

*He is obsessed. Not in love.*

"Maksim!" a man called from behind us.

My stomach dropped. No one called him by his first name.

*Except me.*

Maksim dismissed Petrov and turned to face our approacher.

He was older than all of Maksim's generals, his blond hair thinning at the front. He stood tall and imperious, clad in pristine crimson. His chest shone with an array of medals and pins.

"Boris," Maksim said through a sharp smile. "I wasn't expecting you."

The newcomer reached forward and gave Maksim a quick clap on the shoulder. "Your father wanted someone to check in on your progress here."

*This man must be part of King Joraan Toresav's court. He came all the way from Trenica.*

Boris's amused stare slid over to me, but he still spoke to Maksim. "I knew the Yorke girl was your plaything, but I had no idea you wanted to keep her."

Maksim laughed, but it was tight and nervous. He didn't care for surprises.

"I put her through the tests."

His words had an immediate reaction. Boris's thin lips twitched in surprise as he looked back and forth between us.

"And she survived," Boris ruminated. "I suppose that is reason enough to claim her. If you do not, she will surely be snatched up."

My fiancé shifted closer to me at the comment.

But Boris gently pushed Maksim to the side then stood back, inspecting me. His eyes ran over me diligently, taking in my every detail. Though it wasn't lustful, it was invasive all the same. It was the expression one wore while deciding whether to purchase an animal for slaughter.

His brows knit together. "She's thin. How much are you feeding her?"

"As much as she'll eat."

I fought a scowl. It seemed the trend of speaking as if I couldn't hear them wouldn't end anytime soon.

Boris rubbed his chin, his eyes lingering on my stomach. I crossed my arms.

"You're sure she's fertile?"

A chill ran down my spine. I tried to slow my breathing to keep from gasping.

*It won't matter. It won't happen.*

Maksim straightened, all business. "The stress of the tests interrupted her cycles, but her environment is quite comfortable now. They'll return soon."

The blood completely drained from my face. He had the servants reporting on my cycles. The invasion of privacy shouldn't have surprised me.

*Is that why he's been so tender lately? Why he hasn't given me a third test? To ensure my fertility?*

I swallowed the pernicious nausea crawling up my throat.

Boris finally tore his gaze from me and gave Maksim a clever grin. "Or maybe they won't get the chance to return. You're already surprising your father by being the first son to marry. Maybe you'll be the first to produce an heir, as well."

I blinked away the intense stinging in the corners of my eyes.

*Don't cry. Don't cry.*

Maksim chuckled darkly. "That is my full intention."

My legs were shaking. My rational mind told me our plan would work, and all the talk of marriage and heirs would be irrelevant. It wouldn't matter because Maksim would be dead—slaughtered after being poisoned with his own elixirs.

I willed the thought to comfort me, but their suggestive words rang through my mind.

*I'll die before I let it happen.*

Boris and Maksim continued their conversation for another few minutes, never addressing me directly. It didn't bother me as it had only moments before. I wanted to distance my mind from the situation as much as possible.

The gathering devolved into a raucous celebration as the drinks and elixirs flowed, but Maksim remained sober and steady beside me. As lecherous and debased as he was, I'd never seen him truly inebriated. He clearly viewed the occasion as a political spectacle rather than a real celebration. He sipped from the same goblet all afternoon, occasionally passing it to me. I drank the silver gin without hesitation, knowing he'd notice if the flavor left my tongue.

Though some of the Trenican generals and soldiers had become rather reckless with their women, Maksim kept his affections practiced and controlled. Even when his kisses grew impassioned and his tongue explored my mouth, I could tell he was only tasting me to ensure I was drinking the gin.

I waited for the abhorrent effects of amourelixir to kick in, but they never did.

"What's in it?" I asked Maksim as he handed me the goblet again. To my surprise, the words came out in Vynesic. All of the

Trenicans had been speaking it throughout the afternoon, and it rolled off my tongue easily.

His eyes flashed and his lips parted in surprise. He took my elbow and led me aside, where the crowd was thinning.

"You think I've been drugging you?" he asked, continuing our conversation in Vynesic.

I bit my lip to keep from scoffing in disbelief. "In case you've forgotten, you've done it before. Multiple times."

A droll smile curved his lips. "Ah, touché. But no, this is only gin."

"Then why are you so insistent that I drink it?"

"You seem tense. Gin relieves tension. Besides," he purred, leaning closer. "It tastes good on your tongue." He left a soft kiss behind my ear. "Silver gin, and now Vynesic. It's good to see how well you wear our culture."

I quickly smothered the shame the comment induced. "I'm glad."

He backed away and tucked a strand of hair behind my ear. "Your accent is divine. Who taught you?"

My stomach twisted in knots. As far as I knew, Maksim didn't know the true identity of my mother. I thought of what Lukyan told me about her, and my mouth went dry. She'd fled Trenica to escape King Joraan. Maksim's father.

*She escaped the very family to which I might be forever shackled.*

Maksim clearly suspected my Trenican blood, but my mother changed her name when she ran away to Friese and married my father. In a moment of heavy grief, I realized I never learned her Trenican name.

*I'll have to ask Lukyan... when this is all over.*

"I learned from a tutor. From Grevalst," I lied.

Maksim gave me a look of condescending pity. "I hate to tell you, little gull, but your tutor might also be your father." He pointedly twirled his finger around a strand of my platinum hair.

I clenched my jaw. "Perhaps."

He raised a brow at my casual response. "You don't know your true parentage?"

I thought of my mother, and the secret life she'd had before me. The son she'd never told me about.

"I am a Yorke by blood. That is what matters."

Maksim tsked knowingly. "Your father wouldn't be the first to seek out foreign company. You should be thankful, your northern blood is a credit to you. Our children will be accepted easily among their Trenican peers."

My breath caught at the mention of children. Maksim noticed, and lifted a hand to my cheek.

"Ah, that's why you've been so tense?" he asked, drawing me closer. I tried not to think about the dozens of eyes trained on us, watching closely.

"You simply haven't thought it through. Bearing my heir will protect you," he said.

I couldn't suppress my doubtful expression.

His jaw twitched, and he glanced around. When he was sure no one was close enough to hear, he continued. "Trenican men believe marriage is for a lifetime, but some see that as license to duel. Many a wife has been made to wed her husband's murderer."

A horrified gasp escaped my lips. "That's awful—"

"And Trenican men are less likely to kill each other over a pregnant woman. Few men care to raise the child of a man they murdered."

*These people are monsters.*

But I thought of the Friesian tradition of windblade inheritance, and silenced my judgments.

*In many ways, Friese is just as barbaric. This kingdom enshrined the murder of family members for the sake of inheriting power.*

"It won't matter," Maksim said with a soft stroke over my arm. "No one will take you from me. I'll make sure of it." The last words came out in a zealous Vynesic growl. My skin crawled. Their implication wasn't lost on me.

We stayed only long enough for Maksim to say his goodbyes to Boris, then took the carriage back to the palace.

Blessedly, he was called away to resolve a conflict, and I was left in the safety of solitude.

# *Chapter Thirty-One*

# Jori Volkov

I paced back and forth through the Royal Chambers, anxiety eating me alive. Though Maksim had been called away, I hadn't been able to fall asleep since our return from the Exley mansion. Everything was happening too fast. The walls were closing in on me.

With shaking hands, I poured myself another glass of gin.

*"You're already surprising your father by being the first son to marry. Maybe you'll be the first to produce an heir, as well."*

A shiver ran down my spine. Boris's words repeated in my mind, despite my attempts to silence them. Before I could take another heavy gulp from my glass, I heard Maksim's response.

*"That is my full intention."*

"Less than four weeks. I have less than four weeks," I mumbled, picking at my nails. My eyes kept being drawn to the enormous bed, draped in red velvet blankets and pillows. It was a bed most women would dream of sleeping in.

*With a prince, no less.*

My breaths quickened to gasps at the thought.

The entire Royal Chamber exuded the romantic mood of a honeymoon suite. Bouquets of red roses graced every end table, diligently replaced as soon as they showed signs of wilting. Ambiguous paintings of deep burgundy, black, and ivory hung on the walls, embodying sensuality in their broad strokes. They were far from explicit, but something about the weaving of colors and shapes gave the viewer no doubt of the mood they were meant to evoke. I stared at one particularly vivid piece for too long, and shuddered.

*Think, Eliandre. Think.*

I wrung my hands as I walked past the settee for the hundredth time.

*Find the elixirs. If you find the elixirs, this all goes away. No more sleeping beside Maksim, no more stolen kisses or lingering touches.*

The notion made me desperate. I didn't know how far away Maksim was, but it wasn't far enough. No distance was far enough.

*Maybe death.*

Though the thought of Maksim's death gave me a thrill, I had a nagging feeling his presence would linger.

*Lukyan said the elixirs weren't "just lying around in a bedroom somewhere," but surely he hasn't checked all of them. Maksim would want them nearby.*

I tipped back my glass, finishing it.

*There's only one way to be rid of him. Only one way to win. Find the elixirs.*

My eyes darted to the door. It wasn't locked. Maksim was very confident in the conditioning he'd put me through.

*For good reason.*

I trembled at the thought of what he'd do if he caught me. Wandering the palace in the middle of the night, unchaperoned.

But the lurid reality of my upcoming wedding night terrified me even more.

With only a half-formulated plan and a gin-muddled mind, I strode to the door and opened it.

In the hallway was a lone guard, clad in a full dress uniform and armed with a sword. He turned on me with none of the sluggishness one would expect of a guard tasked with staring at a wall in the small hours of the morning. He was young and handsome, showcasing his golden blond hair by letting it fall loose rather than in traditional braids.

"Miss Yorke," he said in the common tongue, straightening even further. His light Trenican eyes fell to my maroon silk nightgown, but immediately shot back up to my face. "What can I do for you?"

"I need something," I whispered, allowing my true anxiety to masquerade as bashfulness.

The guard cocked his head. "Yes?"

I leaned over, beckoning him to listen. He came closer and lowered his ear to me.

"I need," my whispering voice cracked. "*Feminine towels.*"

The guard's face immediately turned as pink as the austoria flowers blooming in the gardens. "Oh, *oh*. I see."

He backed away and swallowed nervously. Though he was clearly embarrassed, I caught the small hint of a satisfied smile on the corner of his lips. My blood boiled.

*They've been waiting for this. Hoping my cycles would return.*

He'd surely report the falsehood to *His Excellency* as soon as he returned. Maksim would be pleased.

The guard glanced back and forth down the hallway, blinking rapidly as he tried to decide how to handle the situation.

"Stay here. I'll find a maid to help you with your... *condition.*" He said it as if a menstrual cycle was a disease. "Lock the doors. Don't open them for anyone but me or His Excellency."

I smiled and thanked him. He bowed magnanimously, surely thinking himself the most chivalrous man on the continent.

He watched me close the doors, and I made sure to twist the locks with more force than necessary. I needed him to feel very sure of my safety.

The waiting was excruciating, but if I left too soon, he'd surely hear me. So I leaned against the thick doors, trying to ignore the provocative paintings encroaching on me as the walls shrank. I had to escape.

*"When I touch you, you will know."*

My heart hammered in my chest.

*What would Levick think of you sharing a bed with another man?*

*With the man who stole and subjugated your kingdom?*

*You haven't even tried to escape yet.*

"It's part of my mission," I whispered.

*Are you sure it's that simple? You let Maksim kiss you in the hall outside Rynne's bedroom. You pulled him closer and opened your mouth for him.*

I'd tried to forget that lapse in judgment, but the effects of the gin swirled with the panic surging through my mind. I regretted it so much that it made me nauseous. But my thoughts were on a downward spiral, destroying me from the inside.

*Keep telling yourself that you regret it, Eliandre. That you don't enjoy Maksim's twisted games. But maybe it's time to face your demons.*

*You don't want to be saved.*

"No!" I hissed. "I'd rather die than stay here any longer!"

On unsteady legs, I spun around and opened the door to the hallway.

There was no one there. The hallway was completely empty. The only movements were the flickering rays of candlelight dancing over the walls.

*Echna, bless me.*

I wasted no time and started down the hallway, in the direction of the staircase. The palace was eerily quiet—the usual merriment suspended as everyone slept off their indulgences from the engagement celebration.

My slippered feet padded silently down the staircase. It briefly occurred to me that I was wearing nothing over my silk nightgown, but my desperation to find the elixirs and escape rendered me immune to rational thought.

*He'd hide them somewhere quiet. Somewhere that isn't frequented by anyone.*

With the wild urgency of a cornered animal, I raced down the stairs and towards the basement.

I'd never seen the palace so quiet. I briefly encountered a handful of inebriated soldiers in the ballroom, but they were too distracted by their feminine companions to notice me. They kept to themselves as I crept by, propelled by raw determination.

The rear sector of the palace was so empty, it seemed abandoned.

*The perfect place to hide something.*

I opened every single door in the dim hallway, using a stolen sconce candle to illuminate the rooms. Disorganized piles of furniture, linens, and kitchenware lay strewn about, gathering dust.

The rooms were being used for storage.

*This is it. They're here. They must be.*

I rummaged through wardrobes, crates, desks, and even searched under beds. Each room was so haphazardly arranged that I found myself toppling boxes and decor just to make it to the center. Some of the furniture looked like it hadn't been dusted in a decade. My hope began dwindling.

*They'll know I'm gone by now.*

Guards were likely swarming the palace, searching for me.

*And if Maksim has returned...*

I couldn't simply walk back to my room and pretend I'd gotten lost. There would be punishment. So I returned to my search, filled with reckless abandon.

Glass shattered and papers flew as I searched my latest room.

*The elixirs are down here. They have to be.*

As I was rushing through stacks of chairs, my thigh caught on one of their splintered corners. I gasped in pain and reached for my torn nightgown. Blood trickled down my leg. With shaking fingers I wiped the blood away, only serving to smear it over my skin.

*Please, Echna let the elixirs be down here.*

Tears were streaming down my face as I stumbled into the hallway, already eyeing the next bedroom.

"Well, look who it is," an unfamiliar voice rumbled from behind me. He spoke in Vynesic.

*A guard.*

I didn't have time to turn before I was slammed face-first to the ground. My wrist bent backward as I tried to catch myself. A pained wail escaped my mouth.

"Stop!" I cried out. "I'll go back to my room!"

My attacker laughed and yanked my arms behind my back. He pulled too far, and my left shoulder seared in agony.

"Be a good little whore and stay still," he growled.

My stomach dropped. A guard wouldn't manhandle me or call me a whore.

*It's one of his generals. He probably has a windblade.*

"Maksim will kill you for this," I said through tight breaths. I could barely breathe with his weight on my ribcage.

"Not if he can't find us."

*Us.*

He finished binding my hands, then roughly threw me over his shoulder. "Make one noise and I'll slice your toes off."

I'd thought my biggest risk in sneaking out was being caught by Maksim. I was so gravely wrong.

My kidnapper easily slipped unnoticed through servants' corridors and quiet wings of the palace. I couldn't keep track of where he was taking me—my hair hung over my face, obscuring my vision. I tried to keep my composure, but my heart was hammering in my *chest.*

*Don't scream. Don't scream.*

"What do you want?" I whispered.

"Nothing you can give me. Unless you have a vault of gold tucked in that nightgown." He slid a large hand up my leg and over my backside. "Doubtful. But I'll check later, just in case."

I stifled a horrified shriek.

*He'll get caught. There's no way we won't encounter someone on the way out.*

Just as I thought it, someone shouted at my kidnapper.

"By order of His Excellency, drop the girl!"

*I know that voice. It's the guard who was posted outside my door.*

His words were promptly followed by the metallic shriek of a sword leaving its scabbard.

My heart soared at the sound. I never thought I'd be so happy to be pursued by Trenican soldiers.

*They've come for me. I'm safe.*

"You shouldn't have gotten in my way, Antov." My captor swung his arm, and a dull thud echoed from ahead. The sword clattered to the ground.

My hope dissolved as quickly as it appeared.

*He was alone. No one else is coming.*

Then, we were moving again. He carried me down halls and through corridors, slipping away unimpeded. I tried to form a plan of escape, but my fear and residual inebriation made it impossible.

A door clicked open, and cool air rushed over my legs. We were outside. He'd made it out.

*This can't be happening.*

His pace picked up as we passed by the austoria hedges. They were in full bloom, filling the night with their sweet scent.

"Please," I begged. "Just let—"

A deafening screech filled the air.

My kidnapper swore and swatted at something. The soft beating of feathers brushed against my skin.

*It's a bird.*

A string of Vynesic curses flooded from my captor's mouth as he stumbled backwards. More avian screeches erupted, from directly behind me.

*I know that shriek.*

It was Lock. He was attacking my kidnapper.

I quickly shifted my body back and forth, throwing him further off-balance.

*If I can get him to trip—*

The Trenican released a bloodcurdling scream and seized up. I rolled off his shoulders, landing in a breathless heap on the ground. Lock promptly landed beside me, doing his best to swallow the human eyeball in his bloodied beak.

*Echna bless you, disgusting, feral thing.*

The newly one-eyed general hunched over, holding his hand over his face and groaning.

I was about to roll to my feet when something darted in front of me, almost running me over. The dark figure didn't hesitate to tackle the man to the ground. I narrowed my eyes, trying to make out the identities of the men in front of me.

My attempted kidnapper was Jori Volkov, the man who'd killed Rynne's father and took his windblade. Straddling his back was my brother, Lukyan.

A potent jolt of alarm seized me. "Lukyan! He has a windblade!"

But, to my surprise, Lukyan had already pried Jori's hands behind his back. He clearly knew how to subdue a Skylord.

"You despicable piece of slime," Lukyan said, punctuating the sentence with a brutal twisting of Jori's right index finger. Jori screamed and writhed under him, but he didn't stop. One by one, my brother broke seven more of Jori's fingers. I could do nothing but watch as Lukyan worked, diligent and ruthless.

*He's terrifying.*

"Lukyan."

I barely heard the cool voice above Jori's screams, but I knew it immediately.

Maksim was behind me.

My brother looked up, his deep blue eyes hardened with hate. I'd never seen him so infuriated.

After recognizing Maksim, Lukyan concealed his anger and rose to his feet.

"Explain," Maksim commanded.

"An attempted kidnapping, Excellency."

Jori's pathetic whimpering was the only sound echoing around the flower hedges as Maksim walked over to me. He stopped and looked me over. His dark clothing was rumpled and he looked exhausted, but his intensity remained potent as ever.

*What have you been doing?*

His gaze sharpened on my thigh, and rage sparked in his eyes.

It was the gash I'd gotten while shoving past a chair. I said nothing.

"Can you stand, beloved?" he asked, his tone perfectly even. As if he were inviting me to tea.

I nodded and let him help me up. Once I was standing before him, he pulled a knife from his belt and cut my bindings. Then he resumed his close scrutinization of me. He ran his fingers up my arms, over my collarbones, along my jaw. I stood completely still.

"Did he touch you?" he asked. His hardened eyes met mine, and I knew what he was truly asking.

I shook my head.

Maksim's chest fell in a subtle sigh of relief. He reached forward and pulled me against him, tightening his arms around me. After the stress of the night, I couldn't deny the relief I felt to be in Maksim's arms rather than Jori's. I fell into the embrace, resting my head against his chest and wrapping my arms around his back.

"It's alright, little gull. I'm here." He ran his fingers through my hair and stroked my back.

I hadn't realized I was crying. My tears ran down my cheeks and soaked Maksim's dark blue shirt.

*What is wrong with me?*

*The wolf has stolen me back from the fox. This is no victory.*

But I cried anyway, and imagined I was hugging my brother instead of my tormenter.

Maksim pulled away and tilted my chin up to his. "Come, now. We mustn't let such a deed go unpunished." He looked over at Lukyan. "Wouldn't you agree?"

Lukyan nodded. Jori was still beneath his boot, moaning and clutching at his empty eye socket with mangled hands.

"Finish your task," Maksim commanded.

With no hesitation, Lukyan fell onto Jori's back. The latter screamed and thrashed, but he was no match for Lukyan's strength. My brother grabbed Jori's two unharmed fingers and yanked them to the side, snapping them out of place. Fresh shrieks filled the courtyard.

Maksim shooed Lukyan away, then led me over to Jori. He was writhing on his side, his remaining eye wide and locked on Maksim.

"Why, Volkov?" he asked. His hand was wrapped casually around my waist, but his grip was growing firmer by the second.

"It was her idea," Jori stammered. "She offered to sleep with me if I'd help her escape."

Maksim's chest shook beside mine. "I suppose it was also her idea to have her hands bound together?"

Jori paled, knowing his lie was worthless. "Your Excellency, if you'd listen—"

Maksim brought a foot down on Jori's chest, pressing his back into the ground. He bent over and tore his shirt open.

"No, please!" Jori cried, trying to shuffle away. He desperately pawed at the dirt, only to howl at the pain in his broken fingers.

Maksim called for Lukyan. My brother immediately sat down behind Jori and pulled his arms over his head. Jori yelled and struggled against him, but Lukyan had his legs tight around Jori's lower abdomen. Inescapable. He moved with a trained efficiency that told me it wasn't the first time he'd done this for Maksim.

A lump formed in my throat, and I took an uneasy step backwards. The punishment would be severe.

"Come here," Maksim said, beckoning me closer.

I started forward, but hesitated. I'd seen enough pain and death.

"Eliandre," Maksim said, sending a chill up my spine. He rarely said my name.

It was clear—I had no choice. So I did as he commanded, and knelt beside him on the ground.

"How is your handwriting?" Maksim asked.

I looked over at him, confused.

"You were taught calligraphy, I presume?"

My stomach sank as I looked down at Jori. Maksim had torn his shirt open, exposing his chest.

"Yes," I whispered.

Maksim hummed his approval. "Show me."

He took my hand and rested a knife in my palm. It was small and fine, clearly made for delicate work. My fingers trembled around the gleaming silver handle.

"This man is a thief. He should wear that mark for all to see," Maksim said.

My eyes flashed to Lukyan. His face was impassive.

*Why did I have to leave that room?*

Maksim had recently warned me that treacherous generals might try to steal me away. I assumed there was nothing but delusional possessiveness fueling those words.

*I should have listened.*

*Impulsive, arrogant girl.*

I turned back to Maksim. "No," I whispered. "Please don't make me do this."

Maksim's jaw twitched. "Jori Volkov was fully intending to rape you, brutalize you, then sell you for ransom. Do not spare him any mercy."

Jori shook his head and denied it vehemently, but his words turned into screams when Lukyan twisted one of his broken bones.

A finger slid over my jaw, pulling my eyes away. "If you find such a task beyond your sensibilities, I can do it instead. But I promise you this, beloved," he said pulling me close until he was whispering in my ear. "I will draw it out. I will make him beg for death. That is the price for stealing something that I love."

His fingers tightened over the back of my neck. He wasn't simply angry. He was enraged.

As much as I hated Jori Volkov, I wouldn't wish Maksim's unbridled rage on anyone. I took a deep breath, and gripped the knife's hilt.

"Can I kill him first?"

A knowing smile pulled at Maksim's lips. "Of course not."

I worked by the light of the full moon. Jori never stopped screaming, not even when I was adding the final flourishes to the *f* on his ribcage. I wiped the fresh blood away to see if anything needed to be corrected or embellished. Despite the morbid medium, it was some of my best calligraphy. I stilled my shaking fingers.

*Almost finished.*

Lukyan held the thrashing man as I completed my task, but I felt his eyes flash to me every so often. I tried to clear my mind. Self-loathing threatened to consume me.

While Lukyan's eyes were filled with veiled concern, Maksim's eyes shone with something altogether different. He'd watched me carve every single letter, enraptured. His stare would linger on my face, drift down to my blood-smeared hands, then shift back up.

When I finally finished and returned Maksim's knife, he distractedly wiped it off and set it aside. He gazed upon the tortured man, his eyes filled with wonderment. The word *thief* was carved over his chest, complete with dramatic, swirling lines.

"A masterpiece," Maksim said.

His hands found my face. His skin was flushed—invigorated as he pulled me closer.

*He loves it. The horror. The pain.*

But I was too drained to resist him. Too seared.

Our mouths met in a perverted union of ecstasy and despair. He kissed me with a fervor that shook me to my core.

There wasn't enough psychological fortitude in the universe to save me from that moment. I wanted to block out the groaning of my torture victim below me. I wanted to disassociate from Maksim's tongue snaking around mine. And, more than anything, I wanted to forget that my brother was sitting right in front of me, witnessing every one of my reprehensible deeds.

Maksim hanged Jori Volkov from a chandelier the next day, his chest bare for the entire ballroom to see.

*Thief.*

He was making clear the consequence of treachery.

To my relief, he didn't make me watch.

## *Chapter Thirty-Two*

# The Lead

Three more days came and went, and to my relief, Maksim didn't further question me about the incident. There was no one left to interrogate anyway—the only other witnesses of the crime were dead.

Maksim spent most of his days out, and never told me where he was going. I kept waiting for his darker side to come out—for him to twist the ring around my finger and bask in my tears—but it never came. It seemed his desire for a healthy, fertile wife currently outweighed his lust for my suffering. I wondered how long it would last.

Despite the attempted kidnapping, Maksim made good on his promise to give me more freedom in the palace.

"You have a windblade. If someone tries to steal you away, use it," he'd said. "But leave them alive... justice is mine."

I used my new freedom to do some light exploring of lesser-known corners of the palace, in search of the elixirs. I tried to mask much of my searching under the guise of simple curiosity or seeking out Rynne. Though no guards followed me closely, I was certain one always trailed me distantly. It was both a concern and a comfort. I still felt the ghost of Jori's hands sliding over my skin, chilling me to the bone, but I couldn't delay my search. Time was running out.

I was required to be in the Royal Chambers after dark, so seeing Coran became impossible. He could only scale the palace walls under cover of darkness. Rynne claimed she wished we could all meet together like we used to, but I doubted her sincerity. She was enjoying her nights with Coran, that much was clear from her demeanor.

Things were still tense with Lukyan. He'd come by Rynne's room to check on me, but he seemed distant. Like something was bothering him.

*Maybe he's having trouble forgetting about the torture he watched you inflict. Or the demented kiss you shared with Maksim.*

The thought filled me with mortification.

During our next meeting in Rynne's bedroom, I told them about the key Maksim wore around his neck.

Rynne lit up.

"That's probably to the room where he keeps his elixirs!" she exclaimed, her red curls bouncing in her excitement.

I shrugged. "It doesn't do me any good if I don't know where it is. Any leads on that?" I asked, looking at Lukyan.

He pressed his lips into a thin line and shook his head. "Nothing. I've tried to search the less traveled sectors of the palace, but I worry I'm being followed. It's risky to even come here."

My stomach sank. If Lukyan was under suspicion, I was truly alone in my mission.

My brother must've noticed my discouragement.

"The captain has a lead. If we don't find something soon, we'll give up on the elixirs and get you out before the wedding." He took a step closer and clasped my hands in his. "We'll flee. I swear it, Sister."

Another few days passed in relative normality. I continued to search Maksim's rooms during the day, but found nothing new. I'd even resorted to asking Maksim for a full tour of the palace, in hopes he might let slip any clues on where to find the elixirs. He seemed disinterested by the idea at first, and strongly considered outsourcing the task to a guard. But after I dressed myself in one of my more sultry gowns, he abandoned the notion. It was growing abundantly more obvious that Maksim's trust in his guards and soldiers' loyalty was waning.

Maksim took me to every wing of the palace. Art galleries, studies, the library, and even the aviary. He was clearly bored with it, but found ways to entertain himself by occasionally luring me to dark corners and pushing the bounds of our agreement. Eventually the revulsion wore away, but I was never struck with the allure I'd briefly felt in the hallway outside of my room. There was neither disgust nor desire. It seemed I'd shut off those emotions, leaving only despondency in their place. I showed him what he wanted to see—a broken, tamed girl, drowning in a fatal mixture of fear and lust. To my dismay, it was partially true.

The tour was a failure. I learned nothing new of his elixirs, and went to sleep that night filled with frustration and regret.

It was almost two weeks into my engagement when Lukyan passed me in the hallway, discreetly slipping me a note without even pausing.

*Meet me in the old stable.*

I glanced back and forth, then ripped the note to shreds and tossed it in the closest hearth I could find.

The guards at the palace doors expressed doubt about letting me outside. But I was no longer Maksim's prisoner, I was his betrothed. My dress was elegant and dignified, my hair clean and perfumed, and my attitude fitting of a woman of my station.

*Such extravagant polish over a rotting interior.*

"Ma'am, we haven't received express permission to allow you outside," the younger guard argued. He was familiar—one of the guards I spoke to after returning from Maksim's first test.

I took a few steps closer. My priceless shoes granted me height, and he was shorter than his peers, so I looked down on him. "Perhaps you've forgotten who I am," I said, letting some of my pent-up rage edge my tone. I raised my left hand, showcasing the glistening abomination on my finger. "Just yesterday, your viceroy had one of his guards beaten for disrespecting me."

Fear flashed over the young man's eyes. It was true, to an extent. The aforementioned guard had let his eyes linger on me for a second longer than he should have.

I was allowed out the palace doors with no further resistance.

Lukyan was waiting for me at the abandoned old stable, Lock perching on his arm. A smile spread over my face, making my cheeks ache.

*When was the last time I smiled?*

I went to take Lock from Lukyan, but he pulled me into a hug, brushing his hand over my hair.

"Are you alright?" he whispered. "Has he hurt you?"

I buried my face in his chest so he couldn't read my expression when I said, "No."

It was true, but the reason for my comfortable conditions and kind treatment was not a truth I cared to linger on.

"We are following the captain's lead," he said, pulling away. "I think we're close to finding the elixirs. We've been looking in all the wrong places."

Lock climbed onto my arm, his talons scraping over my skin. I didn't even notice the pain anymore, I was just happy to see him again. He seemed no worse for wear after prying Jori Volkov's eye from his head.

"What is your lead?" I asked Lukyan as I stroked Lock's head and neck.

"Maksim's carriage has frequently been spotted in northern Friese—the banking district. The captain thinks he might have the elixirs in a vault."

My eyes shot to his, widening in surprise. "A vault? You'd think he'd want them in the palace, close by."

"Unless he doesn't trust his generals," Lukyan said, giving me a knowing look.

*He thinks there will be a takeover.*

I chewed on my cheek. The concerns were valid. It made sense. Maksim had been gone for extended periods, taking on more responsibilities.

"It's certainly possible," I mused. "What do you need from me?"

Lukyan took a deep breath and fell into his familiar military leader persona. "Stay put and avoid rousing suspicion. We might need you to become a distraction, and we don't want him questioning it."

It wasn't what I wanted to hear. Waiting made me feel helpless.

"Elucia."

I met my brother's eyes. They were dark as the ocean, filled with concern.

"I know we haven't talked about... Volkov."

My body stiffened at the name. I saw his skin splitting easily under my knife, beads of blood trickling over my fingers. His screams rang in my ears, harmonizing with Kiera's.

I shook my head and looked away. "No."

We sat in silence for a long while, but I could tell Lukyan was worried about me.

*Don't worry about my heart and mind. I will fix them later.*

*Once this is all over.*

But I said nothing as I ran my hand over Lock's wing. Unlike before, no dust or grime came away on my fingers. "You cleaned him," I said, giving my brother a faint smile.

Lukyan nodded. "You asked me to take care of him. The least I could do is make him less malodorous."

I shot him a glare and turned away, hiding Lock. "He doesn't mean it," I whispered. The vulture simply nosed around my dress in search of a snack.

*Scavenger.*

That night, Maksim insisted on joining a revel downstairs. He kept his hand firmly on my waist as he mingled with his soldiers and generals. Every so often, Friesian women would come by to talk and bat their eyes at Maksim. They'd lay their hands on his arm, winking and laughing flirtatiously. Though he didn't encourage them, he did very little to ward them off.

The hour was late when the musicians transitioned to their more sultry melodies. I typically tried to avoid watching the dancers when the music shifted, but Maksim didn't lead us to his throne as he previously had. He took my hand and led me to the center of the ballroom. Anxiety swam in my stomach.

"Do you remember what you told me the first time I asked you to dance?" he asked, spinning me in his arms until my back was against his chest.

I nodded, but couldn't find it within myself to speak. The trajectory of the night was taking an undesirable turn.

"You told me you'd rather duel." He laughed, low and cruel in my ear. "Do you still feel that way?"

*Yes. Even more so.*

I didn't say it. There were dozens of eyes on us, watching in curiosity and jealousy. Embarrassing Maksim in front of his courtiers would come with a price.

"No," I whispered.

His chest rumbled against my back as he chuckled.

"What did you call this type of dancing?" he asked, though he clearly remembered the answer. He slid his hand down my left arm, then hugged it over my stomach. His fingers danced over my ring.

I turned my head slightly, until I barely saw his neck in my peripheral vision. "The sway of seduction."

He let his right hand drift over my waist, tugging me tighter against him. "So sway, my dear."

"Excellency!" someone whispered from behind us.

Maksim swore at the interruption, but I could've kissed the man. It was a harried guard with spots of rain staining his shoulders. I barely caught a glimpse of Lukyan behind the guard, his eyes cautiously flashing to me.

Maksim released me and approached the guard, grabbing him by his collar. "Is the palace on fire?"

The guard's eyes widened in fear, and he shook his head frantically. The movement sent flecks of rain flying over us.

"Then it isn't important enough to tear me from my *wife*," Maksim growled.

Lukyan's eye twitched at the word, and I hoped Maksim didn't notice.

I cleared my throat and gently tugged on Maksim's arm. He looked over his shoulder, the fury in his eyes softening.

"*Future* wife," he corrected himself.

"You should come with me. It's—" the guard began, stammering. He motioned for Maksim to come closer, then whispered something in his ear.

Maksim straightened at what he heard, and lifted his hand to his chest.

*The key.*

My heart pounded like a drum.

*It's about the elixirs.*

Maksim stepped away, as if he wanted to leave, but paused. "Go upstairs and lock the door. I'll be back soon," he commanded.

*No!*

I needed to go with him.

"Take me with you," I said, reaching for his hand.

He looked down at our fingers laced together, conflicted.

He pulled away. "No. You'll be safer upstairs." His eyes flickered suspiciously over the drunken soldiers and guards watching us.

A terrible idea came to me.

"Can Lukyan escort me upstairs? Just in case."

Maksim's formerly distracted gaze sharpened on me until it could've cleaved the room in half. He was already suspicious of Lukyan. He thought him in love with me. There was no chance Maksim would leave me alone with him.

I spotted Lukyan behind the other guard, looking like he wanted to disappear entirely.

But my plan worked. Maksim grabbed me roughly by my upper arm and led me from the room. He shoved past Lukyan without a second glance.

"We'll speak in the carriage," my betrothed said, so quietly I almost didn't hear it.

My plan worked, but I would surely pay for it.

I was trembling like a cornered doe when Maksim shut the carriage door behind us. I could barely see him staring out the window in the filtered moonlight, but I could sense his bubbling anger.

"Why?" he asked, his voice tight with restrained emotion.

My mind worked quickly. Though Maksim had learned what made me tick, I'd been learning, too. I took a deep breath, and hoped it was enough.

"I wanted to come with you," I said, shifting slightly so my leg would brush his.

He turned and looked at me, as slowly as a tiger sneaking up on his prey. "You knew I wouldn't leave you with him." He was surprised—bordering on impressed.

*Yes.*

I nodded.

Maksim leaned forward and slid a hand over my knee. I forced my body not to stiffen at his touch. But he was still angry, and his eyes glimmered with bad intentions.

It was a miscalculation. I hadn't considered the implications of my confession—that I was willing to doom another man in order to make Maksim jealous and to get what I wanted. It was exactly the sort of game he loved to play.

*And now I'm trapped in a carriage with him.*

I grabbed Maksim's hand in mine, stopping his advances. He seemed off-put by my perceived rejection, but I wound my fingers with his.

*Time for a distraction.*

"You've changed me, Maksim." I said his name intentionally. It rarely graced my lips, so when it did, he noticed. "I haven't told you because I've been scared of it... of how you make me feel."

He cocked his head, interested but clearly not expecting the conversation. He'd told me he loved me on the night he proposed, but between the mental and physical abuse, I hadn't said it back.

*Nor felt it.*

But that was beside the point.

I brushed a strand of hair behind my ear, feigning insecurity. "When I was trapped in the sea and solving your riddle, I kept seeing things. Visions of you. Of *us.*"

He nodded for me to continue, captivated.

*How long is this carriage ride going to last?*

"We were standing at an altar together, holding hands. I think, even back then, I knew."

I conveniently excluded the fact that I'd been marrying Levick in my dream, and Maksim only appeared once it transformed into a nightmare.

Maksim tightened his hand over mine. My ring dug into my skin, but I barely noticed the pain anymore.

"Knew what?"

*For the love of Echna, please let us be close.*

"I knew that we would have something special. A bond that transcended normal attachments."

He scooted closer on his seat.

"And went beyond normal—" my mouth almost choked on the word, "love."

His lips twitched at the corners. "Admitting the truth wasn't so hard, was it, beloved?" He crossed the carriage to sit beside me, and brushed a strand of my hair behind my shoulder. "Perhaps I'll give you a new ring. One that demands less punishment."

My foolish heart leapt at the possibility.

*No. It won't matter when he's dead and this is all behind you.*

Maksim leaned in to kiss me, but our carriage slowed to a stop, distracting him.

*Thank goodness.*

## Chapter Thirty-Three

# Entirely, Loathfully

Though it was dark outside, I immediately recognized where we were. There was only one house in Friese that stood like a lifeless gray headstone, bare of vegetation and color. It was the Yorke mansion. My home.

Maksim helped me down from the carriage and placed a hand on the small of my back. "Strange to be here, isn't it?"

I shivered, but not from the chilly night air. It was the home my parents had lived in. A home in which I'd considered myself a prisoner.

*Cherished and adored in a home with people who loved me. People who would sooner die than bring me harm. Yet I resented it. I was a fool.*

Maksim noticed my state and pulled me close to his chest. Numb, I fell into him, letting him stroke my back in what he surely assumed was a comforting gesture.

"No need to fret, dear," he whispered. "This isn't your home anymore. Those days are gone."

For a moment, I let myself indulge in the delusion. That Maksim was a decent man, even if I didn't love him. That even if our plot failed and I was made to go through with the wedding, I could still live a peaceful life with him. But Kiera's ripped throat burned through my mind. My ankle ached. My left hand stung. The delusion evaporated, leaving nothing but a grim reality.

He lifted my chin and kissed me so gently that I almost fell right back into that convenient dream. I wondered if it was my love confession that brought such tender words and affection from him.

*A sadist who only wanted love all along.*

It was an uncomfortably convincing absurdity.

He said nothing as he pulled away and led me inside, but I could tell that something had changed for him. I only hoped it would last long enough for me to shatter his rule and sever his head.

The guard from the palace escorted us up the front steps, his demeanor urgent. To my surprise, my cousin Louis greeted us at the door. After Maksim's threat against his life, I had worried he was locked up and languishing somewhere. But he laughed and straightened his blue silk pajamas, an embarrassed smile on his face.

"Sorry, I didn't have time to change," he said, running his fingers over his dark wavy locks of hair. "It's good to see you, Excellency. I was very pleased to hear of your engagement."

I fought back a scowl. He didn't even bother to address me directly.

Louis blathered on. "I heard there was quite a celebration down at the old Exley estate. Although I think you might've forgotten to send my invitation—"

"That's not why I'm here," Maksim said, pulling me around my cousin. "Go back to sleep."

I saw movement from the corner of my eye, behind Louis. A lithe Trenican woman was leaning against the wall in the hallway, clad in nothing but a sultry slip of a dress. It took me a moment, but I finally recognized her.

*Yla.*

It was an effort not to groan in disgust.

*Of course my cousin is sleeping with her.*

Louis didn't even spare me a word before retreating back down the hallway, disappearing with Yla. I buried my resentment.

The guard continued to lead us through my home, winding through hallways bedecked in jewel-encrusted molding and gilded furniture. I tried not to think about the memories tucked into every corner of the place.

The exquisite finery eventually gave way to drab, colorless hallways as we ventured into the servants' corridors. The guard finally stopped in front of an unremarkable door, then turned expectantly to Maksim. My betrothed reached under his collar, slipped the key from around his neck, then unlocked the door.

My heart picked up into a gallop.

*This is it. The ticket to liberating Friese.*

Maksim put his fingers over the handle, but hesitated. He looked back at me, his pale eyes conflicted. He wasn't sure whether to trust me.

I smothered the nerves threatening to give me away, and steeled myself for the most consequential deception of my life.

I cocked my head, stepping closer to Maksim. "What's wrong?"

He let go of the handle and motioned for his guard to give us privacy. The guard retreated down the hall, but surely lingered close by.

Maksim took a deep breath and reached for my waist. I went to him without even a hint of hesitation.

"I need you to wait in the hallway," he said, his expression stern, but slightly unsure.

I twitched my brow and parted my lips. "You don't trust me."

He worked his jaw, but didn't stop me as I came closer to lightly press myself against him. His hand tightened over my back, despite the conflict in his eyes.

"Let me in," I whispered, reaching up to slide my hand over his cheek. "You can trust me."

It was a gamble. In the carriage, he'd shown a faint desire for true affection. True *love*. My ruse banked on the ability of a prideful, selfish sadist to yearn for real closeness.

*Come on. I'm not a threat. I'm your true love. I'm your future wife.*

His eyes fell to my lips.

*That's right. Kiss me. Trust me.*

He slid a hand over the side of my neck and leaned down. I tilted my head to the side, welcoming his affection. I felt his lips press against my skin, just below my ear. A genuine smile spread over my lips.

"To whom does your loyalty belong, Eliandre Yorke?" he murmured.

I let more of my weight fall against him, my body molding to his. His fingers pressed tighter into my back.

"I am entirely yours, my love." The words made me nauseous, but I'd become adept at suppressing it.

He said nothing for a long moment, but made his sentiments clear through the adventurous roaming of his hands and nipping of his teeth. His affections were so slow and sensual that I began to fear he'd taken my words as an invitation. But just as his fingers glided over the buttons on my dress, he stopped.

"You will speak of this to no one," he whispered against my skin.

His hand was back on the door handle. He was going to let me in.

I nodded, the thrill of victory coursing through my veins. He moved to back away, but I grabbed his neck and pulled him down. I kissed him hard and deep, reveling in the feeling of his smile against my lips.

*I have him.*

The room was piled to the ceiling with crates. Despite Maksim's display of trust by allowing me inside, he spoke to his guard in hushed tones a few feet away. I didn't care. I simply walked from crate to crate, admiring the bottles of elixirs packed inside. I'd found it. The elixirs were stored not in the palace, but in a relatively poorly guarded location. I couldn't fight the smile on my lips, but masked its true reason by locking eyes with Maksim every so often, then looking away bashfully. He ate it up without reservation. I briefly wondered whether he'd stop hurting me.

*It doesn't matter. He'll be dead within the month.*

I smiled again, and Maksim smiled back.

*Fool.*

It was a few days before I was able to meet with Lukyan, but they went by uneventfully. Though Maksim still spent most of the daytime away, his nighttime demeanor had changed significantly. When we settled into bed, there was no longer three feet of cold sheets between us. He fell asleep coiled around me like a snake suffocating his prey.

I fought a constant battle against my instinct to squirm free. Maksim's trust was hard earned, and it was inextricably linked to my perceived affection for him. If I wanted to retain my small bit of freedom, I had to remain compliant. So I'd lie in his arms like a complacent little mouse. I trailed my fingers over his skin and fantasized about burying my windblade into it.

I wondered who was more delusional of the two of us. Maksim, who seemed to think he could have a sincere love affair with a woman he'd tortured for months, or me, a woman who assumed she could make it out alive.

*Alive... but ruined.*

An hour after Maksim kissed me goodbye, I dressed myself and started down the hallways of the palace. I took roundabout routes and paused in various rooms to throw off any potential followers. It was mid-morning by the time I slipped into Rynne's room. She was still wearing her kitchen uniform and looked to be scolding Lukyan, who sat beside Coran on her sofa.

They greeted me with intense relief and scanned me for new injuries. In the short time since I moved into Maksim's rooms, my body had begun showing signs of recovery. His new behavior had alleviated much of my stress, and it showed in my complexion. Rynne noticed and asked me what changed, but I dodged the question. I'd rather them not know about the gentle embraces I shared with Maksim before he left for the day, or the amorous lies I whispered in his ears at night. Though I felt very little guilt for the deceit, the shame still made me sick.

I wasted no time in relaying what I'd learned about the elixir stores. Lukyan looked like he might cry with relief at the news. My wedding was ten days away, and the clock was ticking.

I'd hoped my discovery meant I could finally flee the palace with Rynne, but Coran asked me to stay. He was formulating a plan to disseminate the powdered elixirs throughout the palace, and my access to Maksim's bedroom was too valuable to sacrifice.

"We might need you to unlock doors or windows, or do something of that nature," Coran said apologetically. "But don't worry—we'll get you out as soon as we have a solid plan. For now, stay put and keep your head down."

The request was devastating, but I didn't let them see it. It was almost over.

*I can endure a bit longer.*

Lukyan hugged me before I left. He whispered in Vynesic, "I love you, Elucia. Hold fast."

For the next couple of days, my correspondence with Lukyan was very limited. He passed me notes in the hallways, explaining his and Coran's plans to steal the elixirs.

I stood beside the hearth in Maksim's sitting room, fighting tears as I read the most recent letter. It was from Coran, delivered discreetly by Lukyan.

> *We've made a plan, but we need your assistance. Maksim and his generals need to be far from the Yorke mansion when we execute it, to extend our time. There is only one believable reason to gather them together in a distant location.*

I pursed my lips, preparing myself for the answer.

*The wedding. We need you to suggest a wedding outside the palace so we can steal the elixirs while the Skylords are away. It is too risky to attempt a theft while dozens of Skylords are at the palace, a short ride from our target. Extend the wedding ceremony for as long as you can, so we can execute the theft undetected. If we complete the mission successfully, we will strike the night of the wedding. Once everyone at the palace is drunk or asleep, we will scale the walls and drop the poison inside.*

*Leave the door to the Royal Chambers unlocked before going to bed. Lukyan will quietly dispatch the door guard and find you. Either you may kill Maksim in his sleep, or Lukyan will leave a lethal concentration of the powdered elixir in his room. I will leave that decision up to you. But you must wait until after midnight. If you were discovered before we were able to strike, the palace would be placed on high alert, and our plans would be jeopardized.*

*I know this isn't what you wanted to hear, but I am trusting in your strength and dedication to your kingdom.*

*Forever grateful for your sacrifice,*

*Captain Coran Trust*

I ripped the letter to shreds and tossed it into the fireplace, then fell to my knees. After all of my effort, all of my lies, I still had to marry Maksim. I had to let him bring me to bed. There was no way he'd accept any less on his wedding night. He certainly wouldn't let his guard down and fall asleep without having fulfilled his lustful promises.

*I could kill him before midnight... as long as it's completely silent.*

But my windblade was broad and messy. Even if I managed to kill him in one clean strike with no collateral damage, I'd have to catch his body before it hit the floor.

*Too risky.*

*But if he is already lying down, there would be no noise.*

My stomach lurched.

I'd seen so much death and pain. I'd been the victim of torture and the perpetrator of it. My conscience had been so warped that I didn't recognize it anymore. But to kill a man as he was taking me to bed? To cut off his head as he was on top of me?

*He would deserve it.*

*But could I endure it?*

The horror played out in my mind. The kisses turning to choking, the blood pouring onto my skin. The weight of a dead body falling limp on top of me.

I almost vomited at the thought.

Just like that, my fighting spirit evaporated.

It was the killing blow to my dream. The one where Levick would return and save me from the hell I'd been living in, and undo every depraved act I'd committed. If I married

Maksim—only to murder him on our wedding night—it would be the end.

Levick wouldn't come near me. Not because of his own judgment, but mine. Levick was pure. He was good. He deserved better than a woman corrupted by sadism. A woman tarnished by evil.

In truth, it had been a long time since I considered myself worthy of Levick's love. To sully myself with Maksim would only be my final, symbolic commitment to the perversion I'd enabled so many times.

*But if that is the cost for the liberation of Friese?*

I would pay it.

*Do you hate Maksim enough to leave him for dead after swearing to love him forever?*

I hoped so.

It was entirely too easy to get Maksim to agree to an outdoor wedding. I asked to wed on the northern shore, invoking the vision I'd had of my father to justify it. I hated using my father as an excuse for a lie, but it didn't bother me as much as it should have. As much as it would have, before Maksim corrupted me.

The day was fast approaching, and my nerves ate at me. Maksim was often drawn away to tend to his fickle allies, which left me with a lot of time to dwell on my inevitable fate. Instead of wallowing, I hid away at the old stable, feeding Lock and checking on his feathers. His flight would be limited until he grew new ones. Part of me thought Lukyan would show up so I could see him one last time before the wedding, but he never did.

So I spent the last few days of my unmarried life alone, forcing myself not to think about who I'd dreamed of marrying four months ago. The man I was far too corrupted to touch. Levick Roale, my windwalker.

## Chapter Thirty-Four

# Until Death

On the night before my wedding, an indescribable sense of peace fell over me. I had neither pain nor sadness. I didn't think about myself at all. I thought about Kiera, who would never live to have her own wedding day. I thought of my friends, who would face dozens of Trenican Skylords and hallucinogenic powder if I failed.

I didn't think about Levick.

I ran my fingers over my glistening wedding gown, feeling each tiny ruby under my fingers. The gown was a bold statement—made of Trenican-favored velvet rather than Friesian-favored silk and lace. I was becoming one of them.

*You already are, Eliandre.*

A pair of gentle hands slid around my waist from behind. I didn't even jump. He'd become a fixture in my life, even in so short a time. It had only been four months since I watched my friends sail over the horizon.

"You're staying with me, right?" I asked, turning in Maksim's arms and resting my wrists on his shoulders. The act was getting too easy. I wasn't falling for him, but I was losing myself.

*Who am I, anymore?*

He brushed my hair behind my ear and kissed me softly. "Northern men are traditional. I'll be down the hall tonight."

*Traditional.*

I almost laughed.

Instead, a sad smile tugged at my lips, and I traced his cheekbone with my fingers. It was a strange feeling, to split the heart and mind. My heart saw nothing but self interest and cruelty in Maksim's ice-blue eyes. I hated him with a venom so potent it could poison a thousand people. But my mind told me something else altogether. It told me he was my betrothed, the man to whom I owed my fervent adoration.

*And I'll prove it to him tomorrow night.*

Some distant part of myself shuddered at the thought, but it didn't break through the protective delusion I'd built around myself.

Maksim took my face in his hands. "Don't worry. Tomorrow we start something new." He leaned down and started laying kisses over my neck. "A game of love and loyalty. A dance that lasts a lifetime."

*Dance? Or duel?*

Though his touch did nothing for me, I leaned into him. I pulled him closer because once he was gone, there was nothing left except my hideous future and my horrible self.

I hardly slept. My emotions were numb—extinguished by the endless onslaught of death and pain I'd played over in my memories. When I woke the next morning, there was a page of crisp parchment folded on Maksim's pillow beside me.

> *It's time, little gull. Meet me at the northern shore. Everyone is waiting. I've left you a gift in our entry room. Enjoy.*
>
> *P.S., No one will ever love you the way I do.*

I folded the note and returned it to the pillow, then slipped out of bed. I rang for a servant to help me get dressed, but was too restless to wait for her. The velvet gown was heavy as I lifted it up and over my shoulders, then tied the back tight. My muscles were numb as they went through the motions of brushing my hair, braiding the top portion into a bun, then pinning a long flowing veil over it. I didn't even look in the mirror before walking to the bedroom door. I didn't want to see.

But what waited on the other side of the door was far more horrific than anything I could've seen in the mirror.

A pair of perfectly polished military boots hung before my eyes, reflecting the morning sunlight as they spun slowly. Terror swallowed me completely, but I forced myself to look up.

Captain Coran Trust dangled from the chandelier, his lifeless face smeared with blood. His shirt was torn and strewn open, showcasing a grisly declaration carved into his chest.

*Let the dance begin.*

I couldn't prevent the scream from tearing out of my throat. Coran was dead. Maksim had discovered our plot.

My knees hit the floor, but I couldn't pull my eyes away from my dead friend. Blood dripped from his chest, landing in a dark puddle on the gray rug underneath him. Broken sobs racked my lungs as I cried out for him.

*Coran is dead.*

*Maksim knows the truth.*

*Where is Rynne? Where is Lukyan?*

The plot was foiled. We'd failed.

A loud rapping erupted over the door. "Here to escort you to your wedding, Miss Yorke."

The guard's sneering tone told me everything.

*It was all for nothing. The torture. The kisses. The false love confessions.*

*Kiera.*

The door handle rattled, but I didn't register it. Everything was ruined.

I was ruined.

I'd torn myself apart to pass Maksim's tests. To earn his love. There was nothing left of me.

*Nothing.*

*Nothing.*

*Nothing.*

The door opened, revealing the guard I'd stabbed in the back shortly after my capture.

*Stepan.*

"Let's go," he said, a smug smile on his hideous face. "If you want to see your little friend again."

*Rynne.*

The threat rang hollow in my ears. The only sensation I felt was an electric fire burning through my hands, my fingertips. My left hand had never healed correctly after Maksim's first test.

But my right hand was as strong as ever.

All of the hate I'd suppressed came bursting out of me like a flood.

A feral scream erupted from my chest, raw and unfiltered. I lunged forward and threw Isolon for the first time in weeks, then cried as Stepan's blood splattered over my veil.

I made a war zone of Maksim's palace. Trenican men fell apart at my killing touch, soldier and Skylord alike. I dodged swords and windblades as I ran through the halls, down the stairs. No one could stand against me. Nothing could stop me. My very essence screamed out for vengeance.

Three soldiers rushed me at the base of the stairs, but they didn't stand a chance. I dissected them with barely a flick of my wrist. Isolon had been deprived of violence, and she was hungry. I indulged her at every opportunity.

I'd just cut down two inexperienced soldiers when a massive Trenican man rounded the hallway, swinging his arm directly at me. A blade of wind glanced past me, clipping my veil and the shell of my ear.

*They still have terrible aim.*

My eyes widened in unrestrained fury just before I sent Isolon through his head.

After painting the palace's starry tiles in Trenican crimson, I gathered the front of my dress in my hand and started running. More guards met their maker as I charged into the stable, stealing the closest horse. There was nothing left of me.

*Nothing.*

*Nothing.*

*Nothing.*

I saw them before they saw me. Trenican generals wearing their finest military coats stood along the beach, their medals shining in the remaining sunlight. A dark storm cloud loomed to the east.

I leapt from my horse and stumbled in the rocks, but spared no momentum. One of the generals glanced my way, his jaw dropping at the sight. I wasted no time in throwing my windblade, splitting him and his neighbor in half.

"Maksim!" I screamed. My gore-stained dress rippled out behind me as I ran at them.

All at once, the generals converged on me. I threw at them but there were too many, coming from every angle. I couldn't keep up with only one throwing hand. Before I knew it, I was tackled to the ground.

I screamed Maksim's name, but it died on my lips as a sickening *crunch* exploded in my right hand. A heavy booted foot stomped and ground my hand into the rocks. My screams of anger transformed into screams of agony. Terrible stabbing pain shot up my arm, and I knew my hand was broken. Shattered.

A stern shout echoed from nearby and the men backed away, revealing Maksim standing at the water's edge. He had his hand around Rynne's throat and held her tight.

Despite the tears rolling down my cheeks, a disbelieving laugh escaped my lips. "You complete fucking *coward*!" I screamed the last word. I pulled my shattered hand over my chest—it was useless.

Rynne's eyes went wild at the sight of me broken and beaten on the ground. Her dark blue dress was dirtied along the hem, but otherwise intact. I forced myself to take comfort in it.

"Working with rebels? I should've known you wouldn't let things get boring between us," Maksim said, an infuriatingly amused gleam in his hateful eyes.

"Let her go!" I groaned. The fabric of my sanity tore at the seams. I must've killed two dozen people. "Have I not given you enough?"

Maksim's lip curled up. "I told you, Eliandre. I told you I *love* you! And you betrayed me!"

"You don't love me! You torture me! You've destroyed me in every possible way. That is not love." The words felt like knives ripping through my throat.

*Love is selfless. It's gentle and faithful.*

*It's letting someone go, even if you're scared they won't ever come back.*

"This is your third and final test," Maksim growled, reaching down and pulling a stiletto knife from his belt. "Yield. Bow to me. Marry me. Our game will not end here. It will *never* end."

I couldn't speak. I stared at Maksim, blurred through the tears in my eyes, and shook my head.

*I cannot lie anymore. It would be better to die.*

Maksim's jaw twitched, and I could've sworn his eyes were glassy. "If you will not give me your heart, beloved, I will poison it."

He plunged the knife into Rynne's side.

I cried out for her, but she'd already fallen to Maksim's feet, writhing in pain. Her stomach hemorrhaged dark red blood all over the sand.

Maksim tossed the knife to the ground in front of Rynne. "I've stabbed her in the liver—she will be dead within the hour. The knife was coated with a particularly vile elixir. A close relative to appertonic."

Rynne began screaming. Terrible, bloodcurdling screams. She bolted upright and scurried backwards, swatting at some unseen threat.

"Rynne, stop moving!" I yelled through anguished sobs.

"You have *no idea* the horrors she is seeing," Maksim said, kicking Rynne to the ground again. "My bet is on a memory. The one where we kill her lover in front of her."

Rynne didn't get up again, but was seizing and shrieking violently on the ground.

I crawled closer to her. "Make it stop! Please!"

"Ah, you see, I can't do that. This is your third test. Did you forget about it?" He took a step closer and kicked the knife towards me. "I didn't."

My mind ran through the possibilities, but I knew there was only one.

"You can either let your dear friend suffer a most horrific and prolonged death, or," he gestured to the knife, "end her torment."

An inhuman groan escaped my lips. Her wound was fatally placed and coursing with poison. She shrieked and moaned on the ground, rolling aimlessly. Her face smeared into the sand, coating her lips and tongue as she cried. It was hideous. I'd never seen such horrors.

*I wish it was me instead.*

But there was no time for wishes and regrets. I hated caving to Maksim—playing into yet another one of his cruel games—but it ultimately wasn't about Maksim. My dear friend was in unimaginable pain while reliving the greatest terrors she'd ever witnessed. She had no hope for survival. There was only pain and death.

I forced a sense of calm over myself as I accepted what I'd have to do. I crawled to Rynne, my broken hand sending crackling, splitting pain up my arm. There was no choice. I didn't stop.

I clumsily gripped the knife's hilt in my left hand, and cradled Rynne's face against my right. She screamed and wailed wordlessly. Light flecks of rain fell on her cheeks, mixing with her tears.

"I'm so sorry, Rynne," I whispered.

My eyes drifted to her neck, lingering over her unmarred skin.

"You will see him again," I said leaning closer. "Forgive me."

I clenched my fist and tore the dagger across Rynne's throat.

She was dead within seconds. The deep, clean cut gushed over my wedding gown, seeping through and wetting my skin. For a moment, I indulged in the unimaginable despair and misery of the moment. Her light blue eyes stared through me, glazed and lifeless. I couldn't look away. They held me captive, convicting me of my innumerable atrocities.

*It should've been me.*

*I wish it had been me.*

A grating voice sounded from above. "Why can't you see it?"

I looked up to see Maksim standing over me.

"You passed the last test. It's only become clearer to me." He crouched down, tossing away my discarded dagger. "We are the same, my dear."

There was no energy left in my heart to reply. Through my dolorous tears, I couldn't even summon a glare for him.

He dug his fingers into the hair on my scalp and yanked my head backwards. "You are the only woman worthy of me." His cold eyes scanned my face, glistening in unmasked wonder. "And now, I am the only man who could ever love you. Feral, broken girl."

Maksim pulled me from the ground and dragged me closer to the breaking waves. Dead bodies littered the shoreline, fitting witnesses to our damned union. The rain came harder, soaking us both through our clothes. Once we were ankle-deep in the waves, he spun me around to face him. He squeezed my hands in his own, nearly paralyzing me from the pain.

"Look at me," he commanded.

My eyes remained locked on the dense storm clouds rolling in.

"Look at me!" he roared, squeezing my hands tighter.

I cried out and almost collapsed into the waves, but finally complied. His pale skin was flushed, and his chest heaved under his shirt. He almost looked... nervous.

"I, Maksim Toresav, take you, Eliandre Yorke, as my wedded wife."

Unhinged screams erupted in my mind. It was insanity.

Nevertheless, he continued. "To love and to be faithful to you, and never forsake you." He yanked me closer, gripping my jaw in his hand. He leaned in until I could see the crazed mania in his eyes. Then, with an unwavering smoothness, he lifted the bloodied veil from my face.

"Until death do us part."

I caved under everything. Gasping sobs escaped my lips, and my legs gave way. For a brief moment, I entertained the fantasy of being washed out to sea, but Maksim caught me in his arms and held tight.

"Say it back," he whispered, his stare imploring. "Say it. I've broken you. No one else could ever love you. My possession of you is *eternal.*" He growled the last words and squeezed my jaw in his fingers.

The wind picked up, nearly blowing us into the crashing waves. I stared back into the eyes of my enemy, the nexus of my madness, the adulterer of my goodness. His jaw was tight with expectation, the thrill of a kill in his eyes.

I thought of what Lukyan told me about the northern frost tiger. He said they would bite and chase their victims until they were too tired and hopeless to fight back, only to release them and restart the pursuit. The truth dawned on me weeks too late. It wasn't the tiger's eating habits he'd been speaking of.

*He'd been speaking of its mating habits.*

It was so grossly fitting.

"You," I said through waves of trembling. "You will never have me. You may destroy my hope, my spirit, my virtue... but you will never truly have me. You cannot have what's been lost."

His brows furrowed, and for a moment, I thought he'd finally snap my neck and be done with me. But the wind picked up again, knocking us down into the shallows.

It was a tempest the likes of which I'd never seen.

*What is this?*

Maksim lunged for me, but the wind pushed him down again.

Chaos was truly reigning. Heavy rain pelted my skin like a thousand pebbles in a tornado. I collapsed into the waves, heaving fresh sobs into the water. But for the first time in months, the tears weren't from sadness or anger.

The winds caressed me, familiar and exquisite.

Maksim called my name, but I didn't respond. I was laughing and crying into the wind, an exuberant smile spreading over my face.

*It's over. It's finally over.*

"Eliandre!" Maksim yelled, finally close enough to hear. "We're not done here!"

I lifted my face to the sky. "Yes we are. My windwalker has returned for me." My eyes fell shut. "You are going to die."

# Acknowledgements

First, I want to thank my amazing husband. You've tolerated many late nights, read through many **rough** drafts, and listened to countless plot twist ideas. Thank you for being the most supportive beta-reader and editor I could ever ask for.

Next, I'd like to thank my lovely beta readers, Marissa Atherton, Michelle Smart, and Olivia Renner. You knew exactly what I was trying to capture, and helped me achieve that. Your contributions helped make this story stronger, and I'll forever be grateful for that.

I'd also like to thank all of the lovely author friends I've met in the last year (you know who you are). Your support and encouragement have been invaluable, and I hope to see you again soon.

Thank you all for believing in me.

# About the author

Kelly Farina is a fantasy author who enjoys writing stories full of love, magic, and a bit of angst. She is also the wife of an amazing husband, and the mother of two young children who keep her entertained when she isn't reading or writing. When she isn't drafting, editing or brainstorming, she enjoys running and spending time outside with her family.

Connect with Kelly on social media for the latest updates:

Instagram: @kelly.farina.author

www.kellyfarina.com

www.ingramcontent.com/pod-product-compliance
Lightning Source LLC
LaVergne TN
LVHW091250150826
845673LV00006B/1382

* 9 7 9 8 9 9 4 4 1 7 5 0 8 *